"I don't normally poke my nose into field operations."

The President went on, "And I appreciate your candor. But under the circumstances, I'm afraid I'll have to ask you to provide me with as many details as possible as soon as you get them, confirmed or unconfirmed."

"Of course, sir," Brognola replied. "Would it be terribly out of line if I asked why?"

The President appeared to consider Brognola's request a moment and then replied, "I suppose that's a fair question. You must understand that under no circumstances will I permit the outbreak of a full civil war in Cuba without taking significant action. And when I say action, I mean the full-scale military kind. If such hostilities were to ensue and we had exhausted every political remedy to abate them, I would be forced to order the U.S. Marines at Guantanamo to do whatever it took to protect the U.S. and its boundaries."

"War?" Brognola asked. "With Cuba?"

"If necessary, yes."

Don Pendleton's Mack Bolan®
Havana Five

A GOLD EAGLE BOOK FROM
W☉RLDWIDE®

TORONTO • NEW YORK • LONDON
AMSTERDAM • PARIS • SYDNEY • HAMBURG
STOCKHOLM • ATHENS • TOKYO • MILAN
MADRID • WARSAW • BUDAPEST • AUCKLAND

First edition July 2008

ISBN-13: 978-0-373-61524-7
ISBN-10:   0-373-61524-8

Special thanks and acknowledgment to
Jon Guenther for his contribution to this work.

HAVANA FIVE

In revenge and in love woman is more barbarous than man.

—Friedrich Nietzsche,
1844–1900

When revenge steers a person toward murder and deceit, I'll be there to strike a blow for justice.

—Mack Bolan

PROLOGUE

Gulf of Mexico

Two men wrestled the body from beneath the top deck of the small yacht anchored forty nautical miles north of the Cuban coast.

"This wasn't supposed to be part of the plan," Dominic Stein said.

Stein groaned under the deadweight of his load as if to emphasize the point, but his partner took no interest in the conversation. Not surprising, since Leslie Crosse did everything he could to avoid talk of grisly topics. The guy wouldn't even go to a slasher film, although it hadn't seemed to bother him when he'd shot their burden through the head with a silenced .380-caliber pistol.

"At least I bought us some time," Crosse replied.

Stein had to concede that particular point. They certainly hadn't planned on Mackenzie Waterston returning to his Pentagon office minutes after Stein and Crosse picked the lock, broke into Waterston's files, and pilfered every document and

data CD they could find on Operation Gridlock. Nobody
outside of the Oval Office should have even known about the
President's initiative. The U.S. State Department's Plan
Colombia had included covert military actions by specialized
units based out of Guantánamo Bay designed to neutralize
training camps for the National Liberation Army, aka the
ELN. Such operations were particularly lucrative for certain
individuals in the array of criminal trades across Cuba and
the better part of South America. Drugs were only the tip the
iceberg. Precious stones, counterfeit bills and import contra-
band of every kind were also profitable for a group of fabled
crime lords known as Havana Five.

"Okay, so we had to do it," Stein said. "But that sure as
hell doesn't mean I have to like it."

"Quit bitching and keep moving," Crosse muttered. The
flash in his eyes served as a warning he'd about had his fill.

Stein wouldn't have taken that kind of mouth off just anyone; Crosse wasn't just anyone, however, he was Stein's best
friend. They had served side by side in the DIA for more than
a decade. As luck would have it, their long-term partnership
had somehow slipped through the cracks of the DIA bureau-
crats—there were rules about the length of time personnel
could serve together—and the pair had simply decided to
keep their mouths shut about that fact. It turned out fortui-
tously when an irresistible offer practically dropped into their
laps.

"Fine, fine," Stein said. "I just hope to high hell this'll be
worth it."

"It'll be worth it."

They finally managed to get Waterston's body to the top
deck and dragged it over to the polished wood banister before Stein dropped his end. The sudden change in weight dis-

tribution nearly caused his partner to fall onto the corpse, but Crosse managed to regain his balance. He cursed under his breath but said nothing directly to Stein.

Crosse nodded in the direction of the long metal crate in the aft of the boat as his chest heaved with exertion. Stein took the cue and moved to retrieve the crate. He dragged it over to where his friend waited with the corpse and opened the lid. Several rows of silver-dollar-size holes ran along the sides and end of the crate, and after closer inspection Stein realized it was a crab cage. On a three-count, the men hauled the corpse into the cage, closed the lid and then swung the cargo winch into place.

Crosse sat back on a nearby fishing seat while Stein attached a chained hook through a large alloy hole in the top of the crate and winched it up. Stein looked at Crosse who lit a cigarette, dragged deeply on it, then nodded through the cloud of exhaled smoke. Stein swung the winch over the water and engaged the release. The crate hit the water with a splash and immediately sank.

"That should keep his body from ever floating to the surface. Huh?" Stein inquired.

Crosse nodded. "And by the time anybody does find it, we'll have long passed from this hell into the next one, partner."

Stein shrugged and looked uncomfortably at the deck. "Yeah, I'm sorry it went down this way for ya, Les."

"Forget it."

Stein thought about that for a time and then pulled a flask from the back pocket of his slacks. He took a long drink and then passed it to Crosse, who snatched it without hesitation and partook of a couple of long pulls himself. He wiped his mouth, popped in the cigarette and then handed the uncapped flask to his partner. Stein took another swig before capping the flask and pocketing it.

"What now?"

"Now we wait."

They didn't wait long, maybe fifteen minutes, before they heard the sound of an outboard motor buzz in the distance. At first the men didn't see anything and both drew their government-issue Glock 21 pistols. As the seconds ticked by and the drone of the motor grew closer, Stein wondered if this part of their plan had been such a good idea, after all. He voiced his concerns.

"What are you squawking about now?" Crosse asked. "I swear to God, Dom, there's times I think you're paranoid or something."

"Listen, I don't much like these Cubans. I don't trust them."

"Then you should have thought about that before taking this deal. Beside, we're doing what's best for our country. You think those peckerless suits back in Washington would have the guts to do something like this? Now just keep quiet and everything will be fine. Let me do the talking. Okay?"

Stein wanted to protest but thought better of it and clammed up with a nod.

The source of the outboard motor became visible. Right at that moment Stein became more alert to all the sights and sounds around him. The salty smell of the Gulf waters seemed stronger and the cloak of humidity more intense than it had before now. At first he thought maybe the bourbon had started to work on him, but the sudden rise of bile, the churning in his stomach, the hammering of his heart in his chest and ears told him the many sensations were the culmination of one. Fear.

Stein shook it off and tried to regain his composure as the

tiny motor launch came alongside the yacht. Crosse put his pistol away and walked forward starboard. He engaged the ship-side release and kicked out the narrow, steep stairwell that came to rest a mere couple of feet above the water line. Two large Cubans dressed in black fatigues with slung machine pistols boarded first. A man in tailored slacks and flower-print shirt followed them a moment later.

Stein got closer and nodded at the man, who studied the pair a moment with his black eyes—no sign of recognition or friendliness on his face—but then a grin split his features. He had a toothy smile so white it looked stark against his dark complexion and hair.

"Andres," Crosse said, extending his hand.

The man shook it. "Permission to come aboard, gentlemen?"

"Granted." Crosse looked at Stein with a knowing smile. "We were just enjoying a drink and a cigarette. May I offer you something?"

"I would love to, but alas, we're short on time. I trust everything on board is in order?"

"Your men won't have any trouble getting the boat into Havana's port," Stein cut in. "She's totally clean."

The man they knew only as Andres nodded and then something at Stein's feet caught his eye. Everyone else turned their attention there, also, and Stein looked down to see the small trickle of blood run a jagged path between his shoes.

"Oh, yes," Andres replied. "I can see she is very clean. Was there a problem?"

"Nothing you need to be concerned about," Crosse replied. "Just a little side business we had to take care of."

Andres's smile lacked warmth now. "And I trust it's taken care of for good?"

"Yeah." Crosse and Stein held impassive expressions.

"That's fine, I will take you at your word. My men can attend to any last-minute details on their way. So if you gentlemen would come with me, Señora Fuego waits for us."

The men followed Andres into the small launch. The Cuban powered up the outboard motor and within a few minutes they were away from the yacht, its lights barely visible as they faded into the blanket of fog that seemed to settle on them with a swiftness Stein had never before experienced. Despite the fact their rendezvous had gone off without a hitch, Stein couldn't help the burning in his gut. Something told him they had just made a terrible mistake.

CHAPTER ONE

Mack Bolan studied the landscape spread out before him as the Military Airlift Command flight circled for its final approach into Guantánamo Bay Naval Base. He had an almost unobstructed view from his seat in the forward compartment of the huge Boeing 757 cargo carrier, courtesy of one of his oldest friends and allies, Hal Brognola. As director of America's most covert antiterrorist organzation, Stony Man, Brognola had requested Bolan's attention for this mission under the behest of the President of the United States. As a friend, Brognola had asked Bolan to accept the mission. And as one friend would do for another under those circumstances, the Executioner accepted.

Bolan had come to Cuba seeking one thing: information.

"It's very simple," Brognola had told him a few hours earlier in an abandoned hangar at Andrews AFB. "We need you to fly into Guantánamo Bay, question a prisoner named Basilio Melendez regarding the disappearance of Colonel Mackenzie Waterston and then act based on the information provided."

"And when you say you want me to act, you mean…"

"In whatever manner you deem the best interests of this country," Brognola replied. "Colonel Waterston was in charge of military operations related to Plan Colombia. You have some idea of that initiative?"

Bolan nodded. "The President's Executive Order 1-1-7-3-Alpha to the Secretary of State. The State Department is charged with conducting all operations, diplomatic or otherwise, necessary to eliminate the drug and arms-running activities designed to support the FARC, AUC and ELN, and to neutralize such operations deemed a terrorist threat to the U.S."

"I see you keep up with the times," Brognola said with a grin.

The Executioner shrugged. "I have my sources."

"Yeah, and it's not as though this information would be necessarily difficult to come by. Anyway, the Chief of Staff appointed Colonel Waterston to the Pentagon with instructions to monitor the activities of a number of special ops units operating out of Guantánamo Bay. Our boys down there got particularly interested when intelligence reports pointed to the possibility there was an ELN training camp operating full-time in Cuba. Up to this point, we'd never been able to confirm it."

"And this is where Melendez comes in?"

"Right." Brognola pulled the unlit cigar from his mouth, studied it a moment, then stuck it into the other side of his mouth and continued. "All Cuban prisoners were returned to their country back in the mid-nineties when we stopped detaining nationals at Gitmo. Under normal pretenses, any Cuban citizen caught there in a crime is automatically extradited to Cuban authorities."

"Why's Melendez special?"

"Just for the reasons you might have guessed. He had information on Waterston before we even asked. And it's not the first time we've encountered him. You see, Melendez has been picked up many times before. It's how we've managed to make contact with him. Normally, we turn him loose to the Cubans and they just chalk him up as a troublemaker."

"They probably break out the party hats every time he shows up on MP blotter," Bolan concluded.

"Precisely," Brognola said with a frown. "But when we heard what he had to say this last time around, we thought it was probably better to keep him detained for a while."

"Why?"

"Because Waterston's missing and his disappearance fits what Melendez told us. So far, anyway."

"How does this tie to the ELN and their training camp?"

"Don't know yet," Brognola replied. "That's what we need you to find out. Striker, the Man is getting damned nervous about this, and I can't really say I blame him. Waterston isn't the only one to disappear. Two other agents with the Defense Intelligence Agency have been MIA over a week. We have reason to believe they're connected with Waterston's disappearance. We need you at Gitmo as soon as possible. You'll use the Brandon Stone cover, a special investigator with the Criminal Investigation Division."

Now dressed in full Army greens, Bolan considered the mission ahead. He didn't have the first idea what Melendez might know, but the Cuban was his only lead to finding Mackenzie Waterston. How the DIA fit into all of it was another mystery—one he'd probably solve once he located Waterston or at least found out what happened to the missing Pentagon official—as well as the alleged ELN training camp. Brognola didn't have to tell Bolan what to do if he actually discovered the ELN operating inside Cuba. Bolan already knew what to do.

Identify. Isolate. Destroy.

"WELCOME TO GUANTÁNAMO BAY, sir," the Marine corporal said with a salute.

Bolan eyed the young Marine's name tag. "Relax, Northrop, before you strain something."

The Marine eased up and flashed a sheepish smile. "Aye, sir."

Bolan tossed his OD canvas bag in the back of the open-top M998 Hummer—making sure it remained in easy reach—and then climbed in the front. The bag had been loaded aboard the flight and carried two tools of the Executioner's trade: a Beretta 93-R pistol and the flagship pride and joy of Israeli Military Industries, a .44 Magnum Desert Eagle. Spare magazines and holsters accompanied the arms.

"This your first time in Gitmo, sir?" the Marine asked when they were under way.

"No," Bolan said. "But it's been a while."

"It's damn hot down here," the Marine said. Bolan looked at him with disbelief at first but then noticed the broad smile on the soldier's face. "Just kidding, sir. I knew you'd already figured *that* out."

Bolan nodded, acknowledged the quip with a half smile and then decided to take his own advice to lighten up. They made small talk the remainder of their five-minute drive from the airstrip to the main detention facility. The Marine indicated he'd wait until Bolan finished.

"Might be a while," the Executioner said.

"No problem, sir. I'm your escort while you're on the

base. Once we've finished here, I'll show you to the VIP billets."

Bolan nodded and moved inside. He passed through two metal detectors—requiring the removal of all his brass and medals and submission to a hand wand before they cleared him—and then signed in. Once the basics were complete, a Marine cadre escorted the Executioner to a six-by-six room occupied by a bare, gunmetal gray table bolted to the floor and two plastic folding chairs. He waited nearly ten minutes before a door with a wire-mesh window opened and a short man in neon-orange coveralls stepped into the room under heavy guard.

Bolan stood against the wall, arms folded, and gestured to the unoccupied chairs. "Sit down."

He studied Basilio Melendez as he sat. The man had black hair and a matching beard. His brown eyes possessed a beady curiosity. A pair of faint scars ran down the right side of his neck. His arms were grimy and soiled, and his fingers were stained yellow from years of continuous tobacco use.

"You're Melendez," Bolan said.

The man said nothing as he obviously perceived Bolan hadn't meant it as a question. That demonstrated he wasn't obtuse, and the Executioner knew he'd have to tread cautiously on this one. Bolan wouldn't get far being coy with Melendez; the Cuban was obviously intelligent. Besides, he'd met guys like Melendez before and he'd found he could never quite trust them. They were always studying the angles—looking for the best possible way to get ahead—and they had a knack for manipulating even the most unfavorable circumstances to their advantage given the time and opening.

"My name's Stone," Bolan began. "I'm with the Criminal Investigation Division of the United States Army. I'm told you have information that's of great interest to the U.S. government."

Melendez didn't say anything for a minute. He just sighed deeply a couple of times and peered at Bolan from under hooded eyelids. It looked as though he'd been through hell. Bolan wanted to offer him something to drink, maybe get him some cigarettes because he knew prisoners weren't permitted to smoke; *anything* that might help establish a rapport with him. That was assuming Melendez wanted to cooperate.

Abruptly, and in flawless English, Melendez said, "What do you wish to know?"

"That's a start," Bolan said, and he took a seat across from Melendez. "Tell me how you know about Colonel Waterston."

"I spend lots of time in Cuban jails," he said. "I overhear things."

"Okay, fine, but why would Waterston's name come up in a Cuban jail?"

"It seems you know very little about my country, Stone," Melendez replied. "You have heard of Havana Five?"

Bolan shook his head, although he knew plenty about them. The crime lords of the Cuban underworld controlled nearly all the illicit trades throughout the country from their power base in Havana, and had done so for the past three decades. Beginning in the early seventies, Havana Five overwhelmed the Cuban community with drugs, guns, sex and every other profitable vice imaginable. Five men, each with a specific piece of the Cuban island, pooled their resources and built the single most powerful crime cartel in history.

"Many believe they do not exist," Melendez said. "That they have never existed. But I, you see...I know better. I know these men are real. I know they exist and I know what they're capable of doing. And I know exactly what they did to your friend, Waterston."

"And what's that?"

"They killed him," Melendez said. "I hear they shot him through the head and they dumped his body."

"Where?"

"How should I know this? The men I heard talking did not say. Perhaps he was buried, perhaps he sleeps with the fishes. The point is that I hear he's dead and I believe it. And if I say more, then *I'm* dead."

Bolan shook his head. "You're under our protection now, Melendez. We're not going to throw you back into circulation again."

"You? You think you can protect me here?" Melendez scowled and emitted a scoffing laugh. "Don't be naive. Nobody is safe from Havana Five. My days are numbered, of this I'm sure."

Bolan leaned forward. "Then why come to us if you don't think we can protect you? Why not take your chances out there on the streets of your own country?"

"Because maybe in here I have a small chance. Out there, I am dead for certain."

"Why? What makes you think they even know you have this information?"

"Because the people I know, they know other people. And those people are connected to Havana Five. There is much money to be made in their business, American. And they do not like when others interfere with their profit. They will go to great lengths to keep making money, to keep their society secret."

"To the point they think they can hide an ELN terrorist

training camp inside Cuba without us finding out?" Bolan asked.

Something changed in Melendez's expression, but the Cuban quickly recovered. Not before Bolan struck a nerve, however. For a long time they shared only silence. Bolan didn't plan to say anything else. It seemed the better tactic would be to wait for Melendez to speak first, to betray something he thought Bolan didn't know about. Melendez would hold on to every ace he could in the hope of swinging a better deal down the line if things went sour or the scanty information he provided didn't pan out.

"How do you know about this?"

Bolan decided to show his own cards. "Come on, Melendez. It's what Waterston was working on. We both know it. Just like I know it's pretty unlikely you would overhear talk of Waterston's murder without mention of why he was killed. So quit pretending and talk."

And for the next half hour, Basilio Melendez talked of two men—Americans being held in a Cuban jail—who spoke of killing Waterston and how they were betrayed by someone inside Havana Five. He also told how they talked to each other in English because the cops weren't present and he was the only other one in the jail, and how he'd pretended not to speak a word of it. And they talked and talked, and they revealed how they had made a deal with someone to let them in on the location of the training camp, and instead they were betrayed and barely escaped with their necks intact. And finally they had traveled to a remote suburb of Matanzas and purposely got arrested in the hope of evading their unnamed pursuers. It was a wild story.

And Mack Bolan believed every word.

"But you never heard where this training camp was at?" Bolan asked after Melendez finished his narrative.

The Cuban shook his head. "I do not think they knew."

Bolan rose then. "I'm going to look into this, Melendez. In the meantime, I'll see about getting you moved off the base and back to the U.S. I think you'll be safer there."

"Please, Stone," Melendez said with pleading eyes. "I care nothing for myself. Like I said, I'm a dead man. But my little sister…she has been good. Please, you must protect her. I will do anything."

Bolan would only promise he'd look into it and then left the detention facility. He needed to run this new intelligence by Brognola to see what came of it before he'd know the best way to proceed. Stony Man maintained a technological resources network more advanced than anything available to Bolan in the field, and Aaron "The Bear" Kurtzman—a cybernetics wizard extraordinaire and intelligence sponge— could run through the scenarios and come back with more sound leads in one-tenth the time it would take Bolan to run down the old fashioned way.

Northrop waited outside, just as he'd promised. "Ready to go, sir?"

"Yeah, let's head to my billet," Bolan said as he got into the Hummer.

The trip across the base to the VIP billet area took less than ten minutes. Bolan climbed from the vehicle and retrieved his bag. Northrop disembarked and perfunctorily led him to the private quarters due the rank of a colonel. Northrop engaged him in another minute or so of idle chitchat, showed him where to find the basic amenities, but then obviously sensed Bolan's wish to be alone and left him to his own devices.

Bolan waited until he heard the Hummer pull away and then went to the phone on a nightstand. He picked up the receiver and froze. Hairs stood up on the back of his neck and his combat sense screamed at him to…

Duck!

The world around him became a whirlwind storm of broken glass and wood shards as the window above the nightstand exploded. Bolan catapulted his body across the bed, snatching his canvas travel bag as he landed on the opposite side and behind relative cover. He reached inside and retrieved the .44 Magnum.

Bolan crossed to a window at the corner of his billet and peered around the light gray curtain. Two men toting machine pistols made a beeline for him. Bolan pushed out the flimsy aluminum frame of the metal screen, tracked on the closer of the pair and squeezed the trigger. A 380-grain boattail slug punched through the man's chest and blew a hole out his back. He spun under the impact while still in forward motion, and his finger jerked against the trigger of the SMG. A battery of rounds hammered the dirt before man and weapon struck the ground and went silent.

The second gunner realized they had acted hastily and rushed for the cover of a large external air recirculation unit protruding from the ground. He triggered a few volleys of 9 mm rounds in Bolan's direction. The warrior ducked back to avoid perforation and the rounds either slapped the exterior wall or buzzed angrily past his head. He spun and headed out the front door, sprinting from the billet at an angle, intent on flanking his enemy.

It worked. Bolan managed to clear his line of fire and acquire his opposition in the sights of the Desert Eagle before the man could bring his own weapon to bear. Bolan triggered the weapon twice. The first round of his double-tap caught the gunner in the gut, tearing away a good part of his intestine and stopping the man in his tracks. The second .44 Magnum round hit the man at a point just above the bridge of the nose and continued until it blew out the back of his head in a gory spray of blood, bone and gray matter. The gunman toppled to the ground.

Bolan tracked a 360 with the muzzle of his weapon before relaxing somewhat. He'd been in-country less than two hours and somebody had tried to kill him. He'd have a tough one explaining that to the base Provost Marshal, let alone trying to determine how someone could have compromised his cover so quickly.

Before the Executioner could consider his next option, the sound of the phone ringing inside his billet demanded attention. Bolan sprinted back to the building and snatched the receiver from the cradle midway through the fifth ring.

"Yeah, Stone, here."

"Colonel Stone, this is Lieutenant Trundle, I'm officer of the day here at the base detention center. You were here a while ago questioning one of our prisoners."

"Right, Basilio Melendez."

"I'm sorry to report this, sir, but Melendez was just involved in an altercation with another prisoner. He was stabbed. We've transported him to the base infirmary, but he isn't expected to make it."

CHAPTER TWO

Calm settled on Inez Fuego as she stood on the rooftop terrace of her mansion and looked upon Havana Bay.

Whitecaps crested the waves that gently rolled in to splash against the beaches and ships in port. The breeze that blew steadily from the bay warmed her face. She closed her eyes for a moment and took a deep breath. How she loved her country, especially this time of year, and she thought of Natalio and how he'd loved it, too. She missed him. She missed the hours they spent up here, watching the sea as it seemed to dance across the Havana Bay horizon, seeming to twinkle under the blanket of stars. They would drink and laugh, and then make love as the sun rose at their backs. Then they would lie naked beneath a blanket and talk of their plans.

Havana Five had taken that away from her. After they sent their representatives to inform her of Natalio's death—the remaining four not even having the courage and respect to pay their respects in person—Fuego swore she would hold them responsible. For years she had remained a silent partner, pretending to concur with their decisions while she actually plotted to remove them forever. It was their incompetence that had brought about the death of her beloved Natalio, not his own, as they had tried to convince her and everyone else, and Fuego intended to make sure they didn't get away with desecrating the cherished memories of her husband.

The money and good living she had enjoyed at the hands of Havana Five made it only worse. They had ensured she receive the one-sixth payment, Natalio's legacy as a member of the five. Each of them received an equal portion, in turn, and the remaining sixth was kept in trust, reserved so that Havana Five could always remain self-sufficient even in the event one of them fell.

Natalio had been the youngest of the group; ripped from her arms at the prime age of thirty-nine. Nearly seven years had passed since his death and Fuego's soul still groaned for his presence. She had never known a stronger man. They were married when she turned sixteen, an arrangement of convenience at first. It quickly turned to something more, and their love grew and matured. Fuego had known from the beginning the nature of Natalio's business but had chosen to make their marriage work, realizing as time passed that the nature of his business did not necessarily define the nature of him. She'd found Natalio to be a loving and generous man—lending time and money to most anyone in need—and not slothful like his business partners.

Now thirty years old, she remained one of the most eligible widows in all Cuba. She had money, beauty and power; she influenced politicians and business owners; a good many Cuban bachelors longed to possess her body and affections. At nearly five-eleven—a significant height and the gift of lineage in her case—Fuego maintained a figure that looked as if it had been sculpted by Greek artisans. Her tanned, supple skin shown starkly against the cream-colored bathing suit she wore that plunged to a V at the front and exposed her entire back from waist to neck. Dark, wavy hair bounced from her head to her shoulders in a never-ending swirl of cocoa-brown with natural, reddish highlights. The angular line of her cheekbones and jaw gave her an almost Eurasian look while she retained the strong, slender nose of her Spanish roots.

Inez Fuego turned from the rail that ran the length of the parapet wall around the roof. She went to the table where she'd been engrossed in a novel by one of Cuba's most popular writers. She slid into a thigh-length robe made of silk and sat on a padded cedar lounge chair. She tucked her shapely legs beneath her bottom and poured herself a fresh margarita.

Two men emerged from the stairway ascending to the roof from an entertainment room that occupied nearly half of the third floor of the house. They were dressed in subdued silk shirts and casual slacks. Natalio had never let his house guard come off as loud and brash. He expected them to remain quiet and unobtrusive, convinced that the less conspicuous they were, the more effectively they could do their job. After his death, Fuego had decided to maintain his policy and would not let them adopt the dress like those who worked for the other four heads of Havana Five.

One of the men, Lazaro San Lujan, served as Fuego's chief enforcer. He moved with the ease and confidence of a professional, the gait of his tall and muscular body practiced. Fuego watched him approach with admiration tempered with amusement. She had always found him handsome and dashing in a sense, and she could tell that although he'd never made an amorous move toward her—before or after the death of Natalio to whom he'd always remained loyal—he wanted her. She could see it in the way he looked at her. He didn't leer like most men; San Lujan always had too much class for that. No, secretly she felt he harbored a deeper longing for her but he always kept it to himself.

Fuego noticed the disturbed look on his face. "What is it?"

"We have a problem," he replied.

"How many times have I told you that we never have a problem," she said, waving casually at a chair.

San Lujan took a seat but Jeronimo Bustos—his second in command and constant companion—remained on his feet and shadowed his boss.

"I forgot," San Lujan replied. He lit a cigarette before continuing. "Word has it our North American friends were spotted at a jail in Guijarro, just outside of Matanzas. I've sent men to check it out but so far they've come up empty-handed. The Americans apparently bribed some of the local police to move them to another location."

"So, they're willing to go as far as getting arrested to avoid us," Fuego said, mild amusement in her tone. "That's not a problem, Lazaro. That's good, in fact."

"How is that good, ma'am?" San Lujan asked.

"You still don't understand." Fuego shook her head and smiled, then pushed the sunglasses to her head so she could look him square in the eyes. She leaned forward a bit in a conspiratorial fashion. "It means they're afraid. And that is exactly what I wish them to be. As long as they think I'm after them, they'll keep their heads down and stay out of my way."

"I beg to disagree," San Lujan replied.

"Why?" Fuego looked for any sign of nervousness but she didn't detect it. Good. San Lujan had always felt open to speak his mind to her husband, and Fuego wanted him to feel the same way now. Without that honesty, Fuego knew she couldn't trust him and that would spell certain doom to her; San Lujan's advice had saved her husband's life and business many times.

San Lujan took a drag from his smoke and said, "These men…they know too much. We cannot risk them falling into the hands of people willing to listen to what they have to say."

"What they have to say is of no interest to anyone. At least no one inside the country."

"The Americans have spies here."

"True, but they're not aware we're sponsoring the ELN, and they certainly know nothing of the camp on Juventud. Not even those bastards of Havana Five know of this plan. Besides, we only need keep this quiet a little longer. And once Havana Five is eliminated and I have my revenge, then I shall give you charge of the largest business enterprise ever established in Cuba. And you will like that, eh, Lazaro?"

San Lujan didn't try to hide his pleasure at the thought. There weren't too many things that seemed to appeal to him, but the idea of nearly limitless power seemed to be one of them. He, too, had felt the story the men told of Natalio's death seemed like something less than the truth, and he'd always harbored some guilt for not being there to protect his master.

"Your plans will suffice for now," San Lujan replied. "But I still worry that your need to avenge Natalio's death will blind you to other threats. I worry that you'll fail to see what may very well be right in front of your nose."

"And you feel it's your job to protect me from those things. Yes?"

San Lujan nodded.

Fuego reached forward and patted his knee. "You're a

good and loyal man, Lazaro. I hope you never lose those qualities. They are what made you more than just an employee to my husband. They are why you were so valuable to him and why you are valuable to me now."

"Thank you."

"If you feel the Americans pose a threat, then I trust you'll find them and dispose of them properly. I don't want to know about it. It distracts me from more important matters."

"Understood."

"Is that all?"

"For now." San Lujan rose and signaled Bustos to follow.

When the two men were gone, Fuego gestured for a servant to bring her the satellite phone. She had paid a pretty penny to make sure any conversations were totally secured. While she didn't feel much of a threat from officials within the Cuban government, there were other ears belonging to the less discreet. Some of them were foreign ears working for espionage agencies in places like Mexico, Colombia and particularly the U.S. Fuego dialed a twenty-five digit number into the phone and there were several clicks and bursts of static as the communications system kicked in to encrypt the carrier wave. Fuego knew exactly where that signal led: to a similar phone of the National Liberation Army commander who oversaw the training force on Juventud Island.

He answered on the second ring. "Yes?"

"Hello, Ignacio. How are things proceeding with the new clothing line?" Despite her confidence in the secure satellite communications, Fuego had advised the leader of her private army that they would maintain ambiguous communications. They had even developed their own private language style so that each phrase had particular meaning. To anyone listening, and particularly if the communications had to go through a translator, it would sound as if they were conducting simple daily business.

"Well, thank you, ma'am. I believe we shall be ready to deliver your goods within a few weeks."

"And you will meet the quota specified in our supplier's contract?"

"I think so," he replied. "In fact, I believe we shall probably exceed it."

"That's excellent news, thank you. I will inform the board of directors at our next meeting. Please don't hesitate to call me should you need additional resources."

"I understand."

"Good day, Ignacio."

"Good day, ma'am."

Fuego hung up the phone and could barely suppress a shudder of excitement. They would be ready to commence operations against Havana Five within three days, the "few weeks" Colonel Hurtado had actually referenced during their conversation. He also wouldn't need any additional men. His confirmation of delivering the "goods" had actually meant that the weapons and other explosives she arranged to deliver to *him* were in place and had passed inspection to Hurtado's satisfaction. With the last of the pieces in place, Fuego realized she would have her revenge soon.

Yes, she would make them pay for the death of her beloved Natalio at long last.

"WE'VE BEEN COMPROMISED," Mack Bolan told Brognola.

"Lay it out for me," the big Fed replied, and Bolan did.

When he'd finished listening, Brognola said, "How's the pressure from the brass at Guantánamo Bay?"

"They're concerned," Bolan replied. "But without hard evidence to tie Melendez's death to the attempt on me, the Provost Marshal doesn't have much to go on. The base commander did take the PM's recommendation that I not be allowed off base without *official* orders from the Pentagon."

Brognola grunted. "That's no tall order. I can have that in five minutes, if need be."

"I have a better idea," Bolan said.

"I'm listening."

"I was thinking maybe I could use a little help on this one," Bolan said.

"Sounds like a plan. Hold on while I get Barb on the line."

There was a long pause and then suddenly Barbara Price's voice broke through. "Hey, Striker. What's up?"

"I was just saying that some help would be nice on this. What do you have going on with Jack and Rafael right now?"

"Nada," she said. "In fact, Phoenix Force just got back from a mission, and the guys have been in downtime for the past three days. I think they're all starting to go a bit stir-crazy."

"Why not let me take a couple of them off your hands?"

"Sure," she replied. "Hal told me what's happened down there so I can fill them in."

"Do it," Bolan said. "I'd suggest you don't send them through official channels. Is Hal still on with us?"

"I'm here," the head Fed replied.

"Don't worry about getting me those orders," Bolan said. "It's best I make tracks under my own steam. If we start waving too many official documents under the noses of the brass down here, we're likely to create a whole lot of suspicion."

"Understood."

"By the way, Bear's here with some information on Havana Five that might shed some light on the present situation there."

That didn't surprise Bolan in the least. What a single bullet had taken away from Aaron Kurtzman, the man had conquered with intelligence coupled by an indomitable spirit. Bolan had never met anyone better with computers and cybernetic intelligence than the Bear. Kurtzman's body might have been confined to a wheelchair, but his mind knew practically limitless bounds. The man kept things running in the information field for Stony Man and he'd served tirelessly, feeding the intelligence to the field teams whenever they needed it.

"I think you'll find this interesting, Striker," Kurtzman said in his customary booming voice. "Havana Five has quite a history in Cuba, as I'm sure you know. But about seven years ago they had quite a shake-up. One of their alleged members, one Natalio Fuego, was killed by Cuban authorities when he attempted to flee the country illegally. The story was that they caught him dealing in drugs, but nobody could actually prove that charge."

"Any survivors who might have an ax to grind?"

"Yeah, as a matter of fact. His widow, Inez Fuego."

"I talked to one of our CIA contacts in Havana, Striker," Price cut in. "It seems Fuego left his missus quite well to do. On the surface, she's a respected socialite and entrepreneur but under all that beauty and charm she's apparently a shrewd and ruthless businesswoman."

"But she didn't take her husband's place on Havana Five," Kurtzman continued. "In fact, there are rumors that she's actually on the outs with them."

"But she's still making money off her late husband's operations?"

"Yeah," Brognola said. "Apparently, Havana Five has a share-and-share-alike philosophy. All profits are supposedly split equally. But make no mistake about it. They're still the largest single crime syndicate ever known to operate in a country that size."

"Given the fact Melendez made it a point to mention Havana Five to you before he died," Kurtzman said, "we thought this little fact might be of interest."

"It is at that. I'll be sure to follow up on it. Now I'd better run. I have an escape to plan."

"We'll get Jack and Rafael airborne as soon as possible," Price said. "We'll probably have to fly them into Havana. Will you meet them there?"

"No," Bolan said. "I have a very specific place I want to start looking. Melendez mentioned it. I think he ran into your missing DIA guys there. Tell them to pick up some wheels and meet me in Matanzas. We have a jail to find."

CHAPTER THREE

Mack Bolan studied the northwestern perimeter of Guantánamo Bay Naval Station from the cover of a hedge.

The mugginess of the evening air caused him to sweat profusely, but the inner lining of his blacksuit slicked the moisture from his skin. Bolan considered his options. Cyclone barbed wire topped the fifteen-foot-high chain-link fence. The Navy had posted motion sensors every five feet, and Bolan knew from past experience that invisible beams of light ran parallel to the fence. Any break in those beams would cause alarms to sound at the main guard facility and bring down a wave of security forces before Bolan could make egress.

The Executioner knew his escape wouldn't be easy, but he felt his call to get off the base unofficially would raise less questions than calling down an official inquiry from Stony Man or, worse yet, the Oval Office. Bolan operated in an unofficial capacity for his government, and Brognola couldn't afford to let the President get taken to task for authorizing covert missions on a military installation.

No, he'd have to go it alone on this one—as usual.

Bolan studied the fence another minute and considered his options. Even if he decided to risk breaking the barrier, he still had no guarantee of getting past the perimeter obstacles before the MPs managed to capture him. And he sure as hell wouldn't fight them if he did. Long before Bolan had operated against terrorism, he'd gone solo against the Mafia, holding them personally responsible for their part in the death of his father, mother and sister. Even then he'd sworn never to drop the hammer on a law-enforcement officer—he considered them on the same side—and he wasn't about to compromise that policy now.

However, getting off the base without being captured didn't concern him; it's what awaited him on the other side. In the 1980s and 1990s, the DMZ between the U.S. and Cuba had existed as one of the largest minefields in the world. An Executive Order had eventually called for the removal of the mines, but Bolan had to wonder if they got them all; that didn't even address whether the Cuban government had ever disarmed the land they mined. Insofar as Bolan knew, escape via the DMZ posed too great a risk to life and limb. He'd have to find more conventional means.

The hedge line he'd used for cover ran along the perimeter road of the installation. The road terminated at three separate exits, two of them leading to the airfield and a third into Cuba, used only for official diplomatic purposes. That left one avenue of escape for Bolan, and he planned to fully exploit it. Several cays comprised the whole of the Guantánamo Bay region as well as the Guantánamo River, which ran north from its western feed at the mouth of the bay. Patrols ran at regular intervals along the river both day and night. The Executioner planned to use one of those boats as his outbound ticket.

Bolan made it to the boat ramp unmolested. He crawled the remainder of the fifty yards or so to the mouth of the river and quietly settled into the brackish water. Bolan moved through the river as silent and deadly as a crocodile. He reached one of the two patrol boats, slipped aboard on the blind side of the patrol station and found cover beneath a rear tarp tossed over a pair of equipment crates. Intelligence from Stony Man revealed patrols took off every thirty minutes with another thirty-minute rotation that kept two boats in port at all times. Bolan inspected the luminous dials of his watch. He'd have only seven minutes to wait.

And by the time the base personnel discovered he was missing, the Executioner would be deep in the heart of Cuba.

FOLLOWING A HURRIED DEPARTURE from the U.S., Jack Grimaldi and Rafael Encizo touched down in José Martí International Airport and submitted to inspection. Cuban customs officials subjected neither of them to more than a cursory inspection with paperwork and appearances impeccable, practically above reproach, but well-worn enough to satisfy their cover story. Once in-country, they quickly acquired transportation and headed toward their final destination in accordance with Bolan's instructions. Jack Grimaldi, Stony Man's ace pilot, had been a part of the Executioner's War Everlasting from nearly the beginning.

The intense-looking man accompanying Grimaldi on the mission had quite a different history to tell. Quite a while had passed since Rafael Encizo last walked on the soil of his birth country. While Encizo had always taken pride in his Cuban heritage, he owed his life and career to Stony Man. A member of Phoenix Force, one of America's elite antiterrorist teams, Encizo possessed deadly skills as a knife-fighter, demolitions expert and tactician in jungle warfare.

Encizo had passed on the rental car in favor of borrowing a loaner from a local contact. He told Grimaldi, "Rental plates will draw attention. Something we definitely don't want."

Grimaldi nodded. "It's your show, Rafe."

The men also retrieved the provisions left in the trunk by a Stony Man contact, which included a SIG P-239 for Grimaldi, a Glock Model 21 as favored by Encizo and a pair of MP-5 SD-6 submachine guns. They also had a second Beretta 93-R and an FN FNC carbine assault rifle for delivery to the Executioner upon their rendezvous. Stony Man had even included a satchel filled with enough C-4 to level a small house. The men donned their respective sidearms and concealed them in shoulder holsters before embarking on their journey to Matanzas.

Encizo took the wheel, given his familiarity with the country. Grimaldi settled into his role as shotgun and soon the two were out of Havana on a secondary road to Matanzas. Encizo gave Grimaldi a highlighted route on a comprehensive map supplied by Stony Man computers, and the pilot navigated for his comrade. Once they were away from Havana, Grimaldi rolled down the window and broke out a Cuban cigar he'd purchased at the airport. He lit the stogie, pulled it from his mouth with an admiring look and then gazed at Encizo.

"How long is it to Matanzas?"

Encizo shrugged, appeared to give it some thought, then said, "Well, I decided to take the back roads, so it'll be about two-and-a-half to three hours."

Grimaldi nodded. "I really got scant information from Hal and Barb on this mission," he commented. "What's the deal?"

The Cuban chuckled. "Join the club. From what little they said to me at the Farm, I don't think they've got a whole lot to go on. Apparently they sent Striker to Gitmo to question some Cuban national about an ELN terrorist training camp somewhere inside Cuba, and then someone killed the informant and tried to punch Striker's ticket, as well."

Grimaldi let out a low whistle. "Sounds about like the kind of situation the Sarge would get himself into."

"Yeah," Encizo said with another easy laugh. "And us, too."

"So do we know where we're going to meet him?"

"Well, he told the Farm he'd manage on his own getting off the base. Apparently he didn't want to raise eyebrows with official paperwork. His only lead is some jail on the outskirts of Matanzas. Since he wasn't all that familiar with the area, he said he'd call once he got there and then the Farm would contact us."

The beeps of a phone filled the interior of the small car, demanding attention.

"Speaking of which…" Grimaldi said. He reached to his belt and withdrew the phone.

Using a dedicated NSA satellite, Kurtzman's team had arranged an effective communications system. Not only could they use it to track their team members—Price had arranged the installation of a microchip beneath the skin over the left shoulder blade of every member—but all voice and video communications took place through the bursting of encrypted digital data under a 448-bit cipher.

"Eagle, here," Grimaldi said into the phone.

"How goes it?" Barbara Price replied.

"We're in-country," Grimaldi said. "Everything's gone pretty smoothly so far. We're on our way to the meeting place now."

"Good. Striker called and we have a rendezvous point for you. It's a place in the southern end of Matanzas called Las Cocinitas. It's apparently a cantina or something. He said he'll be waiting for you."

Grimaldi repeated the name to Encizo, asked if he knew it, and the Cuban nodded with a comment that he knew the general area. "Okay, we'll find it," the pilot said. "Is that it?"

"Yes," Price said. "He also said to tell you guys to watch yourselves, since whoever's onto him may very well be onto you, also."

"Oh, don't worry. We'll keep our eyes open."

"Good luck, guys."

Grimaldi broke the connection and replaced the phone. He took another puff from the cigar and said, "Barb says the Sarge is concerned we could be compromised since he's already had hostile contact."

"It's a strong possibility," Encizo said. "I've learned Striker's intuition on these things is almost uncanny. If he says we should stay vigilant, I'd listen to him."

MACK BOLAN COULD HARDLY say he felt in his element.

The din of Cuban music blaring from the antiquated jukebox and shouts of drunken men ogling the dayshift of house girls had left him with a slight headache. He'd reached Matanzas very early in the morning and had the good fortune to find a local clothing shop along a deserted street. Bolan paid three times the asking price for a change of clothes— he and the shopkeeper both knowing part of the exorbitant sum would buy the man's silence about seeing a North American inside Cuba—and then he changed in an alley.

Nobody in the cantina had spared him a second glance. Bolan used his limited knowledge of Spanish to order a meal of beans over a tortilla topped with red and green chilies and rice. He also purchased bottled water, not unusual in Cuba, even for the locals, and coffee.

Bolan left for a time and found a pay phone. He contacted Stony Man, gave them a cryptic message about the cantina Las Cocinitas, and then spent the remainder of the morning walking the streets before returning to the rendezvous point an hour or two later. The big American kept his head down and his body hunched to detract from his height. He was nursing his second bottle of beer when two men entered the cantina.

Bolan made a barely imperceptible gesture, but one the pair recognized; they walked casually to his table. The place seemed pretty crowded with very few seats, so Encizo asked politely to join him. Bolan nodded and they sat. A waitress came a few minutes later, took their drink and food orders without any apparent real interest in them, and was gone again in minutes.

Encizo leaned in so only Bolan and Grimaldi could hear and asked, "You okay?"

Bolan nodded. "I'm fine. Thanks for showing up."

"Wouldn't have missed it," Grimaldi replied with a grin.

"Where are things at?" Encizo asked.

"Not here," Bolan said. "You brought wheels?"

Encizo and Grimaldi nodded. "Finish your lunch, then leave before me and pull around back. We shouldn't leave together."

The food and drinks came. Encizo and Grimaldi ate mechanically and didn't say another word to Bolan. Within twenty minutes of their arrival, they paid their tab and left. The place had really filled up with the afternoon crowds who were obviously looking to escape the heat. Bolan even spotted some European tourists. Nobody paid attention to him, and he waited a full ten minutes before leaving. Grimaldi and Encizo waited in a two-door sedan that ran parallel to the alleyway. The pilot sat in back and Bolan took shotgun.

Encizo put the stick shift in gear and sped down the alleyway. He maneuvered the car onto the street, followed that road for two short blocks, then turned onto another street. For the next few minutes Encizo made a series of different turns, twice even pulling to the curb. All three men studied the mirrors and looked out windows to see if anyone appeared to be taking an unusual interest in them. After they were satisfied the coast was clear, Encizo headed toward the southernmost end of Matanzas.

Bolan filled them in on what he'd learned so far, then asked Encizo, "Any idea what jail this might have been?"

Encizo shook his head. "I know it may come as a surprise, but the crime rate in Cuba really isn't that high. In fact, a crime is only classified as an act they call *socialimente peligrosa,* dangerous or harmful to society. Felonies are basically the same here as they are in the States. Armed robbery, rape, felonious assault and murder. What's always staggered me is there are approximately sixty robberies for every hundred thousand citizens per capita. Their biggest problems are drugs, which usually stems from the sex trade."

Prostitution was the oldest profession on Earth. It had continued to be a mainstay of the criminal underworld across the board. Sex for money also led to other things like strong-arm robbery, drugs, black market sales and extortion. Cuba wasn't immune to it any more than any other country, although the heavy-handedness of Cuba's police officials and stiff penalties imposed by its courts acted effectively as an unspoken policy of no tolerance.

"My point in that little lesson on Cuba's judicial system," Encizo continued, "was that Cuban citizens like Melendez getting arrested and tossed in the clink for a few days wouldn't exactly have been headline news. But two Americans getting locked up, yeah, that would've announced like the premier of Russia making a State visit."

"That's what I thought," Bolan replied. "I wonder why they kept it quiet."

"Maybe they didn't," Grimaldi interjected. "Maybe someone kept it quiet for them?"

"Like who?" Encizo asked.

"I'm betting Havana Five," Bolan said. "There has to be some reason Melendez brought it up. He didn't pull their name out of a hat."

"That doesn't make any sense," Encizo replied. "Why would they want to keep the arrest of two Americans secret?"

"I've asked myself the same question a hundred times, and I keep getting the same answer. Melendez said the two Americans talked about killing Waterston. I'm pretty confident those two men are Stein and Crosse."

"The missing DIA agents," Grimaldi added.

"Right," Bolan said. "Seeing as Waterston was charged with finding this alleged ELN training camp, I'm betting someone in Havana Five cut a deal with Stein and Crosse, then backed out at the last minute."

"But why kill Colonel Waterston?" Encizo asked.

"I think Stein and Crosse panicked. I think they killed Waterston to keep him from disclosing their deal with a Cuban criminal organization, one that would clearly violate half a dozen laws if it went public, and they killed him to prevent that from happening."

"I see where you're going," Encizo said. "Then Havana

Five scrubs the deal and now Stein and Crosse are running for their lives. So, if we find our two DIA boys, they should lead us to the head of the operation."

Bolan nodded. "Right."

"Pretty sharp, Sarge," Grimaldi said.

Encizo turned down an unpaved, nondescript street and pulled up in front of a single-story, adobe-style building. Roof support poles of rough, unfinished wood protruded from the front of the building. Visible cracks cut spiderweb patterns through the front facade, which was painted brown and olive drab. The faded outline of a shield filled with blue, red and yellow markings—the symbol of the Cuban police— covered the windowless front of the building.

Bolan looked at Encizo. "Police station?"

"Substation, actually," Encizo said. "I spotted a sign on the main road back there and decided to take my chances. There aren't that many fully equipped jails in the area. Maybe we'll get lucky."

"Better we should wait out here?" Grimaldi asked.

"Yeah. It'll look much less suspicious if I'm alone."

As Encizo started to get out of the car, Bolan said, "Watch your back, Rafe."

He nodded, asked for five minutes, then got out. The Cuban straightened his clothes and ran his fingers through his freshly greased hair as he climbed the three steps. He looked back at Bolan and Grimaldi with a wink before he pushed through the flimsy screen door. Bolan watched as he entered and then turned his attention to keeping vigil on the street, with instructions to Grimaldi to do the same.

If trouble came knocking, they would be ready.

CHAPTER FOUR

The acrid smell of burned fiber filled the cramped bathroom of the run-down motel, the result of a smoldering cigarette butt between Leslie Crosse's fingers.

Crosse could barely stand this wretched humidity. It sure was a hell of a lot hotter here than in Washington, and for a moment, he wished he were back there now. This hadn't turned out as they'd planned. He and Stein had gotten to Cuba as planned, but that's when it all went very wrong. Andres advised them that Inez Fuego didn't want to see them—something about their being sloppy and careless—and next thing he knew, he and Stein were running for their lives.

Stein believed Andres to be at the heart of the betrayal, but Crosse didn't agree. This went well beyond him; Andres was nothing more than a lackey. Fuego had either come to this decision on her own or someone made it for her. There couldn't be another explanation. At least, that's what Crosse kept telling himself. It didn't matter much either way, since they could now write off any hope of finding the ELN terrorist training camp.

"*¡Andele!*" a deep voice boomed just outside the door, followed by a mad thumping on it.

Crosse jumped, woken from his daydreaming. He rose from the toilet seat, took another drag off the cigarette, screwed his face with the taste, then tossed it in the bowl and flushed. He hadn't even bothered to take a dump, since he'd been so preoccupied with their present situation. Well, he was experiencing constipation anyway by refusing to drink tap water, and the cops wouldn't buy them any bottled, goddammit. He and Stein managed to come up with about seventeen hundred in cash between them; not enough for a get out of jail free card, but damn sure enough to bribe the local yokels into letting them wait out a few days in a hotel.

Crosse opened the door and found himself face-to-chest with the biggest of their trio of guards. The guy's shirt was about two sizes too small for him in the sleeves and his muscular arms threatened to rip the seams. He had unkempt, rather long hair, and his teeth were dark and stained from too much booze and cigarettes and not enough brushing. Not that Crosse intended to point that out.

The man gave him a studious look, his face hard and unyielding, and then his eyes softened a bit and he jerked his head in the direction of the couch. Basically, they had made their prisoners eat, sleep and sit on that damn couch while the three guards spelled each other for trips to the single bedroom with a queen-size mattress. Craftsmen had obviously made that couch from splintered wood and old springs, and then covered it in the roughest fabric known to man.

"What gives with Gorilla Face?" Stein asked Crosse, using the nickname they'd dubbed for the big cop.

The fact none of the guards seemed to speak English made it simpler for them to communicate freely. They agreed not to make mention of very specific things, but general conversation didn't seem of much consequence to the guards, and they usually reserved any more secretive talks until night fell and the guards all went to sleep—even the ones who were supposed to be out watching in the front room during their shift. Stein had quipped how the lack of discipline really disappointed him, how he'd expected more from Cuba's finest.

"Aw, I don't know. He's got a stick up his ass or something," Crosse replied.

"When do you think we're going to get out of here?"

Crosse shrugged dejectedly. "How the fuck should I know? I look like some kind of Oracle to you or something?"

Stein shrugged. "Just wondered if maybe you had an idea."

"I don't."

"Fine."

"Good."

Crosse let the silence lapse between them awhile. He really admired Stein in a lot of ways, but sometimes—as a partner quite often does—Stein irritated the living shit out of him. He felt bad taking his foul mood out on the guy, the one guy who had stuck with him for the past ten years. No matter what happened, no matter what kind of shit went down, Stein had been there. Stein backed him when the ethics committee questioned him during a shooting board inquiry, and again one other time when his superiors questioned him about missing drug evidence. In both cases, Crosse had actually been clean. In fact, Crosse had never accepted graft, never brutalized a suspect—at least not that any cop would have considered justifiable. And while he'd bent a few rules, he couldn't ever remember having abused his authority.

But now he couldn't help the uncertainty and irritation of

knowing he'd crossed the line; not once but three times in the past twenty-four hours. They had made a deal with a known criminal in a foreign country, killed an American military officer and stolen top-secret documents belonging to the government. Now, to rub salt in the wound, they had to remain cooped up in this stinking hell-hole with these goat farmers.

"Sorry," he muttered after a time. "I'm a little bent about this shit."

"Forget it," Stein said. "You know, I've been letting this run through my mind since we hooked up with Andres out there. It just doesn't add up, Les. None of it adds up."

"It seems pretty simple to me. We stepped on our dicks. We got sloppy and someone decided to renege on our deal with Fuego."

"You mean Fuego reneged."

"No," Crosse countered, "I mean someone reneged. I don't think she had anything to do with it. I think somebody else made the decision. Maybe she decided to go along with it, but it wasn't her idea."

"What makes you think so?"

"You read the same case files I did on the criminal elements down here. You don't get very far in a business like hers if you go around screwing everybody you meet. She's always had a good reputation as an honest businesswoman, just like her old man."

"Yeah, sure," Stein said. "Look where that got him."

Crosse waved at a big fly with irritation as he replied, "Whatever. My point is if she decided to stick it to us then she did it under the advice of someone else. Not only is going back on your word in her business considered dishonorable, it's a surefire way to gain some very unwanted publicity."

"Just the kind she can't afford," Stein interjected.

"Right."

"So, what do we do now?"

"I say we sit back and wait a little while longer. They'll give up looking for us pretty fast, I think. Once they do, and assuming we can get out from under the thumbs of these Neanderthals, we ought to be able to find someone who can smuggle us back to the country."

"We'll have a lot of explaining to do," Stein said.

"I'd rather have to explain in front of an inquiry board than a Cuban magistrate. How about you?"

Stein merely nodded his agreement.

"Anyway, it won't be too much longer." Crosse experienced a suddenly dry and violent cough. He'd have to get some water soon or he might start pissing blood.

Not too much longer, he thought.

THE FOUR MEN LOITERING in a late-model sedan half a block down on the opposite side of the street tripped Mack Bolan's senses into high alert.

"See that car?" Bolan asked Grimaldi.

The pilot leaned forward in the seat, scrutinized the occupants, then nodded. "They weren't there before."

"I saw it park there ten minutes ago with only the driver. Now I count four inside."

"I smell trouble," Grimaldi replied.

"Yeah." Bolan kept one eye on the vehicle as he looked in the direction of the police station. "Blast it, Rafael. What's taking so long?"

CONVINCING THE SUBSTATION commander at the Cuban jail that he was nothing more than a consulate-appointed attor-

ney for the America prisoners proved a harder task than
Rafael Encizo thought it would be.

In talking with first the cops and then their commandant,
Encizo learned to take anything they said at face value. He
could tell almost from the beginning that they weren't forth-
coming and didn't plan to be any time soon. The Cuban warrior had a careful balance to maintain; he needed to keep them
talking while acting subservient. Attorneys didn't command
the same respect in Cuba as the U.S. Well, maybe it wasn't
the attorneys as much as the "civil rights" of prisoners. The
majority of the populace looked upon criminals as the low-
est form of life, and they weren't afforded more than accom-
modations.

"What has happened to my clients?" Encizo asked as respectfully as he could manage.

"They have been moved to a different location for their…
safety."

The commandant was a small, thin man with curly hair
cut close and streaked with gray.

"You believe they're in danger?"

"What American who is arrested in Cuba isn't in danger?"
That caused him to laugh at what he had to have considered
to be a pretty good joke. "Anyway, for now we have them secured and they aren't going anywhere."

"Well, I must speak with them. The American government
has insisted they receive proper counsel."

"And why would the Americans be so concerned about
these two men?"

Encizo had to think furiously for an answer. He'd probably let the cat out of the bag a little too soon. Encizo hoped
for a faster turnaround but forthrightness didn't seem like a
familiar concept to the commandant. He dealt with thugs and

rapists and other such elements every day. He would therefore be suspicious and untrusting of everyone, despite how honorable their intentions might seem.

"It's not the Americans the magistrate worries about," Encizo said. "He's concerned this will draw attention from the press and other undesirables. He wants to make sure no disinformation is sown, particularly back to the American government."

"And what of it?" the commandant replied. "I have no interest in what the Americans think, particularly the government. They have no jurisdiction here, and their political concerns are no concerns of mine."

"Maybe not," Encizo said. "But they are to the magistrate and I may report back to him that you were fully cooperative?"

Something dangerous glinted in the commandant's eyes, only for a moment, but Encizo pretended not to notice. He realized the risks of such a veiled threat, but it hadn't escaped the notice of either of them this wasn't exactly the Mecca of assignments. Most people of influence and power considered Guijarro the armpit of Matanzas—not that it had any greater or lesser qualities than many of the poverty-ridden suburbs around it—but a magistrate's wishes would always win out over those of a policeman.

"You may thank the magistrate," the commandant finally replied. "And tell him I will be most cooperative. However, I'm afraid I cannot disclose the location of the prisoners at present. Their safety is my responsibility. I will need a signed writ from the magistrate before I can give you that information."

Encizo realized an end had come to more diplomatic methods. Somewhere in the conversation, he heard the two officers who'd been in the station leave on a disturbance of some type. That left them alone in the office, and Encizo decided the time had come to implement more effective means of soliciting cooperation. In an instant he launched from his chair and came across the commandant's desk. Encizo produced his Glock and grabbed a fistful of the commandant's shirt in one, smooth motion. Encizo hauled him out of his chair and stretched him belly-first across the desk to unbalance him.

"I've been nice about this long enough," Encizo told the commandant. "Tact is over and now you're going to tell me *exactly* where you're holding those two Americans."

"Wha—!" the commandant began and then he emitted a squeal of outrage. "You are not an attorney!"

Encizo grinned. "You think? Now I'm giving you a chance to make this easy on yourself. I won't kill you, but I'll definitely leave you hurting if I don't start getting answers."

Oddly enough, the smug and indifferent expression the commandant wore a moment earlier had disappeared. "Okay, okay!"

"Well?"

"They are being held by my men in a room we rent for such things," the man replied so quickly Encizo almost couldn't understand him. "They are under heavy guard, though. They will not allow you to get by with my authorization."

"I'll manage," Encizo said. "Where?"

The commandant gave him the name and address of an apartment complex. Encizo didn't know the place, but the name of the street rang familiar enough that he knew he could find it easily. Encizo looked eye to eye with the commandant, searching for signs of deception, but saw only fear and doubt. The guy figured Encizo wouldn't keep his word. Of course,

Encizo wouldn't have killed the man—just as he promised—and to hurt him now wouldn't be of much benefit. He knew the commandant couldn't tell him anything more of use.

"Looks like your lucky day," Encizo said.

Before either could say another word, a commotion outside the commandant's office drew their attention. Grimaldi burst through the rickety doorway, pistol in hand and face flushed. "We got company."

Encizo nodded and released the commandant. He backed out of the room and kept the muzzle of his pistol in the commandant's direction. Encizo wouldn't have put it past the guy to shoot him in the back if the opportunity presented itself.

The pair reached the door, and Encizo peered out in time to see the Executioner go EVA a millisecond before the windshield of their vehicle imploded under a hail of autofire. The Cuban turned his attention to the source of the firing and saw a car screech from the curb and head directly for the jail.

"Looks like we might have a slight delay," Encizo announced.

THE EVER SO PERCEPTIBLE PUFF of smoke from the tailpipe of the sedan stood as the only clue to Bolan the crew planned to make a move. In that brief lull between the decision and action of their enemy, Bolan instructed Grimaldi to go inside and alert Encizo. The sedan suddenly lurched from the curb just as the soldier had expected. Sunlight glinted on the muzzles of automatic weapons protruding from the passenger windows.

Bolan had set the door ajar a minute earlier, anticipating that kind of move, and his forethought prevented the aggressors from perforating him with a hail of bullets. He rolled out of the vehicle and went prone on the sidewalk, rolling onto his back long enough to slide both Beretta 93-Rs from beneath the folds of the thin, tattered poncho he'd purchased that morning.

Slugs whizzed overhead and ricocheted off the buildings, while others audibly slapped the driver's side of Encizo's borrowed jalopy with metallic plinks. Bolan waited until he heard the squeal of tires and opening of doors before he dropped to one knee behind the solid, metal body of the old clunker. Bolan braced his forearms over the trunk of the car, took aim at the gunners as they went EVA, and squeezed the triggers simultaneously.

The Berettas were both set to 3-shot mode, which in the hands of the Executioner were as effective as the submachine guns being toted by his enemies. A trio of 9 mm Parabellum rounds took the first unlucky gunner in the chest, punching red holes in his sternum, exiting out his back, leaving a crimson spray on the door. The impact sent him spinning and dumped him face-first on the rough pavement. The other burst of rounds shattered the back window and sent the others racing for cover to avoid the deadly glass shards.

In his periphery, Bolan saw his allies join him. Encizo fired from a standing position above the roof of the car and took out his man with a head shot over the roof of the enemy's sedan. The remaining gunner tried to move away from the vehicle and make a beeline for cover, but Bolan and Encizo caught him simultaneously with unerring accuracy. The man danced under the onslaught as slugs drilled through his stomach and chest. Encizo finished it with a round to the neck. Hot blood and tissue erupted from the wound and left a gaping hole where the throat had been. The man toppled to the ground.

Grimaldi focused his attention on the driver. The windshield splintered under the first two rounds, a large part broke away on number three, and two more succeeded in finishing the job. A geyser of blood and brain matter splattered the dash and side window as the driver's head exploded. The echo of gunfire died and in the near distance the wail of sirens signaled the approach of the Cuban police.

"Looks like the commandant got to a phone," Encizo told Bolan as he reached inside the vehicle from the passenger side and popped the trunk.

"I'll fret later," Bolan replied. He jerked his thumb at the car. "Better not to take this. It'll draw too much attention."

"Or this," he said, holding up the satchel filled with C-4 plastique with all the trimmings. "We should be able to lose them on foot."

Once they made some distance, Bolan asked, "You get a location on Stein and Crosse?"

"Yeah," Encizo said with a nod. "They're holed up in a motel not too far from here."

"They're under guard, I assume."

"Of course."

Grimaldi shook his head and groaned. "Our luck just keeps getting better."

"I suppose you realize that commandant will call in reinforcements to ambush us at the motel," Encizo said.

A ghost of a smile crossed Bolan's face. "I'm counting on it."

CHAPTER FIVE

Hal Brognola sat in his office and tried to maintain his cool.

It wasn't often the President of the United States decided to call a personal meet, and particularly not on Stony Man's home turf. The Farmhouse and Annex remained top secret, their locations known by a select few, and the Man rarely opted to pay them a personal visit. With the press and staff constantly nipping at his heels, such a request could compromise the Farm's security.

On this occasion, however, the President had informed Brognola he'd be traveling incognito and even the Secret Service wouldn't accompany him. This didn't worry the head Fed any, since he knew the President came under escort of three of the most capable warriors ever fashioned by hellfire: together they formed the urban Able Team. The President's unconventional request worried Brognola simply because he knew him to be a pragmatist. If he was requesting a personal meeting, then that meant it was damned important.

Brognola left his office and climbed the old secret stairwell that led to the first floor of the farmhouse. Maybe a brisk

walk around the grounds would take his mind off the upcoming meet. Beside the fact, more pressing matters on
Striker's mission—a mission he was sure had prompted the
Man's request for a personal meeting—demanded his immediate attention.

So far, they didn't have much to go on. The fact someone
had tried to terminate the Executioner within hours of his arrival at Guantánamo Bay perplexed the Stony Man chief
most of all. Nobody outside of immediate personnel knew
Brognola had contacted Bolan about the potential troubles
brewing in Cuba, let alone they would have gathered enough
details to pick up Bolan's scent, track him to a secured U.S.
naval installation and then kill him. That left only one possible answer: somebody on the inside of the military prison
at Gitmo knew Bolan had questioned Melendez and decided
to make sure the Executioner took that information to the
grave.

But who and why? Those were two questions for which
Brognola didn't have answers. Even Barbara Price and Aaron
Kurtzman had been left at a loss for suggestions. Well, they
sure as hell needed to find out. And as Bolan had pointed out,
the fact somebody was willing to risk an open killing meant
there was probably merit to what Melendez had told them before his untimely demise.

Brognola walked the perimeter of the wood line and considered their decision to send Grimaldi and Encizo; he
wouldn't second-guess Bolan's request. The Stony Man chief
had learned long ago not to question the men in the field.
They were hardened and experienced warriors who knew
what was what. They were there under the direst of circumstances, not Brognola or Price, hence his reason for a hands-
off policy when it came to making operational decisions at

the field level. Brognola never armchair quarter-backed an operation before and he didn't plan to start now.

Unfortunately they had minimal intelligence up to this point. Operations inside Cuba were always difficult, at best, since they couldn't operate as freely as in other countries. Moreover, the political waves created by the waning health of Cuba's leader caused increasing unrest in the country's citizens. There were social underpinnings to consider, as well, and the talk in certain circles of its bleak socioeconomic and political future wouldn't make things easier for Bolan and his crew. Fortunately, money could still do quite a bit of talking down there, and in context they had an almost limitless supply of cash in the coffers if the need arose for it.

Movement on Brognola's right penetrated his train of thought as effectively as a lithe form penetrated the tree line.

"You startled me," Brognola declared.

Barbara Price half smiled. "Maybe you're losing your edge."

"Maybe I was only kidding and I just wanted you to think you took me off guard."

"Whatever gets you through the day," she said.

They didn't often trade in this type of playful banter, but Brognola guessed Price had indulged in the same recent edginess he experienced at hearing of the President's imminent arrival.

"Out trying to clear the old noggin some?" he asked.

She nodded. "I suppose. You headed back to the farmhouse?"

"Yeah."

"Mind if I walk with you, cool down?"

"Not at all."

Price did a little deep breathing before saying, "This deal

with Striker's recent discoveries in Cuba had me racking my brain most of the morning. I thought maybe a jog through the woods might shake loose a prophetic moment."

"Yeah," Brognola said. "I decided to take a walk in hope of finding an epiphany of my own. I assume you finished your dissemination on Havana Five?"

"Yes. And before you ask, I didn't find much, not of consequence anyway."

"Maybe what we gave Striker will be enough," Brognola said. "Between him and Rafael, they'll figure out the rest."

"Sounds like he's still convinced the two Americans Melendez overheard are our missing DIA agents."

"Right. What I can't figure is why they would have killed Colonel Waterston."

"Doesn't seem to fit the profile of either of them," Price said. "I took a thorough look into their dossiers. Stein and Crosse were both decorated veterans of Desert Storm, ranked high in their respective classes at the federal law enforcement training center and Quantico, and outside of obviously trumped-up charges a couple of times in Crosse's career, neither of them has been in any type of trouble. I even talked to a former supervisor at the DIA. He says they were top of the line."

"Sounds like a couple of regular poster boys for the DIA," Brognola replied with a grunt.

"Indeed."

"Okay, so we can assume one of two things. Either what Striker got from Melendez was flawed in some way or Stein and Crosse really did kill Waterston. If we say the latter scenario's the most likely right now given the fact Waterston's MIA, then that would indicate an act of desperation."

"Or an accident," Price pointed out.

"I hadn't considered that possibility," Brognola admitted. "That's good. Now maybe we're getting somewhere. But even if we're correct, and right now it's all just conjecture, that still doesn't explain how Havana Five figures into all of this."

"Well, Melendez definitely tied those things together when Striker interrogated them," Price said. "Melendez was betting his life on it, which means there has to be a connection."

"Right," Brognola said. "And it's our job to find out what that is. Striker's operating on thin intelligence. We need to come up with something solid, and quickly."

"Well, there's no guarantee they'll be able to figure out what's going on even if they find Stein and Crosse," Price said. "All we can do is our best to find the answers Striker needs. I won't rest until we do that."

"I know." Brognola looked in the direction of the farmhouse with absence. "We'd better get inside and cleaned up. The Man will be here within the hour."

PER BROGNOLA'S INSTRUCTIONS, Able Team escorted the President to the War Room as soon as they arrived.

Brognola and Price awaited him there, and Able Team made a quick exit to nearby posts that were out of the room but still provided them access to the Man in less than ten seconds. Not that they were overly concerned. Nobody knew of the President's visit and he planned to be here for less than a half hour.

"Hal, I know you're all pretty busy," the President began. "I appreciate your meeting me on such short notice."

"Not at all, sir," Brognola said. "It's never a trouble. Although…" Brognola let his sentence trail off, thinking better of it.

"Although you're surprised I'd call a meeting here," the President replied. "Right?"

"It had crossed our minds, sir," Price said coolly and professionally.

"I know it's unorthodox, and normally I wouldn't have risked the security nightmare I'm sure this creates," the President said. "But I felt this was the best way."

"The best way to do what exactly, Mr. President?" Brognola asked.

"To clarify the importance of this mission. You see, ever since the Cuban missile crisis, our relations have been less than stellar with Castro. I know that's hardly a surprise, maybe not even worth mentioning. What you might not know is that one of the main purposes of Plan Colombia was to completely eradicate relations whereby Cuba permitted terrorist training of Colombian guerrillas inside their boundaries. And while it's always been a big risk on Castro's part given our military presence there, it's been an even larger one in recent years.

"I believe Cuba might be on the verge of its very own civil war. It's my hope if this occurs that the United States will be poised to suggest peace talks rather than permit the outbreak of armed conflict between Cuban citizens and their government so close to U.S. interests. If we're successful in that, it could mean friendly political ties between two countries who have been bitter enemies for more than sixty years."

"I see what you're saying, Mr. President," Brognola said. "This is much bigger than any of us."

"It is," the Man confirmed. "So you see, there's more at stake here than I believe either of you might realize. I thought, especially under these most recent circumstances, I at least owed it to you to lay my cards on the table. The disappearance of Colonel Waterston is particularly critical. It's a little known fact Waterston and I served together during Vietnam. He was poised to be our olive branch when and if the time came. There were, or rather are, some men in Castro's regime who respect Waterston because he's a military man. He speaks their lingo, you see, and frankly so do I. They like that. And being military men they're beginning to see Castro as old and weak. They figure it's time for a change in the country, and they figure if whoever succeeds Castro isn't up to the challenge, it'll be up to them to make a better way of life for everyone in their country."

"And you think they see the United States as pivotal to making that happen, sir?" Price asked.

"More than that, Barbara," the President replied. "Crucial would be the more apt word. You see, whatever happens here on out could very well determine the fate of our future relations with the Cubans. I'm not trying to add pressure to you, either personally or to your men in the field. I also know your man didn't have to take this job, although I don't mind saying I'm awfully glad he's on our side."

Brognola couldn't resist a wry grin and a chuckle. "I'm sure he'd appreciate knowing that, sir."

The President nodded. "This isn't my way of tightening the thumb screws, you understand. All I'm trying to do is to impart the fact we're at a very critical juncture. It's important we recover our men if they're in Cuba, particularly Waterston, and it's even more important we do it as quickly and quietly as possible. What we can't afford to do is to expose our supporters there. If Castro found it, there would be public hangings."

"I'm sure," Brognola said. "But, Mr. President, it's very important *you* understand that right now we have it on pretty good authority that Colonel Waterston might be dead."

The President blanched and his expression went flat. Brognola hadn't meant for that little fact to come out quite so indelicately, but there weren't many ways to give the most powerful man in the free world bad news.

"I'm sorry to hear that," the President finally replied after a very long and very uncomfortable minute.

"I don't know what to say, sir," Brognola replied.

The man shrugged. "What can you say? I can only hope this is one of those times where you're absolutely wrong. Does your man in Cuba know?"

"He's the one who gave that to us originally."

"Mr. President," Price interjected, "you can be assured we're doing everything possible to confirm or deny the information. But Striker's operating off scant intelligence as it is. He's playing a lot of this by ear right now."

"Well, I don't normally make it my business to poke my nose into field operations," the President replied. "And I appreciate your candor. But under the circumstances, I'm afraid I'll have to ask you to provide me with as many details as possible as soon as you get them, confirmed or unconfirmed."

"Of course, sir," Brognola replied. "Would it be terribly out of line if I asked why?"

The President appeared to consider Brognola's request a moment and then replied, "I suppose that's a fair question. You must understand that under no circumstances will I permit the outbreak of a full civil war in Cuba without taking significant action. And when I say action, I mean the full-scale military kind. If such hostilities were to ensue and we had exhausted every political remedy to abate them, I would be forced to order the U.S. Marines at Guantánamo to do whatever they had to, to protect the U.S. and its boundaries."

"War?" Brognola asked. "With Cuba?"

The President cleared his throat before replying, "If necessary, yes. A Cuban civil war would threaten an already uneasy balance of power in the Western hemisphere. We cannot afford that. Peace in this region is too important to the greater interests of this country and its populace. I don't want another missile crisis, but I don't want a repeat of 9//11, either."

"I suppose to some degree I can understand this rather precarious position you're in, Mr. President," Brognola said. "But an all-out declaration of war against Cuba seems, well…"

"Don't beat around the bush, Hal," the Man said. "I've always held your opinions in high regard. Say what you have to say."

"I was simply going to say that it seems pretty extreme," Brognola replied.

"Extreme is the situation at hand," the President. "And it may call for extreme measures."

"But we're not there yet," Brognola said.

"Right."

"And you're willing to give us some more time to hammer this out."

"Of course, Hal." He rose. "And now if you'll excuse me, I have to get to Camp David."

Brognola and Price rose accordingly and walked the President, accompanied by Able Team, to the nondescript SUV that awaited him.

Once he departed, Brognola and Price returned to the War Room.

"Barb," Brognola said, "we need to pull everything we have on the situation down there in Cuba. Names, faces, the whole kit and caboodle. I want to know what we're up against as soon as possible."

"Understood," Price said with a nod.

"Also, get Able back here as quick as possible and put Phoenix Force on full alert."

"You're not going to give Striker and crew a chance to resolve this?"

"Certainly," Brognola said. "But we both know if this thing goes south we need to have a backup plan. I don't want to get caught asleep at the wheel on this."

"What about Waterston?" she asked.

"I don't think there's much we can do to confirm his status. We'll have to rely on Striker to get that information. We should focus our efforts on the political end of this. If we stick our finger in the dike, I want it to hold, not spring another leak somewhere else. Also, I want you to pull all the plugs with the NSA. I want to know everything we have on this Havana Five, past or present. Call in favors, go over heads, threaten jobs, but do whatever you must to get us some answers. I want to know who's running the operation down there and what they're into. Maybe we'll shake something loose, get a line on this ELN training camp."

"And if we don't?"

"At least we'll get close enough to start making people nervous. Maybe they'll make a mistake and expose themselves in some way."

"Then what?"

"Then we'll send Striker their way to do what he does best."

CHAPTER SIX

Mack Bolan studied the layout of the two-story motel through binoculars. An innocent inquiry by Encizo revealed the motel had no air conditioning, and these July days were sweltering in Cuba. Soon the sun would start to set and with the dissipation of heat would come drowsiness for the occupants.

Dusk or dawn was the best time to conduct a military assault against any type of stronghold under any type of guard. Such an assault wouldn't be difficult under the circumstances if what the Cuban police official had told Encizo was true. The men were being guarded by three officers. But if his plan worked there would be a lot more men there in a short period of time, and a lot of cops with a motel filled to capacity would create just the kind of confusion he needed.

Still, Bolan didn't intend to assume either way—he liked to deal with the facts.

He swung the binoculars from his view of the motel entrance to Encizo's position approximately fifty meters down the street. The Phoenix Force veteran held position inside a primer-gray 1984 Olds Ninety-Eight they procured from a vendor's used lot. The vehicle would have been a find to some car enthusiasts, but it had the worn and unobtrusive look required to divert attention. Encizo sat low behind the wheel, head canted back with sunglasses to hide his open eyes. To any other observer, he would appear as just another local copping a siesta.

Bolan grinned behind the field glasses and then swung them past the motel entrance in the opposite direction. He could barely make out the lines of Jack Grimaldi. The pilot sat at a table in a sidewalk café adorned in the ridiculous poncho and hat Bolan had purchased early that morning. Grimaldi would serve as eyes and ears, with Encizo providing backup. This was Bolan's show and his alone, and when he'd pointed that out, neither man argued with him.

Bolan studied the street, which seemed totally devoid of movement. In the past twenty minutes of his reconnaissance, he'd noted a half dozen cars had driven by. It seemed like things should be busier—much as they had been at Las Cocinitas—but surprisingly there didn't seem to be much activity in this part of town. Then he remembered it was Saturday and this was the calm before the storm. Very shortly, the place would be teeming with people and the entire area would turn into a hubbub of activity.

Bolan stowed the binoculars and then stepped from the darkness of the rickety building into the twilight, now fading into night. The Executioner dashed across the street and reached the motel entrance unseen. He took a quick look inside, taking in the layout of the lobby—just as Encizo had described it. A petite Cuban girl, no older than sixteen or seventeen, maintained the front counter. Encizo indicated he'd spied a larger person in an adjoining office, male, maybe mid-to late-forties. Bolan figured a father-daughter team, although such an age difference in a married couple wouldn't have surprised him.

Bolan opened the door and moved silently indoors. He crossed the lobby in three steps and withdrew the Beretta 93-R from shoulder leather. The girl looked up just as he reached the counter. She sucked in a breath and her jaw dropped, but a finger to his lips while he kept the pistol in plain view extinguished any thoughts she might have to cry out. Bolan vaulted the counter and gently steered the girl into the office by the arm. A man scribbling furiously at the desk looked up and surprise mixed with panic registered on his face. At that proximity, Bolan could see he was older than the Executioner originally surmised. The man started to speak to Bolan in Spanish.

"Quiet," Bolan ordered him. He softened his voice as he put the girl in a chair against a nearby wall.

"*¡No lastimar por favor a mi tío,*" she said. "He no speak English."

So he was her uncle. "I won't hurt him. Will you tell him that?"

She did, and then Bolan said, "There are two men upstairs, Americans, under police guard. Yes?"

The girl nodded.

"How many?" he asked.

"What?"

"How many policemen?"

She held up three fingers and replied, "Three."

Bolan nodded. It looked like the commandant had told Encizo the truth. The three cops weren't really the problem, though, as much as the fact he had no idea on the conditions of Stein and Crosse. If they were injured in some way, a quick and quiet escape was out of the question. Bolan would simply have to run the plays as planned and look for the best results.

The Executioner noted a phone on the old man's desk. He unsheathed a Ka-Bar combat knife on his web belt and with a rapid slash cut the line. He told the girl to wait five minutes and not to come out of the office before then, and closed the door behind him. He took out the cord on the lobby extension and the pay phone against a dirty, brown wall. Bolan started toward the steps and then froze in his tracks when the clack of decorative shells hanging from the front door sounded.

He ducked into an alcove and watched with interest as four men entered the motel. From their mode of dress, Bolan could tell they weren't here for a room. He instantly identified the leader of the pack by his cocky walk, short and stocky build, and ridiculously oversize mirrored sunglasses. The man shifted inside the linen sports coat he wore and Bolan saw a gun butt peak from beneath it. The other three men who accompanied him were bruisers who all carried themselves like men used to being armed carry themselves.

Bolan considered taking them then and there but decided to hold off. While the possibility seemed remote, their presence may have had little or nothing to do with his mission. The Executioner didn't believe in coincidence, and if these men were members of either the Cuban police or Havana Five, then things were going as planned. In either case, they hadn't stopped by for a little chat—at least not packing the kind of hardware they were.

For a minute or so they loitered in the lobby and waited, but when nobody showed to greet them a brief conversation between the trio and their leader led them to some decision, because they split into pairs with two headed to the elevator and the other pair by stairs. Bolan still couldn't be sure who he was dealing with but he didn't think these men were cops. Police officers, even in Cuba, would have bothered to investigate a desk with no clerk.

Bolan waited a full minute, then headed to the stairs and quietly opened the door. He stuck his head through the doorway and looked up the stairwell. In the dim lighting, a shadow was visible on the wall. Smart. They had left a lookout on the stairs. Bolan would have to deal with that first before he could get down to business. The soldier pushed inside the doorway, closed the door behind him and ascended the stairs.

He rounded the midfloor landing and crouched. The sentry had wedged his body between the half-open door so he could monitor the second-story hallway. That left him blind to anyone approaching from the stairs. Obviously, the guy hadn't done this kind of thing before. The Executioner took the second flight of stairs as quiet as a mouse and grabbed the guy's collar. He yanked down and back, which effectively took the sentry off balance. A hard blow behind the man's right ear finished the job. Bolan wouldn't take any lives at this point unless absolutely necessary. He didn't think these men were policemen, but he wouldn't risk killing a cop.

Bolan dragged the body to the corner of the landing and stuffed it into a janitor's closet. The door had no lock, rather just a flimsy bolt on the outside to hold it closed. It wouldn't prove much of a barrier, but it might provide enough time for Bolan to complete his mission here. The Executioner went to the door, looked onto an empty hallway, then reared back when he heard the ding of an elevator bell.

After checking his flank, Bolan opened the door a crack

and tried to see as far down the hallway as he could. Two men, the pair he'd seen take the elevator downstairs, rounded the corner. The third man passed the door where Bolan stood guard, stopped a moment as if he were planning to get his partner, then seemed to change his mind when he spotted the other two. The threesome converged on a door near the end of the hallway. The leader of the group immediately pounded on the door and yelled in Spanish. His guns moved to either side as he pulled his pistol and kept it low and behind his right thigh.

Bolan heard the door open. The leader smiled, made some quiet comment, then leveled his pistol at whoever answered and squeezed the trigger. That one act of cold-blooded murder told Bolan all he needed to know about these men.

The Executioner un-leathered his Beretta 93-R as he burst into the hallway, snap-aimed the pistol at the leader while on the move and squeezed off a double tap. The subsonic cartridges emitted a report not much louder than a discreet cough. The first round drilled through the leader's side and spun him to face Bolan's direction; the second blew a hole in his forehead and knocked him off his feet.

The remaining gunmen turned with surprise on their faces. They hadn't expected to cover their flanks, assuming any trouble from that direction would have been handled by their scout. It was a fatal assumption for both. While the gunners had their pistols drawn they were not accustomed to the skilled resistance Bolan offered. The Executioner sighted and triggered a single shot that took one man through the throat. A bloody spray washed the wall to the man's right. The second tried to zigzag for some type of cover but to no avail in such narrow confines and under such keen marksmanship. Bolan caught the guy with two rounds to the chest.

The slugs slammed the man's corpse against the wall with enough force to damage the plaster.

Movement to his right caused Bolan to track on the front door and two men in rumpled slacks, filthy suit shirts and shoeless feet dashed from the room. Bolan knew them immediately by their dossier pictures.

"Stein! Crosse! Let's move!" Bolan called.

He gestured for them to come along and the two men didn't hesitate in rushing to follow him.

"How the hell did you find us?" Crosse asked as he sidled up next to Bolan and struggled to keep up with the Executioner's purposeful strides.

Bolan didn't reply, instead keeping focused on their next task, which was escape. He led them to the stairwell, but as he pushed through the door he heard the door below open and the slap of boots on the stairs. Bolan pushed back and closed the door—so much for taking the stairs. Stein and Crosse started to protest at the sudden change of direction, but Bolan didn't bother to stop and argue with them.

"This can wait," the soldier replied flatly. "Now, you want to play twenty questions and die or would you like to get out of here alive?"

They stared at him dumbfounded, and Bolan continued down the hallway. The stairwell had been on the front end of motel, which meant there had to be some type of back entrance. Whoever was coming up those steps in force—and Bolan had every reason to think it was the cops springing their trap—might have all sides covered. That was okay, though, because Mack Bolan had a couple surprises of his own.

LESS THAN FIVE MINUTES after Rafael Encizo observed three heavies and their boss enter the motel, trouble erupted.

Encizo hadn't been real big on Bolan's plan, but he didn't try to argue. This was Bolan's show and they were under strict orders to do exactly as he said. Not that Encizo would have it any other way. Bolan had been at this game longer than just about all of them, and he trusted the man implicitly.

So Encizo waited and watched as the four men disappeared inside the motel. He didn't have long to wait as Cuban police showed up a few minutes later. The commandant had taken the bait and sprung a trap—just as the Executioner predicted—but the earlier arrival of the as yet unidentified parties might introduce a complication into Bolan's plan. Either way it didn't much matter. He had his orders to follow as soon as the Cuban police made entry.

Encizo yanked a big cigar from the seat next to him, lit it, then cranked the radio full-blast and put the Oldsmobile in gear. He swung out onto the otherwise deserted lane and cruised slowly past the line of police vehicles parked in front of the motel. A pair of Cuban cops left to watch the front entrance swung their attention toward him as he passed. Encizo tossed them a salute—just another man out in his slum-mobile looking for a distraction—but the cops didn't acknowledge him. By the time they passed into view of his side mirror, Encizo could see they had returned their attention to the motel.

He rounded the corner at the end of the block and stopped as soon as he was out of sight. Grimaldi slapped some coins on the table of the café, then vaulted a velvet rope cordoning the café from the sidewalk, dashed across the road and jumped into the passenger seat.

"Need a lift, sailor?" Encizo asked.

"Yeah, but just become I'm easy doesn't mean I'm cheap," Grimaldi joked.

Encizo smiled. "I'll keep it in mind."

The Cuban took off with a squeal of tires and headed to the narrow alley at the back of the motel. This wouldn't be quite the subtle exit they'd hoped for but neither of these men was a stranger to the quick getaway. If all went as planned, the Executioner would have two DIA agents in tow, bringing them one step closer to the goal.

Encizo cranked hard on the wheel and swerved into the alley. The vehicle fishtailed a bit on the gravel but Encizo maintained total control. He brought the vehicle to a skidding halt at the back door of the motel, leaving a cloud of dust in its wake that threatened to choke them both out.

"Come on, Sarge," Grimaldi muttered. "We're running out of time…."

"Uh-oh," Encizo cut in.

Grimaldi looked sharply at him. "What?"

Encizo didn't reply, instead pointing directly ahead of them. Through the haze of dust Grimaldi saw a number of police cruisers turn into the alleyway from an entrance at the other end.

BOLAN IGNORED THE PROTESTS of Stein and Crosse who continued to demand answers where he had no time to give them. The Executioner gritted his teeth. He had conducted many a rescue mission, and he couldn't remember playing nursemaid to a bigger pair of whiners than these two.

Locating the stairwell, he descended three at a time and stopped once to check the progress of his charges. Bolan watched with mild amusement as the pair stumble-bummed their way down the steps like a comedy team duo. When they caught up to him, Bolan continued the remainder of the way and stopped short at the rear exit. A heavy chain with a padlock secured the door.

"What the fu—?" Crosse began.

"That violates the fire code!" Stein sputtered.

Bolan looked at the pair disbelievingly. "Well, maybe we should stop at the front desk and complain."

The sound of the second-floor door opening could barely be heard above the rush of footfalls coming toward the rear hallway running the length of the building. A quartet of Cuban officers raced around the corner at the far end. Bolan fired several warning shots above their heads, causing them to scatter for cover, then drove the butt of the pistol against the padlock several times to break it. Bolan disengaged the chain and pushed open the door, then waved the DIA agents through.

As Stein and Crosse passed, Bolan looked back to see the sentry he'd knocked out staggering down the steps, a machine pistol in his grip. The Executioner didn't know where the guy had managed to get such a weapon on short notice, but he didn't have to guess how he planned to use it from his expression. Even as the Cuban police fired on him, Bolan thumbed the Beretta to 3-shot mode and squeezed the trigger. A trio of 9 mm Parabellum slugs punched through the submachine gunner's chest and lifted him off his feet. His back struck the wall and he left a bloody streak against it before he tumbled down the steps. Bolan was out the door before the man's corpse hit the floor.

The Executioner, less than two steps behind Stein and Crosse, looked up the alleyway and saw more troubles headed toward the waiting Oldsmobile. Bless Encizo and Grimaldi for sticking to the plan. One of the cops had to have leaned out the window and triggered a blast of autofire because the rear-door window shattered as Crosse opened it and leaped inside. One of the rounds ricocheted and struck Stein in the meaty part of the shoulder.

The agent yipped like a dog. Bolan shoved him inside the relative safety of the vehicle and then followed. "Go!"

Encizo, the gearshift already in Reverse, tromped the accelerator before Bolan could close his door. A retaining wall smashed into the door and nearly knocked it from its hinges. Thankfully, the solid metal body held under the torsion and it only managed to rip away a good part of the vinyl interior panel. Bolan got a viselike grip on the door, ignoring the shards of broken glass that bit into his callused hand, and yanked it close.

"Sorry..." Encizo said, head over shoulder, eyes glued to the rear window.

"Let's try shooting out their tires!" Grimaldi suggested.

Bolan shook his head. "No. We might hit one of them."

"Who the hell are you guys?" Crosse finally demanded.

"Later," Bolan said as he pulled a thick gauze pad from one of the slit pockets of his blacksuit and slapped it on Stein's bloody shoulder wound. He instructed Crosse to apply pressure, then pulled out a second one and wrapped his own hand.

"Well, if anyone's got an idea, now would be the time to speak up," Encizo said.

CHAPTER SEVEN

"We need a diversion," Bolan said. "Get something between us so we buy enough time to lose them."

"Any suggestions?" Encizo asked.

"I have an idea," Bolan said. "Get onto the highway and head for the coast."

Encizo nodded and whipped a hard right at the next intersection. Not many major highways ran through Cuba, but a good number of them led to water. Bolan figured the Cuban police would expect them to stick to dry ground, but the Executioner had other ideas.

"You think we can get into open waters, Sarge?" Grimaldi asked.

"No," Bolan said. "But I'm betting we can make them think we are."

Encizo steered them onto Highway CC, then immediately flipped onto the interchange for Highway CN as it ran along Bahia de Matanzas. The traffic had become heavier, and the breeze blowing through the back seat cooled the sweat on Bolan's face despite the mugginess of night. Things would cool quickly now, considering they were so close to water. It would be difficult for the Cuban police to stay on their tail given the traffic and darkness. The Executioner's plan would prevail.

Encizo poured on the speed, accelerator to the floor, and the Olds' engine roared in protest.

"We might actually lose them if we don't throw a rod first," Encizo noted.

"Not a chance," Grimaldi countered. "This puppy has four barrels riding in a 307 V8. Classic!"

"This is insane," Crosse muttered.

"Quit your bellyaching," Stein said. "We're alive, aren't we?"

"Why don't you both keep still," Bolan said. He leaned forward in the seat and peered out the front windshield. He pointed to a bright blue sign. "There's an exit for the bay. Take that."

"Aye, aye, captain," Encizo quipped. The Cuban waited until the last second, then pumped the brakes and swerved onto the exit. As they dropped toward the underpass, the flashing blue lights of Cuban police vehicles disappeared from view. By some miracle, it appeared they were slowly outdistancing the cops. Not surprising given the small police vehicles were no match for the Ninety-Eight's engine. As Grimaldi had pointed out, this was one powerful ride.

Encizo blew the red light at the bottom of the heel but executed a perfect power slide into the intersection and didn't hit a single vehicle. He accelerated smoothly toward the bay amidst an angry blare of horns and swearing drivers. Bolan could feel the floorboards vibrate as the Ninety-Eight effortlessly powered its five passengers toward freedom.

"The guys we ran into back there," Bolan said to Stein and Crosse. "Any idea who they were?"

"No," Stein replied.

"Why are you asking us?" Crosse said with a snort of disbelief. "Don't *you* know?"

Bolan's face took on a hard edge. "We'll get into that later, Crosse. Right now, you two have some explaining to do. Where's Colonel Waterston?"

"How the hell should we—?"

"Dead," Stein said. "We killed him."

"Shut up, Dominic!" Crosse snapped.

"Why? What the hell difference does it make now?" he asked his partner. "They obviously know what's up, or they wouldn't have sent someone to risk their necks pulling us out of this."

"Shut up, Dominic," Crosse repeated.

"Enough," Bolan said, making the threat implicit in his tone. "Neither of you is up for a medal."

"End of the road, Striker," Encizo said.

Ahead, the road terminated at a small, deserted parking area bordering Bahia de Matanzas. Encizo started to slow, but Bolan placed a hand on his shoulder. The Cuban locked eyes with him in the rearview mirror and knew immediately what the Executioner had in mind. He gunned the accelerator and jumped the curb. The wheels bit into the sand and spun, but a repeated jerking of the steering wheel gave them traction.

Directly ahead, a large group of citizens lounged along the sand, enjoying the evening breezes, and one crew of Cuban youths even had a bonfire blazing. Amid those crowds were a dozen or so vehicles including trucks, cars and ATVs. As Encizo got close to the makeshift parking lot, he slowed to a stop and killed the lights. All five men went EVA. Bolan looked around and quickly spotted a tall culvert pipe running under the highway. He pointed and they all sprinted directly for it. They were just far enough away to be indiscernible by the police units now rounding the corner. The sudden arrival of law enforcement had the congregation of beach partiers convinced their festivities were over. They scrambled. Some dumped out bottles of booze while others closed the trunks—a few of which were filled with ice and liquor—or buried their variety of drugs and paraphernalia in the sand.

Encizo took the lead, followed by Stein and Grimaldi. Crosse came next with Bolan at the rear. They made it inside and were able to crouch-walk to the other end. Bolan intermittently checked their flank to be certain the police weren't pursuing them. The shouts of surprise by those on the beach were drowned by the sound of Cuban officers speaking through megaphones.

Crosse slowed once to look over his shoulder.

"Keep moving," Bolan commanded.

They emerged on the other side and happened upon a tree-lined road. Fate smiled on them as Encizo pointed out an unmarked panel truck parked on the narrow shoulder, engine running and cab unoccupied. Probably some type of delivery vehicle. Bolan urged them toward it once he verified the road was clear of traffic. They reached the truck safely and Grimaldi hopped into the cab first on the driver's side. He went over the driver's seat and stepped into the open back end. Encizo helped Stein up via his good shoulder followed by Crosse. Then he hopped aboard and took shotgun as Bolan followed him in.

The Executioner made a five-second study of the controls, disengaged the emergency brake, depressed the clutch and dropped into second gear. A coordinated trade between accelerator and clutch got the truck moving. Encizo checked the side mirror but didn't see anyone rush out to protest their hasty departure.

"Well, looks like we've bought a little time," he told Bolan.

"Where to now, Sarge?" Grimaldi asked from the back.

"We need to get this pair on ice. At least until they can get out of the country."

"Then what?" Encizo pressed.

Bolan looked his friend in the eye and replied, "Then we shut down whatever's going on here."

WHEN LAZARO SAN LUJAN heard four of his men were dead, he slammed the telephone receiver so hard into the cradle it cracked the casing and sent chips of plastic flying. Mother of God! Four of his most loyal men were dead? He could hardly believe his ears. And according to his informant, an American had done it. Not one of their competitors, not the police, but an American. It didn't make any sense, and San Lujan knew it wouldn't until he got some straight answers.

Obviously he couldn't trust this to just anyone—he'd have to handle it himself. He decided not to tell Inez. She'd skin him alive if she discovered he'd disobeyed her directly by keeping his men on the search for Crosse and Stein. Then again, she didn't pay him to obey orders; she paid him to protect her interests in Havana Five and see to the security of her property and person. He never had the heart to tell her he didn't think much of this half-baked revenge scheme or her blaming Natalio's business partners for his death.

San Lujan had the biggest problem with this Colonel Moises Hurtado, code name Ignacio, who headed up the private little army Inez had built. The joke was on her in some respects. San Lujan had done some checking. Hurtado was little more than another Colombian stoolie in the rebel forces. His interests rested with the ELN and he didn't give a damn about Inez or her vendetta against Havana Five except for the benefits: funding and support for training a private army he could use to elevate his own personal status within the ELN. Hell, the Hurtado wasn't even a real colonel, and near as San Lujan could tell the man had never served in a recognized military unit.

San Lujan decided to forget that for now and focus on the problem at hand. He descended the wide marble steps of the mansion and pushed through the doors of the main parlor. Several of the house guards were lounging there with cigars and drinks of sparkling water. San Lujan didn't tolerate any sort of drinking on duty, and his men weren't allowed to consume alcoholic beverages within twelve hours of coming on shift.

"Kill those smokes and get ready. We have a job to do."

The men got serious, stamped out their cigars and rushed to make preparations to leave. One of them would get the SUV warmed up, while the others would head to the special armory and secure sidearms. The Fuegos had never permitted their house guards to carry guns. Natalio had always felt it best to dissuade as many signs of impropriety as possible— especially since the police were not required to solicit a warrant to enter a private residence if they suspected either drugs were on the premises or occupants possessed concealed firearms.

Off the property, however, San Lujan insisted all of his men be armed. They weren't in the laundry business; they dealt with many criminal elements, some with much less class than those who oversaw Havana Five. To go into these realms unarmed was tantamount to suicide, and San Lujan had no intention of ending his career by being too stupid to take the necessary precautions of personal protection. Besides, he'd found there were times where a gun could get things accomplished more quickly than simply saying "please" and "thank you." Many of the dregs with whom he interfaced didn't give an accounting to such niceties.

The men hustled to their preparations and within five minutes they were in the SUV and headed toward Matanzas. San Lujan didn't have any idea what to look for, or even where to start, but he knew the Americans would stand out like a sore thumb. Surely one of his contacts would know something. He would start with his street-level people, and if that didn't yield anything then he'd move up to the cops.

Either way, the American who had killed his men was as good as dead.

ONCE MACK BOLAN AND comrades got south of the urban areas, they ditched their stolen truck in some woods off the highway and walked the last quarter mile or so to a small town that consisted of one small grocery store, a run-down service station and three paved streets. The town didn't appear to be much more than a poor village in some Third World country, although the surrounding fauna and sights were apparently breathtaking—in the daytime anyway, according to what the station attendant told Encizo. The Phoenix Force pro gave the man an unrehearsed sob story about his car breaking down, and did he perhaps have some temporary transportation?

The man eyed Bolan up and down suspiciously, but Encizo explained how he was a Cuban escort for the gringo journalist who was in the country legally doing a story on the traditional ways of living in Cuba. While his story didn't appear to the impress the older man, he seemed to buy Encizo's tale. He offered to take them to a larger city first thing in the

morning for a few hundred pesos, which Encizo happily produced to prove he had the cash.

The man agreed to leave at first light, and they were welcome to sleep on some old mattresses he piled up in the out-
building at the back of the service station. Encizo acted
eternally grateful and they made their way to their makeshift
quarters after retrieving the others under cover of darkness.

"Why don't you two get some rest," Bolan told Encizo and
Grimaldi. "I'll keep an eye on these guys."

"Thanks, but I'd be more interested to hear their story,"
Encizo said.

"Me, too, Sarge," Grimaldi said. "I'm betting this will be
interesting."

"My shoulder is killing me," Stein moaned.

"Better your shoulder than your head," Grimaldi said with
a sour expression. "I can't have much empathy for a couple
of guys who turn on their own country."

"We didn't turn on anything," Crosse interjected. "And
I've just about had it with the self-righteous bullshit of all of
you. We're only in this predicament because we were trying
to help our country."

"By killing an unarmed Army officer?" Encizo asked with
a raise of his eyebrows. "Funny way of showing it, don't you
think?"

"Agreed," Bolan said, pinning both men in turn with ice-
blue eyes. "You guys have some explaining to do."

Crosse let out a snort. "I wouldn't even know where to
start."

"Let's start with how Plan Colombia and intelligence gath-
ering turns into one dead officer and two DIA agents on the
run from Havana Five."

It was Stein's turn to raise eyebrows. "You know about that?"

The Executioner decided not to show his hand too early. "I know about the training camp and that you were fingered for dealing with Havana Five."

"You don't know why, though."

"Explain it to me."

"Well," Crosse said, "you look like you've been around awhile. And since you knew where to come looking for us, you've obviously got a top-secret clearance. So we can all agree it's no secret the Cubans have opened their borders to the ELN and FARC for years. They've admitted these guys and allowed them to train, take refuge, and live here under the auspice of political asylum."

"So what?" Encizo said. "That's not exactly a newsflash."

"Well, maybe this is. Recently we found out the ELN had a massive training operation under way here."

"Basically, we stumbled onto the information by accident," Stein supplied helpfully.

Crosse gave him a look, then continued. "Anyway, you don't really care about that. At first we didn't think much of it. At least not until we managed to get someone inside who took digital pictures and e-mailed them to us before he turned up dead in a back alley in Havana."

"Pictures of what?" Grimaldi pressed.

"An army of ELN trainees, a huge load of weapons, and an explosives cache. Basically, there were enough men there to practically start a private war. And that's exactly what worried us they might be preparing for. Not against some force in Colombia, but maybe against U.S. targets here in Cuba."

"Gitmo?" Bolan interjected.

Crosse shrugged. "Sure, maybe, although we're thinking the most likely target would be a civilian one."

"Why would ELN terrorists want to launch an attack against Cuban citizens?" Encizo asked. "I don't think that gains them much."

"Not Cubans, Americans," Stein explained. "You have to remember that the average American is unwelcome here in Cuba. Only those traveling for official purposes are allowed into the country, like journalists, athletes and members of an international organization."

"And students," Bolan said with a nod.

"And later this week, there will be a massive influx of American students from the U.S. as well as a dozen other countries."

"The First Annual Congress for Diversity in Education."

"Right," Stein replied.

"So what makes you think the ELN is interested in killing a bunch of college kids?" Grimaldi asked. "And, anyway, it still doesn't explain why you killed one of your own."

"We discovered that all of the documentation got into Waterston's hands," Crosse said. "Including the deal we made with Inez Fuego to disclose the location of the training camp."

"In return for what?" Bolan asked.

"Our help in bringing down Havana Five," Stein said. "We saw an opportunity to keep American citizens alive!"

"And if we had to shed a little blood to save a lot, we figured it was worth it," Crosse continued.

"That's insane," Encizo said. "Why didn't you two idiots just take this through official channels? Maybe they would have let you cut the deal anyway. At least you would have had government support."

"We knew they'd never go for it," Crosse protested.

"Doesn't matter," Bolan said. "You're not a law unto yourselves. You killed a fellow American and withheld intelligence. That borders on high treason."

"You don't understand," Stein said.

"I understand better than you think," Bolan replied. "Like Crosse says, I've been in this game awhile. You should have walked the straight and narrow. But you can at least make it right and tell me where this training camp is located."

"We don't know," Crosse said. "Once we did our part, Fuego betrayed us."

Encizo cleared his throat, a signal he wanted a moment with Bolan, and the pair found a corner where they wouldn't be overheard. "If what they're saying is true, Striker, we're dealing with one of Havana Five. Inez Fuego's a widely known figure here. She's a socialite and very influential both politically and financially. Inez is the widow of Natalio Fuego."

Bolan nodded. "I wondered if there was a connection. I'm familiar with that name, as well as the others."

"You got an idea for our next move?"

"Yeah. If we can't get useful information from these characters, we'll have to go straight to the source."

"Guess it's time to pay a visit to Havana."

"Exactly," the Executioner replied.

CHAPTER EIGHT

Pirro knew the meaning of hardship, mainly because it was all he'd ever experienced on the mean streets of Havana.

From his earliest years, Pirro learned how to survive on his own. His mother—a woman who lived such a pathetic existence that one day she finally took her own life—didn't make many appearances at the run-down studio apartment on Havana's worst side. Her extended absences taught Pirro her trade and how to survive on the streets, but it also taught him the hardest lesson he ever learned: Pirro could only rely on himself. The purpose of everybody else in the world was to serve Pirro in some way.

In spite of the loneliness and occasional hardships, this policy worked for Pirro and he learned how to exploit it to his maximum benefit. Prostitution, male and female, remained a major player in the Cuban underworld. In some parts of the country, Havana in particular, the sex trade workers kept things going on the streets. Prostitutes not only provided the usual services but were also a major buying and selling vehicle for the black market.

Pirro remained a proud member of that crowd. It was just a job that needed to be done to meet the basic necessities like food, clothing and shelter. And Pirro wouldn't have complained about it, because he lived well above the standard. He had a three-bedroom apartment, a car with an automatic transmission and plenty of pocket cash whenever he needed it. Canned and boxed goods lined the shelves of his pantry, and he kept his compact refrigerator/freezer filled with juice, meat, eggs and milk.

Occasionally, Pirro shared his good fortune with those in his profession when they needed a place to stay, shelter from the rain, some food or just a place to come down off a bad high. Most of the time, though, Pirro kept to himself and never admitted visitors—and he *never* took a client back to his place.

His biggest trouble had been with the pimps. Pirro hated them because they'd created significant problems for him when he first got into the business. Then Pirro met Lazaro San Lujan, enforcer and bodyguard to Natalio Fuego, and that single event changed his life.

San Lujan sought Pirro out by pure reputation—something Pirro had always done his best to keep—and offered him a business proposition. Pirro knew a good thing when he saw it and he immediately accepted San Lujan's offer. After that, the pimps never came near Pirro, and they certainly didn't try to squeeze in on any of San Lujan's action. It wasn't until much later, though, that Pirro found out just exactly why. Despite what anyone thought, Havana Five had total control over the criminal elements throughout the better part of Cuba. There was almost no corner they didn't darken or have their fingers into. Those who thought they operated independently, even the Havana pimps, merely fooled themselves and most of the time they paid dearly for such delusions.

None of that concerned Pirro now that he worked for Natalio Fuego, and he felt total allegiance toward his benefactors as long as it benefited him. The day it stopped, then he would move on to something better. Still, he didn't see that would ever be the case because he'd worked for them almost ten years now, and never had any problems.

There were definite advantages to operating under the protection of such a powerful organization. Not that anyone had a choice. Still, it was nice to know someone of influence had his back. So when Pirro got the call from Lazaro San Lujan to keep his eyes open on the streets for the Americans he didn't hesitate to put out the word to everyone he knew. There wouldn't be a corner they could darken once it got passed along.

Yes, Pirro would contact San Lujan as soon as he had any information. No questions asked.

THE CONGREGATION OF Havana Five overlords was short one member.

When they heard of possible treachery by Inez Fuego they didn't hesitate to convene an emergency summit to discuss options. The meet was scheduled for 0400 in the basement of a local business that belonged to the group. The lighting in the room was poor, illuminated by red bulbs, and for very good reasons. An outside observer wouldn't notice the light shining from the basement windows high above the attendees, and the red light also made observation through an infrared device close to impossible.

Chairing the discussions was Santiago "Chago" Famosa, who to the best of their knowledge was a descendant of Spanish nobility. Famosa carried himself with a cocky air, even among his colleagues, but his power hold alone on the various business enterprises of his crime empire throughout Cuba was enough to keep the rest of his associates in line. Nobody had dared challenge his authority simply due to his far-reaching influences. Still, Famosa was a loyal and astute member of Havana Five and had earned their respect for his allegiance.

Eduardo Valdese sat directly across from Famosa and picked at his teeth with mild disinterest. He specialized in drugs and money laundering, the two activities fitting well with each other. The gangster had built his own empire predominantly on the export markets, and had a reputation as a ruthless and methodical businessman. He also hated non-Cubans, and held a special disdain for Blacks and Asians.

To Famosa's right sat Macario Lombardi, the child prodigy of a Cuban father and Sicilian mother. Lombardi, who had taken his mother's maiden name at a young age to avoid some legal trouble, possessed the most mild-mannered personality of the group. In most circles Lombardi's reputation was that of a gentleman, soft-spoken and demure, and generous to a fault. But deep inside boiled an unsatiable greed, and a very select few knew Lombardi capable of slitting another man's throat if it meant he could get his hands on a few extra pesos.

The final Havana Five member present was Nicanor Armanteros, overseer of all the rural provinces in Cuba, appropriate since he hailed from the "old country." The Armanteros family owned land and a good number of the natural resources used for power and manufacturing throughout the country. Additionally, his land holdings brought him tremendous wealth and influence in the export industry. A large percentage of nearly all monies received for exports of tobacco, sugar, nickel and coffee products landed right back into Armanteros's vast coffers, and while he didn't yield the social or political hammer Famosa did, Armanteros had always served as a sort of counterpoint to any one member gaining too much power.

"Gentlemen," Famosa began, "I know you're tired and anxious to get back to your families. Let's call this meeting to order and discuss our options."

"I, for one, don't see as we have any options," Valdese interjected, lightly pounding his fist on the hardwood table. "We must kill Inez Fuego and we must do it now, Chago."

Famosa raised his hand. "Let's not be hasty. Whatever we may think of our beautiful companion, we have to consider her contributions to Havana Five."

"We must also consider these rumors could be unfounded," Lombardi added. "Without more proof, I am not comfortable issuing an edict for the head of Natalio's widow unless we can confirm the information we have now."

"What more proof do you seek?" Armanteros asked. "I have triple-checked my sources, and I can assure you that she's building a private army. My spies on Juventud confirm that she's contracted Moises Hurtado to train ELN terrorists. She's disbursed monies to them from her private offshore funds."

"And let's not forget she chose to go outside Havana Five to get weapons for these Colombian mercenary dogs," Lombardi said. "If she didn't care we knew about it, why not go straight to Chago for the arms? Why contract with a different supplier? You can't tell me she got a better deal."

Famosa knew he couldn't argue with either of these men. What they said was the absolute truth. He couldn't understand Fuego's need for additional manpower.

"These are facts, to be sure," Famosa admitted. "I, too, don't understand why she would feel the need to go behind our backs on this."

"Because she plans to turn against us!" Valdese said. His face flushed. "You simply don't get it, do you? We all know she blames us for Natalio's death."

"And why not?" Lombardi asked quietly. "We were responsible for sending him to his grave."

"Are you suggesting we did this without good reason?"

"I am not suggesting anything."

"Good," Valdese said with renewed vehemence. "As I would hate to think any of you suddenly find it acceptable to betray Havana Five simply for the purpose of avoiding prosecution."

"Put it back in your pants, Eduardo," Famosa warned. "We all know Natalio had to be sacrificed."

"Yes, of course," Armanteros. "It doesn't really matter to us, of course, that it was you who came up with the idea to make those particular arrangements for the rest of us."

Something went dangerous and dark in Valdese's expression. Finally he said, "Only because we know you didn't have the intestinal fortitude to do your own dirty work."

Famosa slapped his open palm on the table to get their attention. "Enough! This bickering among ourselves is utterly pointless. What we have to do now is figure out whether there's any truth to the allegations we've heard, and to determine how we plan to deal with Inez."

"You don't honestly believe she's simply an innocent pawn in this," Valdese replied with a scoffing laugh.

"I don't know what to think, yet," Famosa said. "And I refuse to act on simple conjecture. We must deal with her in the same way as we would deal with the treachery of any member, yes. But we must also remember she is one of us until proved otherwise. She contributes to our cause, and she is rightful heiress to a seat as one of the Five."

"Then why is she not here now?" Lombardi asked. "I would like to hear how she answers to these accusations directly. Then, and only then, do I believe we can tell if she's lying or if someone is simply trying to discredit her reputation."

"I agree," Armanteros said.

"And if we are to assume you're correct," Valdese said, "I would ask for what purpose? Why would someone try to impugn her reputation with us?"

"To break us up," Famosa answered for them all. "To drive a wedge between us. And if that is what's happening, we will have enough to deal with that these personal and petty squabbles will abate themselves, I assure you. Together we are nearly invincible, but apart we are vulnerable. And what makes us vulnerable makes the Five vulnerable. And if there is an enemy attempting to drive us apart, then they have figured this out and that makes them a very dangerous enemy indeed."

"You speak well of this," Valdese said after a long silence, apparently placated for now. "It shall be as you wish...for now."

"Good then," Famosa said. "It is settled. We shall advise Inez of our need to meet and have her personally answer to these allegations. If they are unfounded, as I believe they may be, then we will turn our attentions to finding out who it is that's attempting to break us apart."

"And if they are found to be accurate?" Lombardi asked.

It was Valdese who responded evenly in a bare whisper, teeth clenched. "Then she shall burn."

AT FIRST LIGHT, THE station attendant took Bolan and Encizo to a neighboring city, with Grimaldi, Crosse and Stein stowed away in the bed of the man's old truck.

Encizo managed to procure a set of wheels and soon the five were headed up Highway CA and straight for Havana. Encizo figured the trip would take them about two hours, so Bolan decided to check in with Stony Man. Despite the secure communications satellite phone he carried, Bolan hadn't wanted to risk contacting the Farm before that time, concerned Cuban officials might somehow track their signal. Aaron Kurtzman picked up midway through the third ring.

"Striker, here," Bolan said.

"At last," Kurtzman replied with enthusiasm. "Where have you been, big guy? You don't call, you don't write…"

"Busy. I hooked up with the boys, but somebody made us almost immediately. Anything more on that end?"

"Yeah, Hal wanted me to put you through to him as soon as we heard from you. Hang loose a second."

Less than fifteen seconds of silence followed before Brognola's voice came on the line.

"Striker, you okay?"

"We're fine," Bolan said. "Couple of close calls, but we found your missing agents."

"And Waterston?"

"Dead," Bolan replied quietly. "I'm sorry, Hal."

"Not as sorry as me," Brognola replied. "We got a visit from the Man, and I can tell you the situation just went real ugly. He won't take to hearing such news lightly."

"What's happened?"

"Well, it might have been nice to have this information before now, but apparently there's a bit more riding on this Plan

Colombia. The natives are getting restless. The Man thinks this thing may spill over into full-blown civil war if negotiations don't resume between Waterston and some of Castro's people. If that happens, he's committed to a full-blown invasion with Gitmo spearheading it all."

"He may not have to worry about civil war," Bolan replied. "We've got something else fueling the fire."

The Executioner laid out the information Crosse and Stein had given him, along with the reasons for Havana Five's potential involvement. He also told Brognola about the educational conference, and the potential disaster they faced if the ELN planned a terrorist attack within Cuban borders.

"That might not make them too popular with the Cuban government, actually," Brognola said.

"It will if only Americans are casualties," Bolan reminded him.

"You think they'd be that selective?"

"If it stood to benefit their cause? Yeah. Your average terrorist would only care about a spectacular target. These home-grown types are something else, though. They know good relations are a key factor to their survival."

"So they tend to be more selective of their targets," Brognola concluded.

"Right."

"What do you want to do about this?"

"We're heading to Havana now," Bolan said. "See if we can run interference and get on the inside of this thing. Meanwhile, I need to get our two boys here to a safe location until we can arrange an exit strategy."

"I'll have Barb get on it pronto."

"Thanks."

"By the way, she's here now with some additional information that may help in your hunt."

"I'm all ears."

Price's voice filled his head and sent a block of warmth to his gut. No matter where he was or what he was doing, it was always good to hear her voice. "Striker, we pulled everything we could find on this Havana Five, and we're downloading the encrypted files with the details. But the most important information we found has to do with their involvement relative to this ELN training group."

"Which is?"

"That's just it," she said. "There isn't any involvement by them, near as we can tell, and I'll tell you why. Normally this sort of thing goes through Havana Five. They have their fingers on the land, the weapons, everything a private little terrorist army would need. But whoever's running this training camp didn't utilize those resources. There have been no major arms shipments or purchases of military equipment."

"You're thinking if Havana Five was involved in this, it would have funded the operation."

"Exactly."

And yet according to Encizo, the widow of a prominent member in the group had known enough about the camp to disclose its location. Inez Fuego had also planned to expose whatever these ELN terrorists had planned in return for American assistance in bringing down those responsible for murdering her husband. And yet, if intelligence was correct, Fuego actually belonged to Havana Five. To bring down her own organization would mean an end to her livelihood, as well as her only source of income.

"Okay, I'll keep that in mind," Bolan finally said. "Out, here."

"What did they say?" Encizo asked.

"They'll make the necessary arrangements so we can off-load our cargo," Bolan replied as he jerked a thumb in the direction of Crosse and Stein.

"Then what?"

"Then I need you and Eagle to start running down the major areas of Havana Five's operation. Meantime, I'll be making an appointment."

"With who?"

"Inez Fuego," the Executioner replied.

CHAPTER NINE

Colonel Moises Hurtado looked on his army with great pride.

He took a deep breath and studied the clipboard in front of him as his men ran through their drills.

Inez Fuego would be pleased. Originally the idea of working for a woman hadn't set well with Hurtado. It wounded his manhood, denting the machismo on which so many like him prided themselves. Unfortunately these were the kinds of business arrangements sometimes required to facilitate the greater cause, so Hurtado considered his work mere matters of duty and patriotism. So he would continue to act subservient until it no longer suited his purposes, and then Hurtado would turn his efforts toward the true cause.

First, he needed the weapons so vital to completing their operations; he could only obtain them from the cache awaiting his men on the island. The task itself seemed simple. They had four targets, all fairly accessible and none possessing the capability to resist his army on any grand scale. These were overlords of a criminal syndicate and Hurtado had plenty of experience dealing with their kind. They tended to be overconfident and their self-appointed states of grandeur blinded them to their own vulnerabilities. Hurtado planned to exploit those vulnerabilities.

Hurtado turned from the railing of the observation tower and proceeded inside. He descended the winding staircase and through a doorway that led to his headquarters adjacent to the tower. His office and living quarters furnishings were meager, essentially a prefab hut with a cot, plain wooden desk and a full field kitchen. Adjoining the field kitchen was a mess hall capable of feeding fifty hungry men, about half Hurtado's fighting force.

A lone picture on the wall caught Hurtado's attention, and he smiled. A large, burly man had his arm around the more lithe and wiry Hurtado. The man's mustache stood as wide and broad as his grin. Hurtado studied the picture of his father and recounted the many good times they had together, fighting side by side against the regime of the Colombian government.

Freedom—his single greatest desire and the basis of his platform—remained the mainstay of the National Liberation Army's efforts to overthrow the government traitors. Hurtado's life had been a hard one with his father becoming involved with the liberators when Hurtado was young. Then government soldiers came, raped and killed his mother, and Hurtado saw the opportunity to find his father and join in the fight to free their people.

Now, many long years after his death, Moises Hurtado didn't feel they were any closer to victory. The fighting continued, despite the fact the ELN hadn't made much headway, and their FARC allies were practically nonexistent now. The best they could do would be to make a statement in other countries, primarily those of their supporters, and find the backing they so desperately needed to carry on their struggle. And if that meant the elimination of a few Cuban criminals for personal reasons—Hurtado didn't really consider this any of his affair—then he could live with it.

"Colonel, there is someone here to see you," an aide said from the door leading into the kitchen.

Hurtado looked up from where he'd taken a seat at his desk with surprise. He frowned and replied, "I'm not expecting anyone. Tell them to make an appointment."

"It is not one of your officers, sir." The aide looked over his shoulder, then leaned forward and in a quieter voice added, "This is…a woman, sir."

Hurtado wanted to tongue lash the aide in outrage, but he curbed his temper. Only one woman could know he was here: Inez Fuego. He hadn't planned on seeing her again until they arrived in Havana the next evening. There wasn't any reason for her to be here now unless something had gone wrong.

"Show her in, Vega," he replied. "And then see that we are undisturbed."

The man moved away quickly and a moment later Inez Fuego's sultry form filled the door. Hurtado could not deny her beauty. To be sure, she possessed all of the finest qualities of a South American woman. She looked particularly attractive in the pair of cream-colored stirrup pants that clung to her shapely thighs and knee-high boots of brown leather swathing her legs. A tan, short-sleeved blouse tugged seductively at the ample curves of her upper torso. She had pulled her black flowing hair into a long ponytail and a sweat-band encircled her head. Just the hint of dampness gave her evenly tanned skin a luminous glow in the bare-bulb lighting of Hurtado's office.

"Thank you for seeing me, Colonel," she said.

The man showed her a chair in front of his desk. She sat and with smooth, effortless practice crossed her legs.

"Of course," he said with an incline of his head. He tried to remain impassive as he continued, "Although you take a terrible risk coming here. This might compromise the operation, you know."

"I understand this is a violation of protocols," Fuego replied, "but I must beg some of your time. I think our operation could already be in jeopardy."

That didn't sound good but Hurtado kept his cool. "Oh?"

Prompted by his inquisition, Fuego said, "Just before we talked, I was informed the two American agents from the DIA had escaped from our men. They are now in hiding, presumably under the protection of the Cuban police."

"With all due respect, Ms. Fuego," Hurtado replied with an intermittent chuckle, "I would hardly consider two Americans in a Cuban jail to be secure. In fact, I wouldn't doubt they are dead already."

"They had the means to bribe the police," Fuego said, her voice strained. "You must know that a good number of the law can and usually are bought if the price is right."

"I did not know that," Hurtado replied with a bit of caution. He wasn't exactly sure yet where they were going with the conversation, but he decided to play along to see how it unfolded. "But I hardly see how this should be of concern."

"They might know of our plans," Fuego replied.

"And how would they know that?"

"I have my sources." Fuego looked with feigned interest at her long, manicured nails before giving him a hard stare. "Anyway, we need to be cautious. My men are looking into it now, although they probably don't think I know what they're up to."

"What men?"

"You remember Lazaro?"

Hurtado nodded, although he wished he could forget. He didn't trust Lazaro San Lujan, and he knew the feeling to be mutual. The last time they'd met, when Fuego had first engaged Hurtado's services, the two men were immediately distrustful of each other. He could understand why, considering the fact that Havana Five—a group that had a reputation for its loyalty—had betrayed Fuego's husband and destroyed him, hence her reasons for vengeance.

Hurtado tendered a cool smile. "No disrespect, Madam Fuego, but your personal affairs are really your own, and of no concern to me. We had an agreement. I can assume you plan to stick to it."

"Of course," she said, acting a bit offended. "But I thought it necessary we discuss a contingency plan in the event something goes wrong. These men don't know about our plans but they have enough information they might be able to interfere with them. This shouldn't happen if Lazaro finds them, but I felt it prudent to prepare you for any eventuality."

"And I appreciate your making this visit in person. But as I've said, it is really of no concern. Whatever these men know, I do not think they can harm our operations. I doubt your police would believe these men, even if they exposed our plans, and I hardly doubt the Americans could make any kind of response."

"Ah, yes, under normal circumstances I would agree. But my people inform me that the Americans may have already responded. Word travels quickly in my country. Maybe the authorities won't do anything about this, but it might get back to the others of Havana Five. That would not be well for your operations."

"Your concern is noted," Hurtado said, rising from his chair. "And now I must ask that you return to your home and await our rendezvous. I have many preparations still before we commence operations."

"Of course." She rose and turned to leave, then on after-thought said, "Thank you for your time, Colonel."

"It is my pleasure," he said.

When she was gone, Hurtado sat and contemplated the visit. Strange that such a woman would come all this way, risking exposure, just to tell him that the Americans may have information regarding their operations. But the Americans didn't concern him. They were too wrapped up in their ter-rorist war against the Arabs to be interested in what was hap-pening in Cuba.

Still, Fuego's visit had stirred him enough that Hurtado felt it best not to make any assumptions. The most logical choice would be the same as he would do back in his own country. He would send an advance team of his best covert operations squad to assess the situation and feel out the enemy ahead of time. That should be sufficient to deal with any potential interference from outsiders.

"Vega!"

Hurtado's aide showed his face a moment later. "Yes, sir?"

"Find Captain Aguilera and tell him to report to me im-mediately."

LAZARO SAN LUJAN AND his crew arrived in Matanzas just be-fore dawn broke and proceeded straight to the police jail in Guijarro. He didn't like what he found or heard. A beat-up ve-hicle riddled with bullet holes sat in front of the jail, and a fol-low-up inquisition led to a commandant who was less than willing to cooperate. Until San Lujan advised him of exactly who was interested in knowing everything the commandant did.

It didn't come about too often when he dropped Inez Fuego's name, but when he did the most miraculous change came over people. Suddenly they wanted to cooperate with him. It wasn't that anybody really didn't know about Fuego's connections to Havana Five as much as that they chose to do nothing about it. The widow of Natalio Fuego had a significant reputation throughout the country, and was particularly known for her affiliations with some very powerful political figures. In some respects, it was said that there was little difference between Inez Fuego talking and President Fidel himself.

Still, San Lujan didn't risk such exposure unless it became absolutely necessary. So he heard the entire story of how the two American DIA agents had been taken by force. And yes, it was very tragic that some of San Lujan's men were murdered in cold blood, and they were exercising due diligence to hunt down those responsible. And of course they would keep San Lujan advised of how the investigation proceeded and any information they had they would be glad to pass on to him; any hour of the day or night would be fine for him to call on them for an update.

The commandant's chief investigator tried to convince San Lujan and his men that they believed the suspects were still in the area, but the security chief wasn't convinced. They didn't stand to benefit from sticking around. The insurgents had gotten what they'd come for and now they would make every attempt to get their prized package—two murderous scum who would kill men in their own army for a chance to make names for themselves—and that meant selecting a port of call.

As they drove from Matanzas, San Lujan's lieutenant suggested, "Maybe they will head for Guantánamo Bay, Lazaro."

San Lujan shook his head. "I doubt it. I think they will attempt to get the Americans out discreetly. We may not be able to stop them from escaping, but we can certainly make it harder."

"What do you suggest?"

San Lujan didn't reply at first; he needed to think about it. The most logical and least conspicuous method of sneaking out of the island country was by boat. The Cuban army and police force couldn't possibly monitor every segment of their shorelines every minute of the day, although they managed to do a competent job. As representative of the Fuego legacy and a chief enforcer inside Havana Five, San Lujan had complete access to the maritime patrol lanes, schedules and capacities. He'd acquired this information because of more than a few operations that required complete avoidance of law enforcement; even bribe money went only so far. It was this knowledge that led him to draw conclusions relative to the suspicious circumstances surrounding Natalio's death.

San Lujan didn't trust anyone. A hardened realist from childhood, he expected simple facts and data before making a decision; he considered anything less unacceptable. So now he had a decision to make. Spearhead a massive search-and-destroy operation, or put the feelers out to see what came up. It wasn't a difficult one to make. He'd already put word on the streets of Havana, Matanzas and Cienfuegos, primarily because they were the closest and largest ports.

If San Lujan had to dig deeper and stretch out the blanket of influence, he would, but for now that would be enough.

"We should return to Havana," San Lujan finally told his men. "I think the Americans will try to find haven there first."

The men seemed to silently agree with him and the driver pointed the car toward the capital. San Lujan had been born and bred in Havana, and he knew little else. He knew Havana like the back of his hand, every corner, every street, every alleyway. The enforcer knew its citizens and its criminals; he knew the dregs and the elite. The Americans were there—he could feel it. Sooner or later they would turn up. And when they did, San Lujan would make sure they paid for killing his men and threatening Inez Fuego's livelihood.

PIRRO SAW THEM. At first, he couldn't believe his eyes, but when he looked again he realized that it was really the Americans.

They'd parked their clunker of a car at the curb and four men exited. A man with brown hair and dark sunglasses got out of the back and climbed behind the wheel, replacing another man who looked Cuban but didn't carry himself that way. He had a chiseled jaw and looked to be in great physical condition beneath his casual silk shirt, trousers and loafers. The other three looked completely out of their element. One was tall and muscular, and wore jeans and a black T-shirt outside his pants. Pirro noticed a slight bulge at the man's waist; he knew the outline of a gun when he saw one. The other two were attired in suits that looked as though they'd been worn the past week.

Definitely these were the men San Lujan was looking for.

Pirro cursed himself for not bringing his cell phone. Actually, he wasn't really working. Marisol had come by to stay last night and Pirro had decided to go down to the local market to get her some milk. She was five months pregnant and could barely afford food, let alone the expenses of a medical specialist. While Cuba had socialist medicine, only the elite could access the very best physicians, which left the large majority of the population in the hands of the butchers and quacks. The lack of adequate housing and unsanitary conditions in many of the crowded urban areas contributed to poor health. The regime had also done nothing to curb the tide of disease with its loss of subsidies from the Communists in the former Soviet Union.

Well, it didn't really matter much at the moment. Pirro knew he couldn't solve those problems. All he could do was keep his friends close and his enemies closer, and at the moment they were about as close as they would get. Pirro knew the small beauty shop the four men entered, and he knew the shopkeeper, Isidora, quite well, which is why he'd never trusted the fat bitch.

Pirro turned on his heel and headed for his apartment just half a block away. He couldn't believe his luck. San Lujan would pay him well for this! Pirro ignored the cat calls of a couple of regular customers and vaulted the steps leading into his apartment building. He skipped the elevator—not that he ever took it anyway because he didn't trust the rickety thing—and ascended the steps like a gazelle. He burst through the front door and slammed it behind him, then headed directly to his bedroom nightstand where he remembered leaving his phone.

"Pirro!" a voice called from a back room. "Is that you?"

Pirro ignored Marisol and dialed San Lujan's number, which he had programmed into his phone.

A voice answered on the first ring. "May I speak with Mr. San Lujan?"

"Who's calling?" the gruff voice asked.

"Please tell him it is Pirro."

There was a pause and then San Lujan's familiar voice came on the line. "Yes, Pirro, what is it?"

"I have seen them!"

"The Americans?"

"Yes, sir."

"You're sure?"

"I promise you, it is them!"

Marisol came through the bedroom door. "Pirro, where is the milk? What are you doing back so soon?"

"Shush!"

"What?" San Lujan's voice demanded.

"I'm sorry, sir, I was not speaking to you."

"Pay attention, Pirro! Tell me exactly what you saw."

Pirro gave him the information and a good description of all the men. "It is just like I remember. Are these not the men you are looking for?"

"It may very well be. You have done a good job, Pirro."

"Thank you, Mr. San Lujan, thank you! What do you wish me to do?"

"Nothing. Do not make your presence known to them. These men are very dangerous. They have already murdered my associates. Simply keep an eye on them from a distance. I will be there soon. If they leave, all of them, you will follow. Otherwise, you shall stay where you are at and wait for me. I will be there within the hour. Do you understand?"

"Of course, Mr. San Lujan. I shall do as you say."

"See that you do, Pirro."

A click sounded in his ear. He hadn't even said goodbye, but Pirro was too excited to care. He would see a grand reward for this. He turned toward Marisol, saw the inquisitive expression on her face, but then decided not to tell her what he was up to. She might want him to share whatever money he got. He pitied her. Poor Marisol...poor, poor Marisol. Her brother was missing, supposedly picked up by American policemen and detained at the Guantánamo Bay military detention facility, and she hadn't heard from him in weeks. Well, he'd buy her food and medicine but he wasn't about to share in the wealth. No, that was a reward he would reserve solely for himself.

After all, friendship went only so far.

CHAPTER TEN

"Get the feeling we were being watched?" Encizo asked Bolan as they entered the salon.

Bolan nodded. "Kid near the grocery store? Yeah."

Encizo nodded. "I thought he took a little too much interest in us."

Bolan lowered his voice as a heavy-set Cuban woman wearing gobs of pancake makeup emerged from a back room. A couple of chairs in a makeshift waiting room along with two customer seats mounted in front of water-stained sinks and a dusty shelf packed cheap salon products and equipment completed the cramped salon's decor.

"You look lost," she said. "Do you need directions?"

Bolan recognized the challenge phrase and returned it with the confirmation. "I think we are lost. We're trying to find Bahia de Havana."

The woman nodded and then waved them toward her. "I can show you on a map in the back room."

The four men proceeded to follow her through a curtain into a much smaller back room. She opened a closet door and stepped inside. It looked like she disappeared from view but as they followed Bolan discovered it actually descended into a dimly lit, brick-lined corridor. As they went deeper, Bolan felt the natural cool of the underground passage chill the sweat on his forehead.

The idea of Stein and Crosse getting trapped by potential enemies in these narrow confines didn't make Bolan feel any better, but for now he didn't see they had much of a choice. He began to consider their options. If that kid on the street, one whom the Executioner actually believed to be a male prostitute, saw only two of them come out after watching four go in, he might get curious. And he would definitely impart his observations to whomever he worked for.

At the end of the passage was a small, wooden door set in the side of the wall. It was so low and narrow all four men actually had to duck to go inside. It opened onto a cozy room that sported a couple of cots, a desk and chair, and a television. A shelf bolted to the wall had a few books and magazines on it. Bolan found it perfectly functional.

"Ah," Crosse said with a scowl. "Home sweet home."

"You were maybe expecting the Biltmore?" Encizo asked.

"No, but—"

"But nothing," Bolan cut in. He'd had just about enough of Crosse's attitude. "Our job is to get you out of the country alive. In return, you'll cooperate fully. Understood?"

Crosse's complexion reddened, but one look into Bolan's grim visage was enough to keep him quiet. Considering their treachery—and despite their attempts to protect their country—neither was expecting a warm welcome in the States. But prison in the U.S. would be much better than prison in Cuba or a watery grave just offshore.

"I am Isidora," the woman said in flawless English. "I will

take care of you until we can arrange to smuggle you out of Cuba. It may take a few days, but we'll make it happen. In the meantime, you are welcome to stay here. It may not be fancy but it's safe."

"No offense," Stein said, "but it looks pretty open to me."

"Up at the front there is a false wall that slides over the back of the closet. Very heavy door, metal core and covered with mortar and brick. Anyone who looks at it or even beats on it would think it's a solid wall."

"A panic room," Encizo said.

Isidora nodded.

"We think we might have been observed coming in here," Bolan said. "I'm concerned what will happen when we come out with two less men."

"Tell me what this person looked like," she said. Bolan gave her a quick description and she nodded, expressing recognition. "Yes, that sounds like Pirro. I know him well. He is a prostitute."

"Yeah, we know," Encizo replied.

"Who does he work for?" Bolan asked.

"For himself," Isidora replied with an almost engaging laugh. "But I know that he operates under the protection of Señor San Lujan."

"Who's that?"

"Oh, you don't want to mess with him, mister," she said. "He's part of—" she looked at each man conspiratorially "—Havana Five."

Encizo looked at Bolan and said, "Well, at least we won't have to guess."

"If they're onto us already, that means they know about these two," Bolan said with a gesture to Stein and Crosse. "We'd better go."

"Wait a minute!" Crosse demanded. "You're not going to just leave us here with the dragon lady."

"Yes, we are," Bolan said.

Crosse didn't look happy, but the Executioner couldn't do anything about that now. Not that he would if he could; Crosse, especially, hadn't won a special place in Bolan's heart. He considered them traitors and murderers, and would have just as soon killed them both and been done with it, save for the fact that would have made him no different from them.

"Maybe one day you'll learn the way to solve problems isn't to run away from them, Crosse," Encizo said.

"Or murder them," Bolan added.

Bolan and Encizo bid all of them farewell and were soon back on the street. The Executioner looked for Pirro but didn't see him. The guy had probably gone to report to his masters. Well, odds had it they'd encounter him soon enough. Meanwhile, they needed to push ahead with the mission; maybe he could infiltrate Havana Five before they realized the threat.

As they got into the vehicle and Grimaldi started the engine, Bolan said, "Wait a minute. Don't leave yet, Jack."

"What's up?"

"I have an idea." Bolan turned to look over his shoulder at Encizo. "I'm sure this Pirro kid has orders to keep an eye on us."

"Yeah?"

"Likely he doesn't have wheels."

Encizo nodded. "Most can't afford them."

"So I get him to follow me on foot," the Executioner said.

"Sounds risky, Sarge," Grimaldi said. "We don't really

know what we're up against. We'll have better odds in numbers."

"Not of getting to the heart of the matter," Bolan said. "Maybe this Pirro can lead me to Inez Fuego more directly. The two of you continue as planned. I'll contact you when I can."

Bolan went EVA, gave his comrades a reassuring gesture and headed down the sidewalk. He didn't really know if his plan would work but he didn't see any other options. If Pirro was young and inexperienced, he'd surely trip up and Bolan would exploit that to his advantage. The Executioner had two disadvantages: he didn't know the terrain and he didn't speak the language well. He had two things on his side: experience and a plan.

PIRRO COULD NOT BELIEVE IT!

Everything went wrong after he called Mr. San Lujan. Four men went into Isidora's place but only two came out. The two men got into the car and the engine started. Pirro began to panic. His orders hadn't addressed this particular situation. He was to follow the group if they left together, otherwise observe if they split up and advise. But in this case, they were splitting into more than just two groups. He supposed for a moment he should stay; that would be the most sensible. He suspected the two men in suits were the ones that interested San Lujan the most.

Pirro's heart raced even more, his pulse thudding in his ears, when the muscular American got out of the car once more and headed down the street. The vehicle pulled away from the curb. Pirro became immediately suspicious. Two possibilities existed. The men either knew they were being watched and split up to shake any tails, or they had accomplished whatever they'd set out to do and were now parting company. Pirro considered it a moment more before making a decision. He would follow the big American.

Pirro started to shuffle along and he risked a glance in the direction of the Americans in the car as they rode past. Neither of them even looked in his direction. Good. They hadn't spotted him, after all. He could feel his confidence return; Marisol called it cockiness but Pirro preferred to think of it more as assertiveness. Anyway, that didn't matter at the moment. He didn't need to worry about what Marisol thought; he needed to focus on his quarry.

Pirro followed the American for a few blocks. The guy looked back once or twice but not for any particular reason. The young man knew that a lot of people could sense if they were being followed, but the American looked like he had professional training in covert operations. He wouldn't make the mistake of underestimating the man; Pirro had grown very streetwise over the years.

PIRRO HAD SCREWED UP.

Mack Bolan caught it immediately when he looked back and Pirro averted his eyes. Unfortunately, his attempt to look conspicuous and disinterested made it impossible for him to ascertain if Bolan made him. Not that it made a difference. Pirro's orders might have been to stay on Bolan's trail whether Bolan knew it or not, in which case it didn't matter what the Executioner did.

It didn't matter, anyway, since young Pirro had performed just as expected.

Bolan rounded a corner and broke into a jog. He had to get as far down the street as possible before Pirro made that corner. Bolan got a couple of blocks and then slowed to his initial pace. His eyes roved along the sidewalks on both sides of the street. Cars bustled with regularity along this particular thoroughfare. Fine, it would make this much easier.

Bolan waited until he saw a shop ahead, a convenience store of some sort, and dashed across the street between the slow-moving cars. He continued to the store and walked inside. He didn't see a soul in the place save for a young boy tending the counter. Bolan looked along the walls and spotted an opening covered by some type of colorful tapestry, like a rug or blanket. Bolan went behind the counter. The kid's eyes got wide but Bolan put up both hands just to show he meant the young man no harm. He jerked his thumb toward the door, put his finger to his lips and then moved behind the curtain.

Lazaro San Lujan called Pirro as soon as they reached the city limits of Havana. The first time he called, the phone rang and rang but Pirro never picked up. San Lujan muttered a few curses. Maybe he shouldn't have put that much trust in the kid. He'd only brought Pirro into the fold for more reasons of nostalgia than anything else. Pirro reminded San Lujan of himself at that age, although he'd never succumbed to being a prostitute, because San Lujan knew what it meant to be alone. He remembered a bitter childhood—he had worked long and hard to forget—and how Natalio had taken him under his wing. His attempt at bringing Pirro into the fold, however limited that attempt might be, was his way of giving back.

San Lujan tried a minute later and the young man's voice came on immediately. "Yes?"

"Where have you been?"

"I—I follow him, sir," Pirro replied. "Just like you told me."

"You followed who?"

"One of the Americans."

"Pirro, I'm disappointed," San Lujan replied. "I told you to follow them all if they stuck together and otherwise to stay put if they split up."

"I understand, sir, but I had no choice." The tone in Pirro's voice changed to a high-pitched whine, which had the motorized quality of one of those miniature rotary tools.

"Tell me everything you know."

"Two of the Americans are at Isidora's place," he said. "You know Isidora, yes?"

"Yeah, I know of her. What else, Pirro?"

"Two of them left in a car, and I followed a third on foot. He went into Alberto's, it is the convenience store near my house. I do not follow him in."

"Good, don't," San Lujan ordered him. He looked at his watch and said, "Just keep an eye on the store. We'll be there in five minutes. You understand me? Don't go into that store for any reason."

"Yes, sir! I will not go in, and wait for you."

San Lujan disconnected the call and ordered his driver to head in that direction. He sat back in the rich leather seat of the SUV and allowed himself a smile of satisfaction. He knew exactly what was happening here. The Americans split up purposely—Pirro probably gave himself away in some fashion—and they were now trying to draw the young man into a trap. Oldest trick in the book: divide and conquer.

Well, they didn't have anything to fear from one man. A lone American in a foreign country was hardly a threat. Not to mention that they now had Stein and Crosse trapped like rats. San Lujan would deal with Isidora's betrayal; yes, he would make an example of her by blow-torching her face in front of her close friends. That would teach them not to step out of line with Havana Five. Then he would kill Stein and Crosse, thereby eliminating the last links to Inez Fuego.

But first, he would deal with this American once and for all.

INEZ FUEGO BREATHED DEEPLY to calm her nerves.

She omitted telling Colonel Hurtado of the summons she received from the other members of the Five. To make matters worse, Lazaro seemed unreachable by now and she really needed him to accompany her to the meeting. For a moment Fuego considered her chief bodyguard and enforcer might actually have something to do with this sudden call to appear before the others, but she quickly dismissed the idea. Lazaro stood to gain nothing by siding against her with the others in the Five, and she didn't believe him to be that kind of man, anyway. He had ethics…just like her Natalio.

After calling Lazaro about a dozen times and no success in reaching him, Fuego grabbed his right-hand man, Jeronimo Bustos and a detail to accompany her to the meeting. Fuego didn't bother to change her clothes following her return visit to Juventud. She rather liked the outfit—a number of people had remarked how it enhanced her beauty in a sporting way—and such allure seemed one of the few remaining ways to exert some control over the men of Havana Five. The fact all but Macario Lombardi were married made little difference to them, so why should it make any difference to her? A lot greater women than she had used their feminine wiles for centuries to influence powerful men, and she considered it little more than another tool in her arsenal.

She arrived at the estate of Santiago Famosa on the fringes of the city within twenty minutes. A pair of servants showed her to the formal sitting room, which included a full bar and snack buffet.

What a gluttonous beast, she thought.

Famosa always had lacked any sort of control when it came to fine living. He ate and drank constantly, lived a sedentary lifestyle and smoked cigars incessantly. Fuego had once overheard his wife at a party talk to her friends about how she could hardly stand to be in bed with the man at night. Was it any wonder she took about five or six trips a year out of the country, those usually for weeks at a time? The thought of Famosa's sweaty, fat body even sliding between the same sheets at night with her made Fuego want to retch. She couldn't imagine having to pleasure such a slob and still find any of her own.

Natalio had always kept in top physical shape. His dark hair had started to gray around the temples just a bit in his later years, leaving him more handsome and distinguished than ever, and his skills in bed were unparalleled to any other lover Fuego had ever known. Not that she knew many. Since his death, Fuego had only twice slept with other men. Most of the time she felt content to simply pleasure herself— quickly and unemotionally—to satisfy the basic urgings natural to any woman her age.

A few minutes later Famosa came into the room along with the others of the Five. Macario Lombardi, the Cuban-Italian for whom Fuego had the most respect, smiled and planted a fashionable, gentlemanly kiss on her cheek in way of greeting. Neither Nicanor Armanteros nor that bastard, Eduardo Valdese, came anywhere close to making such a gesture. They took seats next to each other at the table across from her.

Famosa patted her shoulder and moved to kiss her hand, but Fuego pulled away with a mock expression of righteous indignation. "What's this all about, Chago? Why have you called me here like a dog?"

"I wasn't aware the request of a meeting constituted such treatment," Valdese said. "We were all called here in haste."

Fuego looked at him with the sensation of ice coursing through her veins. "I believe I was addressing Chago." She looked back at him expectantly.

Famosa took a seat and lit a cigar, a half-full glass of brandy clutched in his other hand. Through the tendrils of smoke he said, "I'll come right to the point, Inez. We've come into some information that you are planning a, how shall we call it? A coup, perhaps?"

"A what?" Fuego asked.

"We have it on good word that you might wish to betray us," Armanteros said. "That you blame us for the death of your husband."

Fuego kept the tone in her voice measured and casual. "My beloved Natalio, may he rest in peace, was killed conducting business for the Five. I have never made it a secret that I suspect all of you might have contributed to his death. But I haven't any proof. Therefore, I must assume you have all acted honorably and that you had nothing to do with Natalio's death."

"But you think we did nothing to stop it," Famosa said.

"I don't trust you to watch my back, if that's what you mean," Fuego said. "But I haven't done anything to betray the Five. I haven't told our secrets or taken anything that wasn't mine. So what is your charge against me?"

"Let's cut this shit," Valdese said. "We know about the little army you are building on Juventud. We've been told it's for the purposes of destroying us."

Fuego burst into laughter. "You're stupid, Eduardo. Too

stupid for your own good, I think. Do you believe I would need to raise arms against you to destroy you? If I wanted to eliminate the Five, I could simply walk away…or even better, destroy you from the inside. The particulars of what you're talking about I am not yet at liberty to disclose. But I can tell you that I paid for it solely out of personal funds, and I have no intention of eliminating this enterprise."

"We hear otherwise, Inez," Famosa said. "And it disturbs us."

"What proof do you have?" she asked.

Silence ran through the room. Fuego made sure she locked eyes with each man in turn. "Well? I'm waiting for someone to show me proof!"

"We have none at present."

Fuego rose and headed for the door. "Then I assume we're done. When you have something better, you know where to find me."

"Inez!" Famosa called. She stopped and turned to face him. He said, "Whatever it is you're planning, think very carefully before you act. You cannot win against us. Let this go and find forgiveness. We can take care of you."

"I need no one to take care of me, Chago," Fuego said. And as she turned and walked out the door she added, "Ever."

CHAPTER ELEVEN

The Bosa Nova rhythms of the Latin American rock music blared throughout the club, and Rafael Encizo moved through the place with relative ease. It wasn't that crowded considering the time of the morning, although that was about to change. Grimaldi had dropped him off fifteen minutes before, and Encizo elected to case the joint before venturing inside. He didn't trust anyone right now, considering everything that happened to this point in the mission, and he wasn't about to let his guard down.

Actually, his visit to this particular place seemed like a long shot, but Bolan was counting on him and Encizo knew he had to come through. He searched for someone in particular: a man named Andres, aka Umberto Andres-Ituarte. The same man that Stein and Crosse confirmed they had been dealing with; the man who claimed to represent Inez Fuego. The truth about this man went a little deeper. It always did in these kinds of things.

Andres hadn't always been a member of the Cuban underworld. At one time he'd served as a trusted member of the

Central Intelligence Agency. Born in Mexico and raised in Honduras, Andres became a political refugee of Cuba to escape death after it was discovered he'd acted as a double agent between the Contra and Sandinista factions. He managed to get into the U.S. on a Cuban visa and soon gained naturalized citizenship. His knowledge of operations in the Central American regimes, not to mention his intimate acquaintance with Cuba, served him well in his cover training at Langley and subsequent reinsertion into Cuban society.

Of course, Crosse and Stein would have known all this about the man named Andres if they had taken the time to do their homework. While Andres had long severed any official ties with the U.S. government—he decided to become a freelancer and officially "resigned" from the CIA by mailing the charred remnants of his credentials to the deputy director—he still plied his trade quite profitably to the highest bidder. This made him a valuable asset to members within the Cuban underworld, mostly because of what Andres knew about U.S. operations in and around the country. However, that knowledge also made him vulnerable, susceptible to the suggestion that the government might think it worth coming after him if he didn't lend his cooperation, and that's the angle Encizo planned to play.

Despite the small crowd and its sparse seating, it still took the Cuban nearly ten minutes to locate Andres. He found the man in a large, semiprivate booth that gave him almost a perfect view of the entire club. Two large men stood guard at the edge of the slightly raised dais on which the booth sat. Andres appeared to be enjoying some type of late breakfast, supplemented with an ample supply of margaritas and a dark-haired woman who was trying to wriggle her way onto his lap.

"Hello, Andres," Encizo said in perfect Spanish.

Andres looked up—a moment of surprise followed by recognition—and then muttered something under his breath. Encizo didn't catch the entirety of what Andres said, but he recognized intents in the swift and threatening movements of the bodyguards. Encizo ducked in time to avoid a ham-size fist from one of the bruisers that, unfortunately for them, connected with the other bodyguard. Encizo moved easily to the side and jumped into the air while firing a two-finger jab to the attacking bodyguard's right eye. Something wet and sticky spread across Encizo's hand, followed by a scream of agony from his opponent a moment later. The man reached up to his injured eye with both hands at the same time his knees hit the carpeted dais. Encizo fired a front snap kick that sent the guy rocketing down the steps.

The other bodyguard quickly recovered from the punch landed by his comrade and charged Encizo. The Cuban crouched and fired a rock-hard uppercut that caught the bodyguard in the groin. Air whooshed from the man's lungs and he bent over. Encizo jumped to his feet, slapped the man's ears between his palms, then executed a spinning side kick that fractured the bodyguard's jaw. The man's form went slack and slid down the steps to land next to his unconscious partner.

Encizo turned in time to see Andres reach inside his coat. He rushed for Andres, pinning the man's hand beneath his jacket before he could draw his weapon. Encizo produced the Glock Model 21 and shoved the muzzle under Andres's chin.

Encizo looked at the woman and said, "Get lost."

She did.

"Let go of the heat and take your hand out, Andres," Encizo ordered him. "Slowly, or I swear I'll blow your brains out the top of your head."

Encizo felt Andres's hand go slack inside his jacket as the man slowly removed it. He came out empty-handed, just as instructed. The Phoenix Force pro reached into Andres's coat until the butt of a pistol filled his hand. He yanked it free from the former CIA agent's holster and tossed it across the room. Encizo hauled the man out of the booth and steered him toward the hallway that led to the bathrooms in the back.

When they got inside, Encizo locked the door by the flimsy bolt. It wouldn't keep anyone out who really wanted to get in, but the average person would probably come back later or notify the manager. Encizo planned to be long gone by then. He shoved Andres into the farthest stall and sat him on the dirty toilet seat.

"Spread your legs," Encizo ordered him in English. "Wider. Good. Now, I'm going to ask questions and you're going to answer them. If I think you're lying to me, Andres, I'll shoot your balls off. Understand?"

Andres nodded. "Yeah, I understand. I know it has been a long time, but there's no reason to treat me like this."

"Shut up," Encizo said. "You brokered a deal between two DIA agents and a member of Havana Five for information."

"I don't—"

"Don't bother denying it, Andres. You were never that good of a liar."

"Fine, what do you want to know?"

"I want to know who was behind it and why?"

"Her name is Inez Feugo," Andres said. "She is one of Havana Five."

Encizo nodded. He hadn't bothered to ask questions right off to which he didn't already have the answers. He needed to test the waters first, see if Andres would tell him the truth. He didn't have any reason to trust a guy who would sell out his own mother for just a few pesos. Guys like Andres really had no moral code to live by; mostly, they got on with their wits and their ability to keep secrets, most of the time anyway, and somehow they managed to weasel their way into enough deals they could often make a pretty decent living at it. Such men disgusted Encizo because they didn't know the meaning of loyalty, and Andres was just one of those men.

"The ELN terrorist training camp Fuego told you about," Encizo continued. "Where is it?"

"I do not know."

"Did Fuego fund their operations?"

"I think so," he said. "But there's no way you're going to find it. Not that easily. I haven't even been able to learn of its location. The rest in Havana Five, I think they found out about it but they kept it quiet."

"If you couldn't learn of its location, and you worked for Fuego, what makes you think *they* could find out?"

Andres chuckled. "Come on, even you aren't *that* stupid. In fact, if I remember correctly, you were born in this country. You know there isn't anything Havana Five doesn't have a hand on here. They have connections all over the country. I don't know if they actually learned of the location, but I do know that one of them managed to get spies inside the operation itself."

"What's Fuego planning to do with them?"

"She's going after the other members of Havana Five."

"No dice," Encizo said. "She'd be cutting her own throat that way. Get ready to lose a testicle, Andres, because I don't believe you."

"No, wait!" he said, raising his hands. "It is true what I tell you! If the others in Havana Five are out of the way, all of it reverts to her. Anyone who could wipe these men from existence…do you think anyone would dare challenge such power? If she destroys Havana Five, it all becomes hers."

Some of what Andres said made sense. Fuego would have to face up-and-comers in those territories, maybe a few who might take to challenging her authority, but on the whole she would gain control of their shares. On the flip side, the entire thing could backfire on her. The balance of power among Havana Five was its main strength, and had been for more than three decades. To think that balance might be shaken, that the scales of power might tip in the favor of anyone— particularly a ruthless and influential woman like Fuego— seemed a pretty frightening prospect. Never mind changing the balance of power, it would also create unrest in Cuba, maybe even lead to the civil war the Man feared, if the current power structure under Fidel knew Fuego had built a terrorist army right under their noses without them even knowing about it.

What everyone feared most in Cuba, but nobody would admit to, was the idea of change. Particularly if it meant an end to the regime that had ruled with an iron hand so long— it had maintained its stranglehold through intimidation and brutalities best not left scrutinized by the polls of public opinion—because such a change could send the entire country into economic and social turmoil. The lines would grow fuzzy, and citizens might actually try to take back what they had been unable to possess for so long.

"I still don't see how this could end up being anything but a disaster for Fuego," Encizo finally said.

"It won't matter to her!" Andres protested. "All she can see is her blind hatred of the men who killed her husband. She has had years to let this fester. She has saved her resources, every dime she could manage, and built her influence among the politicians. She won't suffer from this at all. Even if she doesn't seize control of the other territories, nobody would dare challenge her or even question her involvement."

The whole scenario seemed entirely unlikely, but Encizo couldn't make that judgment alone. He needed to get the facts as best he knew them and deliver straight, hard intelligence to Bolan. The Executioner couldn't operate efficiently or be expected to make a strategically sound decision without the correct information. There was only one way Encizo saw of doing that. It expanded the original parameters of his mission but he didn't see he had much of a choice.

"I'll tell you what, Andres," Encizo said, lowering his pistol. "For now, I'm going to let you live and assume you're telling me the truth."

Andres's body went slack and the relief spread visibly across his expression. "Thank you, Pascal. I owe you one."

"Yes…you do." Encizo grinned. "And I'm glad to hear you say that, because I know exactly how you're going to pay me back."

"And how is this?" Andres now looked worried.

"You're going to introduce me into your little circle of friends," Encizo replied. "You're going to get me inside Havana Five."

THE MEN WHO CAME THROUGH the door of the shop were not what Mack Bolan expected.

He didn't worry about it, though, since he actually liked surprises—especially when he was the one springing them, which is exactly what he did. The four men fanned out through the small store and Bolan came through the curtain with full vengeance. The Executioner took the first one with a single shot to the chest. The Beretta's report thundered inside the confines of the small shop as the 9 mm Parabellum round punched through the gunman's heart and exited below his right shoulder blade.

The second target managed to pop off a pair of shots from a .45-caliber pistol before Bolan silenced him with a double-tap to the gut. The man's body reeled backward, sending him flying through the shop window and onto the sidewalk. That would, unfortunately, attract attention from those outside, which would surely bring the police all the quicker.

The other pair produced SMGs slung beneath their jackets. In that brief moment Bolan recognized the deadly lines of the weapons. They were Mini-SAFs, manufactured in Chile and based on the SIG 540. The weapon had a cyclic rate of 1,200 rounds per minute and the Executioner knew he wouldn't have much room to get clear when they opened up. Particularly not when he noticed the panicked boy behind the counter step directly into the line of fire.

With any thoughts of his own safety gone, Bolan leaped for the boy and pulled him behind the counter milliseconds before the remaining pair of gunners opened up. A fusillade of 9 mm slugs slammed into doors, counters and cabinets. Glass shattered and frozen goods imploded under the onslaught of autofire. It sounded like the very insides of the building shook under the blaring, eardrum-popping reports of the twin Mini-SAFs. Bolan sheltered the boy's body with his own as shards of glass and bits of plaster rained on him.

When there was a lull in the firing, Bolan got to his feet. The men had mistakenly opened fire simultaneously and sustained their assault until both weapons ran dry, perhaps hoping the volume of rounds would take down their quarry. It seemed like the actions of untrained thugs rather than elite enforcers for a group like Havana Five, but Bolan would take whatever good fortune he could find wherever he could find it.

The Executioner set the Beretta for 3-round-burst mode and squeezed the trigger on the closer target. Fumbling with a fresh magazine, the man looked surprised to see Bolan up so quickly and firing on him. Surprise flashed to pain and then nothingness as his head exploded under the unerring aim of a seasoned marksman.

The remaining enemy gunman managed to get his weapon up and tracking before Bolan brought him down. Two rounds caught the guy's weapon and blew it from his grip; the last entered his right lung, bounced off the breastbone, perforated the right kidney and lodged there. The impact drove the man off his feet and dumped his corpse on the dusty floor.

Bolan looked at the boy who still laid facedown, hands covering his ears and mumbling what had to have been prayers. The Executioner didn't bother to check on him; the boy was frightened but uninjured. He whirled and headed for the front door, intent on doing the most unpredictable thing he could think of. Bolan landed on the sidewalk outside and looked in all directions.

It didn't take him long to spot the panicked face of the young boy named Pirro.

The young man turned and sprinted away. Bolan set off in pursuit without hesitation. He couldn't let him get away. Pirro would know who had sent him, and why, and that remained Bolan's one lead in getting to Inez Fuego. Pirro would have information nobody else would, and the Executioner didn't plan to let such an information goldmine slip through his fingers.

Bolan pushed the wail of police sirens from his mind, intent on making sure it didn't detract him from his pursuit. Pirro was definitely fast and in other circumstances he would have given the average man a run for the money, but he lacked Bolan's physical stamina and training.

For only a moment the Executioner wondered exactly where this trail would lead.

CHAPTER TWELVE

Eighteen seconds.

That's how long it took the American to wipe out four of San Lujan's men, and two of them had been armed with stutterguns. He knew because he timed it. He then watched with utter shock as the guy leaped through the broken window of the store and sprinted down the street. San Lujan saw the American chase after Pirro, but he couldn't do anything about it between the traffic and swift arrival of police cars.

With no other choices, San Lujan slid into the driver's seat, started the SUV's engine and got the hell out of there. Where to go? He figured he could call for reinforcements but by the time they arrived he would have lost Pirro and his tail. Pirro would have to fend for himself on this one; San Lujan couldn't risk drawing that kind of exposure or attention. As he left the neighborhood and got onto the bayshore drive that led home, his cell phone buzzed for attention.

San Lujan looked at the number on the LCD. Shit. It was Inez. He thought about not answering at first, then changed his mind and picked up. "Yes, ma'am."

"Where the fuck have you been, Lazaro, hmm?"

"Watching the American cut down four of my men single-handedly."

A long silence followed before Fuego asked, "What American?"

"The one I told you about, Inez. The one I told you would be a problem." Indeed, as he proved it with each passing hour. So far, this American agent and his friends had been in-country less than twenty-four hours—at least that's what he assumed—and they had already retrieved Stein and Crosse. Now San Lujan could feel them rapidly closing in on their operations.

"Have you identified him yet?"

"No, there wasn't any time. He's apparently secured Stein and Crosse, probably hiding them until arrangements can be made to get them out of Cuba. They won't be a problem, though. I know where they are and I will eliminate them soon enough."

"That's only the beginning of our problems, Lazaro," Fuego replied. "I just came from a meeting with the Five. They have someone inside the colonel's group, and they're getting close to discovering my plan. I'm going to contact him now, tell him to speed up the timetable."

"None of it will make any difference if any of what's happened in the past few days gets back to them," he reminded her.

"What do you suggest?"

"I would feel better if you return to the estate and don't leave until I contact you again."

"What are you going to do?"

"These Americans are professionals," he said. "At least the one I've seen. He has killed eight of my men and walked away unharmed. It is obviously going to take more than one of our security details."

"You have a plan?"

"Yes. Is there someone you trust most inside the Five who might be able to supply me with men and weapons."

"If I had to choose, I would suggest you speak to Macario first. I think he's the most trustworthy of them, and he's always been my greatest supporter inside the group."

"I will do it," he replied. "I think your idea to push the operation forward is the right one. If these men are as good as your colonel is boasting maybe they'll have better luck stopping the Americans."

"All I can do is ask," she said. "From my meeting with the colonel today, he seems anxious. Is there anything else I can help you with?"

"No, ma'am," San Lujan said. A lump began to form in his throat but he choked it back. "And I want you to know something, Inez. There is always a possibility I will not survive an encounter with this American."

"Nonsense!" From the tone in her voice, San Lujan knew his use of her first name wasn't lost on her. "You are one of the most ablest men I know, and I will not hear you talk like this again. Do you understand?"

"I do. But I have seen him fight, and I can assure you he is very good. I just wanted you know of this possibility. And if I should die, I didn't want to go without telling you that I've enjoyed serving you. And Natalio before you. You have been my closest friends."

"You will come back," she said quietly. "That's all there is to it."

"Goodbye." And he hung up.

San Lujan shook the eerie feeling that ran through his

body in the form of a shudder. He suppressed the urge to vomit. Somewhere out there the Americans were making a mockery of their entire operation and killing his men without hesitation. There wouldn't be any reasoning with men like this. Given a choice, San Lujan would have liked to solve this with a simple bribe. His mistress certainly had enough cash to make an attractive offer. But he hadn't called the game here and the big American had already made his point loud and clear. There wouldn't be any compromise. So now San Lujan had to find and eliminate these men before they did more damage.

It wasn't the operations by Hurtado at risk in this particular instance. No, the Americans were preoccupied with something else; they seemed driven by something more important. He knew the key to finding them would be to discover what exactly had them so scared. Maybe they were on a mission to take down Havana Five, perhaps something else. Whatever their reasons, San Lujan would start by getting the best and most skilled soldiers he could from Macario Lombardi.

And then he'd hunt down the American bastards like the natural prey they were.

"END OF THE LINE!" Bolan called as Pirro reached the adobe wall of a dead-end alley.

The young man turned and raised his hands. Bolan approached with caution, the muzzle of his pistol aimed center mass. The Executioner had to wonder a moment if the kid's choice to take an alley to nowhere was simply the product of fear, or if he might have led Bolan into a trap.

Bolan's eyes roved along the tops of the three-story multifamily dwellings, watchful for any possible threat. He considered that threat might lurk behind any one of the dirt-streaked windows that lined the tenements. There were no stairs to basement doors, so he didn't have to worry about a threat from below. Bolan looked over his shoulder and saw nobody approaching. Even with it nearing midday, it was still pretty dark this far back in the alleyway.

"Do you speak English?" Bolan asked.

"No," Pirro replied.

"A lie," Bolan countered. Pirro's eyes betrayed truth in that observation. "No prostitute in Havana wouldn't know English. Too many European and North American customers. So spare me."

"You think you're smart," Pirro finally said. "Don't you?"

"I could just put a bullet through your head for sending those thugs down on me," Bolan replied. "But I figure everyone deserves a second chance."

"I no help you!" Pirro said. "No way!"

"You help me or I kill you here and now," Bolan said. He wouldn't have shot the kid unarmed, but he figured Pirro didn't know that. Not that he took Pirro for an idiot; far from it, in fact. Bolan had to give Pirro credit for one thing: the kid had some spirit. Not that it would buy him an out with Bolan and certainly not that the Executioner approved of the lifestyle he'd chosen. Still, the best he could do was try to guide young men like this one, show them the error of their choices.

"Now's your chance," Bolan said, taking a couple of steps closer. "You seem smart. Maybe you do the smart thing now and live to tell about it. So decide now."

Bolan stopped within a couple of feet to make sure the youth stayed out of reach but had plenty of room to avoid a move. He'd chased Pirro for better than a half mile and despite his excellent shape he had to admit the kid gave him a run for his money. Bolan could feel the exhaustion set in but he didn't let it distract him.

"Time's up," Bolan said. "What's it going to be?"

"Not today," Pirro said simply.

The whack to his head came out of nowhere. A second blow drove him to his knees before he fell forward. Bolan tried to maintain the grip on his pistol, but Pirro suddenly rushed him and stomped on his hand while punching him in the head. Bolan forced the pain from his mind but the stars continued to dance on a backdrop of gray.

Then his world shimmered from gray to green, and finally black.

RAFAEL ENCIZO SAT IN THE CAR, watching the massive house for quite a while, and considered his options. When he first convinced Andres to get him inside Havana Five he hadn't really thought the guy could do it. His profile said Andres always talked big, and although he had the ability to deliver the goods there were other times when he'd failed miserably.

It didn't seem like this would be one of those times.

Encizo had to wonder if Andres was leading him into the proverbial lion's den. The guy had many connections and friends in Cuba. Some of those friends might have seen what went down in the club and decided to contact other friends. For all Encizo knew, an entire army of machine-gun-toting hoods were just waiting for them to make an entrance so they could blow his guts all over the place.

And then maybe he was just becoming paranoid.

Grimaldi spoke up from behind the driver's seat as if he'd read the Cuban warrior's mind. "You sure about this?"

"Not really," Encizo replied. He showed his friend a grin and added, "But then, that's part of the fun. Isn't it?"

"You've been hanging around the others too long," Grimaldi said in reference to Encizo's fellow Phoenix Force members.

"We'll be back," he said. "Don't wait up."

"Remember your ten o'clock curfew," Grimaldi quipped.

Encizo got out of the backseat with Andres—never a bad idea to keep an eye on a guy like him—and they walked casually to the pair of tall, wrought-iron gates of the driveway entrance. Some of the locals considered it a veritable sin to live like this in Cuba. Castro's regime didn't generally tolerate the flaunting of one's wealth, particularly when done in plain view of the government, although there were a few notable exceptions. Friends of the regime, for one, and few would argue that Santiago Famosa wasn't one of them.

Four heavies converged on the men and immediately frisked them—Encizo had insisted they leave any firearms behind—and then Andres managed to talk them into seeing Famosa on an urgent matter. The walk up the drive didn't fail to impress. Verdant flora lined the massive house painted in earth tones. Four large adobe pillars running along the front supported the portico. Stained-glass windows gleamed in the late-morning sun, set in floor-length window boxes emerging at the corners and along the front of the facade. Terra-cotta tiles covered them along with the remaining roof. Based on what he saw just from the front, Encizo estimated the house and grounds in America would probably fetch at least eight or nine million dollars. Down here, Famosa had probably paid half that.

Encizo wasn't unfamiliar with the infamous "Chago" Famosa, as his friends knew him. Some even still referred to him as Don Famosa, and not too surprising given his family history. In Encizo's book, though, Famosa was little more than just another dirt-bag crime lord with an overinflated ego; a man who thought the money and success from plying his filthy trades had somehow bought him a divine license to impose his will, by whatever means, on the helpless and innocent.

Encizo looked forward to the day he would kill this man, and he knew that day was coming soon.

The house guards led Encizo and Andres into a sitting room. The place looked comfortable and nonthreatening. Encizo had to admit that Famosa's interior decorator had impeccable taste. He decided to take a place on a settee covered in rich, red-velvet upholstery fringed with hand-woven tapestries of gold and purple threads. Andres seemed fidgety and paced the whole time they waited.

"Relax," Encizo finally muttered after five minutes of watching Andres nearly work himself into a nervous breakdown.

The door opened and two guards entered followed by a lumbering Santiago Famosa. Encizo immediately got to his feet in respect. He tried to look as dapper as possible in the cream-colored linen suit he'd bought and had hurriedly tailored by a man Andres knew.

"Chago, thank you for seeing us," Andres said hurriedly.

"What is it?" Famosa barked impatiently. "My men said you told me this was urgent."

"It is," Andres said. "To be sure, Chago, it is definitely urgent!"

Encizo felt immediately on edge, worried that Andres would give away their entire game before he got a word in.

"Well, then, what is it?" Famosa now noticed Encizo

standing there, hands folded in front him like a mild-mannered car salesman. "And who the fuck is this?"

"This—this…" Andres stammered.

Encizo decided not wait any longer. He stepped forward and offered his hand. "Don Famosa, my name is Segundo Pestos. I am sorry to intrude like this. I know you're busy so I'll come right to the point. I understand that you may be in the market for some information."

"I have plenty of spies, man," Famosa said with a dismissive wave.

He looked at Andres and in a less easy tone said, "This is what you bother me for? Some peddler of information?"

"I beg your pardon, sir, but I—" Encizo began.

Famosa put a finger in Encizo's face and said, "Say another word, Pestos, and I'll have your tongue cut out."

Encizo thought furiously. He knew unarmed he didn't stand a chance against the house guard. He could probably take the two bruisers here, they didn't look any bigger or meaner than the pair who had been guarding Andres—and not doing a very good job of it in Encizo's humble opinion—but to go up against the whole entourage without some backing would have been the work of a brazen fool. No, the best thing to do would be to let Andres, probably the smoothest tongue in all the Western hemisphere, talk him into Famosa's good graces.

"But, Chago, you will want to hear what this man has to say!" Andres protested. "May I talk to you a moment?"

"You *are* talking to me!" Famosa's face visibly reddened. "What is this bullshit?"

"I mean privately."

"I don't do business in private," he said. "Unless it's with one of my own."

Famosa didn't know Encizo knew it, but he knew the man was actually referring to the other members of Havana Five. Trust remained a mainstay of their operations according to what Andres had told him, and it was this fact that gave Encizo the idea to play out the hand to see where it got him. But he wouldn't get an audience unless Andres stopped sputtering and got to the damn point.

"But that's what I'm trying to say," Andres pressed. "That's what Segundo's here to talk to you about. One of your own." Andres's voice dropped to a whisper on that last.

Famosa looked a moment at Encizo, who remained passive, waiting in the same position he had before but a bit more respectfully now. Famosa looked at his two bodyguards, looked at the coquettish, almost shy, expression on Encizo's face, visibly came to a decision, and then ordered his guards out of the room with instructions to wait just outside the door and not let anybody in.

When they were alone, Famosa took a seat and gestured Encizo and Andres toward the settee. When the men were seated, he said, "All right, tell me what you have to say."

Encizo chose each word carefully. "I have come into some information that I think will be of great value to you. My connections have learned of a plot against Havana Five."

"What kind of plot?"

"One of the Five is planning to kill the rest of you," he replied.

Encizo had decided to take this risk in the hope of getting inside the organization. Role camouflage was a technique the Executioner had used many times against the Mafia, and even on occasion against select terrorist organizations, with great success. Part of it required good acting skills, but part of it required the role player to know something of that society, to have lived and even breathed it in some way. Well, maybe Rafael Encizo didn't know Havana Five but he certainly knew what it meant to be Cuban.

Famosa burst into laughter. After he caught his breath he said, "So what? You think we don't already know this, Pestos? We have know this for quite some time now. We even know which one of us has planned this."

"Do you?" Encizo said with a cocksure smile.

"Why do you ask that way?" Famosa inquired with a frown. "You act as if you know something I do not."

"That is exactly what I've been trying to tell you, Chago," Andres chimed in. "This is not what you think it is."

Encizo cleared his throat and continued. "I would bet you've been told that Inez Fuego is behind this whole thing."

"Yes. How do you know this?"

"Because it's a lie," Encizo said. Now he had Famosa where he wanted him. "A lie started by one of the others to throw you off guard. Think about this, Don Famosa. Who of all the Five do you trust the least? And who would stand to benefit from your death more and the deaths of the others?"

A harsh expression came over Famosa's face, mixed with the dawning of a revelation. Encizo had used Andres's intelligence regarding other infighting among Havana Five and played a hunch. He didn't really know who the other members of Havana Five were, but then, he didn't have to. All he had to do was to plant the seed and let Famosa's imagination do the rest. It didn't take much to spook men like this; theirs was a dark and shadowy world of murder and betrayal, where those who called themselves friends waited in the wings for just the right opportunity to draw a razor across the exposed throats of those same pathetic victims.

"I think I may know who you mean," Famosa said.

"Then it's important I tell you right away," Encizo said, nailing the coffin shut. "He plans to make his move. Tonight."

CHAPTER THIRTEEN

It felt like a freight train ran through the Executioner's head.

As he regained consciousness, lancing needles of white-hot pain burned through his eyeballs and made him feel like he had to vomit. Bolan forced the sensation from his mind while choking back the rise of bile. A few deep breaths calmed his stomach and left him feeling good enough to raise his head to view his surroundings. At first Bolan thought his eyes deceived him, but as the world came into focus he realized the figure seated next him was anything but a dream.

The young woman wore her long, dark hair in an unkempt fashion, although that did nothing to hide the graceful and heart-shaped lines of her face. She had a strong chin with the blackest eyes Bolan could ever remember seeing. As she watched him, he could tell she seemed neither fearful nor anxious. Instead she seemed to study him with a mix of mild amusement and curiosity. The image faded and Bolan couldn't be sure how long he was out but he didn't think it was long because the young woman remained seated in the same position.

This time, Bolan had all of his faculties and the pain in his head subsided. He reached up to feel the back of his head and he encountered a damp cloth.

"You okay," she replied. "I no hit too hard."

Bolan didn't bother to hide his surprise. "You speak English."

"Yes."

"And you're admitting to whacking me in the back of the head?"

She delivered a curt nod and replied with a stronger, "Yes. You try and shoot my friend."

"I wasn't going to shoot him," Bolan said, and he rose slowly at the waist.

His surroundings came into focus. The room couldn't have been more than eight by eight, and Bolan realized his feet dangled over a cot. To his surprise, he still had his boots on; he would have at least expected his captors to strip him down. Either they weren't professionals—not a hard thing to believe considering the fact Pirro left a young woman to stand guard over a full-grown adult male—or he hadn't been here long. It would have taken quite a bit just for them to haul his deadweight from the alley to wherever he was now.

"You point gun at him," the young woman replied, then repeated, "You try and shoot my friend."

"And why would someone like you be friends with a guy like Pirro?"

Bolan got the flinch of a reaction he hoped for. Obviously, Pirro didn't know that the Executioner knew his identity and neither had this one. They wouldn't have expected this since Bolan only came into the information because he spotted Pirro tailing them. That would at least keep Isidora's cover for a little longer, in turn keeping Stein and Crosse alive. For now he didn't have to worry about them and could focus on the most important thing to any man in his position.

Escape.

"What's your name?" Bolan asked.

"I no supposed to talk to you," she replied hesitantly. "I no say more till Pirro come back."

"I'm afraid I won't be around for that," Bolan said.

The Executioner sat up fully and swung his legs off the cot. He started to rise and then heard the unmistakable click of a hammer cock. Bolan looked at the girl and saw she'd scooted back her chair and now stood at the door. She held a .38-caliber snub-nosed revolver. Bolan took immediate notice of her swollen belly, obvious only because the maternity blouse she wore looked about three sizes too small. So, maybe Pirro was a bit clever after all—no guy in his right mind would harm a pregnant woman.

Bolan considered his predicament. Not even he would be fast enough to reach the young woman before she pulled the trigger, *if* she could pull it, although that wasn't a risk he planned to take. The Executioner didn't have any delusions of grandeur, particularly with some notion of invulnerability to bullets. Bolan tried not to look at the gun, preferring to keep his ice-blue eyes locked on his antagonist.

"Now you plan to shoot me," he said in a level voice.

"You no leave," she said simply.

Her hand wavered just a moment, and in the dim light something about the pistol caught Bolan's eye. Something about it seemed familiar although he couldn't immediately place it. It was almost as if he'd seen the weapon before. Bolan thought furiously, a bit puzzled that sight of the weapon would trigger so many alarms. Then it came to him. The cylinder on the pistol was too narrow long-wise. There was no way it could hold .38-caliber shells, and he knew he hadn't misidentified its configuration. A heartbeat later he realized he'd been duped. So had this young woman because she obviously didn't know the weapon in her hands was a starter's pistol.

Bolan stepped forward and in one blinding moment ripped the pistol from her shaky grip. He thumbed the release catch and flipped out the cylinder. Five gold circles occupied the holes but they weren't the ends of .38 shell casings. Bolan pushed back the rod and out dropped five powder blanks. Bolan whisked the weapon across the room, gently moved the young woman aside and opened the door she no longer blocked.

She let out an ear-piercing scream and a few seconds later Pirro appeared in the hallway. The youth watched Bolan a moment, indecisive, and then he rushed the Executioner with a blood-curdling shout of his own. The soldier waited until Pirro was nearly on top of him, and then he sidestepped and caught the youth with a clothesline to the chest. Pirro hit the ground hard, but Bolan didn't give him quarter. He reached down and hauled the guy to his feet. Bolan looked to his flank to ensure the young woman didn't blindside him again, and then dragged Pirro kicking and screaming into a main living area.

Bolan threw him across the room and onto a couch that was way too big for the space it occupied.

"Who do you work for?" Bolan asked.

"Fuck you!" Pirro said in Spanish, and he began to hurl additional curses at his captor.

Bolan simply stood there, arms folded, and waited for Pirro to get over his tantrum. He'd actually meant what he said to the young woman in not planning to kill Pirro, but right at the moment he felt his patience begin to wear thin. Bolan turned and went back to the room where he'd been. He reached for the young woman, who shied away, grabbed her arm with enough force to let her know he meant business, and steered her out to the couch where he set her not-too-gently next to Pirro.

"I want you where I can see you," Bolan said.

He turned back to Pirro and said, "Now, we're going to try it again. Who are you working for?"

Pirro remained silent with a resolute mask of defiance. Bolan stepped forward and grabbed the youth around the throat. He picked him off the couch and pinned him to a nearby wall. Pirro tried to emit a growl of outrage but with the pressure applied to his throat it came out more like a squeal. This wasn't the kind of tactic Bolan preferred in situations like this but he didn't have any time, and this pair had already demonstrated quite effectively how treacherous they could be.

"Sorry, not the answer I wanted. One more time, who got you onto us?"

Bolan released the pressure enough for Pirro to talk while still keeping him pinned to the wall. "You do not know who you are messing with."

"I'm petrified," Bolan deadpanned.

"You will be dead by sundown."

"You've been watching too much TV," Bolan said. "Is it Havana Five who sent you?"

For a long moment Pirro didn't say anything but then he appeared to change his mind. The look of fear left his face— at least Pirro tried to pretend it had but he couldn't seem to control the tremors in his body—and his disposition became almost cocky. "Yes, they did. And when they find out you've done this they will come and kill you. You are dead, American."

"So Inez Fuego sends a boy to do work she's too cowardly to do herself," Bolan said.

"I'm no boy, mister," Pirro said.

"Yeah, sure," Bolan replied. "My weapons…where are they?"

Pirro didn't say anything, trying to avert his eyes, but Bolan watched carefully and saw Pirro's eyes flick just once in the direction of a nearby cabinet, about knee high. The Executioner turned and walked to the cabinet, detected it was constructed of cheap wood, and swiftly put a boot through the twin doors. The flimsy construction shattered under the force of Bolan's kick. Inside the cabinet lay his Beretta 93-R and combat knife. He snatched the weapons, tucking the knife into his boot, and then checked the Beretta's ammunition level and action before secreting it in the waistband holder beneath his T-shirt.

He turned on Pirro and the young woman and pinned them with an icy stare. "Now, let's talk about how I might get in touch with Inez Fuego."

AFTER NEARLY A HALF HOUR of discussions, Santiago Famosa permitted Encizo to leave with the promise he would be in touch by late afternoon. As Encizo squeezed into the front seat of the cramped vehicle alone, Grimaldi gave him a strange look.

"Where's Andres?" he asked.

"He's staying behind."

"What?" Grimaldi expressed surprised. "Won't he tell Famosa what you're really up to?"

"Not if he wants to live," Encizo said. "Especially if he

knew he just let me get away and didn't say anything before that, not to mention that Andres would actually bring someone into the fold who intended to set up Havana Five. No, he'll keep quiet, guaranteed."

As they pulled away from the curb Encizo asked of any word from Bolan. Grimaldi shook his head. "Nada, and I'm getting concerned."

"Striker can take care of himself," Encizo replied.

"Of course," Grimaldi said. "But whatever he was up to he surely would have some answers by now."

"Let's just keep our eyes and ears open," Encizo said. "He'll get back to us."

"So, how did it go with Famosa? What did you tell him?"

"Not much, actually, which made this a little easier. It seems he already suspects treachery from one of the other members."

"Bet that made it easier," Grimaldi said.

Encizo nodded with a devilish grin. "You said it. I got the impression things aren't quite as copasetic as they used to be among the tribe. Famosa showed me his cards pretty early, and based on what we knew from Andres, I figured it's better to let him ride on that mistrust. I'm sure Famosa is calling his connections right now to validate my story. Let's just hope that little disinformation campaign we've got the Farm working on pays off in a big way real soon."

"So, where to now?"

"Now, we need to set up a temporary base of operations, and I know the perfect place."

LAZARO SAN LUJAN SAT patiently in the spacious, comfortable parlor of Macario Lombardi's mansion home.

Unlike his affiliates in Havana Five, Lombardi elected to

live in the country, well away from the everyday hustle of urban life in Havana. The mansion sat on about forty acres of land, a good part of which Lombardi had left in its natural state, another portion—mostly the lands around the house and his massive private vineyard and coffee plantation—kept pristine by an army of outdoor architects and groundskeepers.

Most of the land and resources Lombardi acquired came from his friendship with the Armanteros family. Naturally, Nicanor profited from that fact by taking a percentage from a number of Lombardi's personal investments as compensation for the land deeded to him. Of course all of it had been done under a perfectly legitimate deal, with the government taking its cut. If anything was at a premium and had remained so in Cuba it was land, and even those with strong political and economic allies paid through the nose to get it.

Personally, San Lujan didn't place Lombardi in the same class as Inez Fuego. While he might truly have been her greatest ally, San Lujan couldn't really trust anyone who had a good relationship with Armanteros. The two men came from completely opposite backgrounds. Lombardi didn't go much for making his money by completely criminal means; he'd always tried to capture the majority of profits from legitimate business dealings and subsidize it with questionable but inconspicuous activities. But Armanteros…well, Armanteros was simply a con man and a shyster, and everybody knew it because the guy didn't hesitate to flaunt it.

Left to his own devices, San Lujan would have sought the help of Eduardo Valdese. While his affiliations didn't exactly stand up to the social graces of the others, San Lujan could at least trust to take Valdese completely at his word. They'd grown up in the same neighborhood, had known the same kinds of troubles, and they spoke the same language. San Lujan had never known Valdese to be mealymouthed about anything. Sure, the guy was a brutal and sadistic murderer, but at least he knew what he was and didn't try to hide it. San Lujan always preferred to know where he stood in these types of dealings and at least there weren't any questions with Eduardo Valdese.

The double doors to the parlor opened and Lombardi stepped through, a tanned beauty on each arm. The women split away from him like banana peels, one heading to the bar to pour him a drink and the other straight to a stereo system where she put on soft music.

San Lujan tried to curb the smile. It had been a while since he'd seen Lombardi—at least a year. Most of the time Bustos handled security at any regular meetings, and San Lujan only went if the members of Havana Five called a special session.

"Lazaro!" Lombardi said, pulling the enforcer to him and hugging him ceremoniously. "It's good to see you, boy. You've stayed away too long! Why?"

"My apologies, Don Lombardi," San Lujan replied formally. "It was not out of disrespect, I assure you."

Lombardi's bushy eyebrows rose high. " 'Don', it is? This is how you address me? So proper… Why, however, I do not understand. I had great respect for Natalio, you know, and I realize how close he was to you."

"Close doesn't describe it, sir. He and Inez treated me like one of their own, a son. They took me off the streets, cleaned me up and taught me their business. Now their holdings and well-being are in trouble, and I've been sent to ask for your assistance."

Lombardi looked first puzzled and then a bit mistrusting. "Me? Inez Fuego sends you to me to ask for help? Help with what?"

"She says that the accusations of the Five aren't true. She wanted me to tell you that she won't bother to deny she's financed a private army, but she also wants you to know it's not for the purpose of destroying the Five. She's done it to protect all of you."

"From whom?"

"From the Americans," San Lujan lied. "She tried to broker a deal with two men from their Defense Intelligence Agency, but they betrayed her. They misused the information she gave them by twisting it to make their government think that Havana Five was sponsoring terrorists. By the time she realized she'd gotten in over her head, it was too late. Now these men are hiding in downtown Havana under the protection of a woman named Isidora. *This* woman is the traitor. And do you know who she works for?"

Lombardi shook his head.

"Chago," San Lujan replied. Another lie—these kinds of things came very easy to him because he had much practice in manipulating the truth—as he didn't have a clue who she worked for. By doing so, she had betrayed the Five and would now suffer the consequences.

Lombardi sat silent for what seemed like an eternity. Finally he asked, "What do you want from me?"

"Men and guns," San Lujan replied. He sat forward and said, "Inez is afraid if she moves in some of her own now to take care of this situation that the others will consider her intentions hostile and take radical action. But with your men... well, you are trusted and respected. And if we don't do something now, all will be lost. We need your help, sir. Will you help her?"

"I have always had the utmost respect for Inez," he said. "And while I haven't spoken up like maybe I should have, I have always felt her to be at a disadvantage where the rest of the Five are concerned. I don't think they even wanted to give her a fair chance."

"When I asked her who I should go to, she named you without hesitation," San Lujan said, covering it with frosting just to make it more tasty. "She trusts and respects you. And she needs you now more than ever. Will you answer her plea?"

Lombardi set his drink on the table, leaned forward and clamped a friendly hand on San Lujan's shoulder. "Inez Fuego has done me an honor today. She is one of us and asked for my help. And she shall have it."

CHAPTER FOURTEEN

Captain Ciro Aguilera knew only one thing: duty.

As head of Moises Hurtado's black ops unit, Aguilera's experiences were considerably vast. He'd spent most of his childhood inside an ELN training camp, and during that time he met Hurtado. From nearly the beginning of their friendship, Hurtado demonstrated superior leadership skills. But Aguilera made up for what his friend and superior officer lacked in the swift and decisive actions required during field operations.

Hurtado never considered this a point of contention between them. In fact, he would have been the first to agree with Aguilera's assessment. Hurtado possessed the traits of a spit-and-polish soldier with a keen tactical mind; Aguilera knew how to transform Hurtado's plans into practical, effective action.

This latest mission seemed almost beneath his abilities, however. Aguilera had never been particularly interested in accepting financial support from the Cubans for their cause, and particularly not from a woman. To even think that a woman would be in charge of them bordered on the detestable to Aguilera, and especially under the circumstances. Still, both the National Liberation Army and their brothers in the FARC had to get the support wherever they could. Aguilera understood this concept, although he didn't like it, which is why he left these kinds of decisions in the hands of Hurtado.

In some ways, Aguilera was glad for the assignment and a chance to get onto the mainland. Not only would it get him out of the training camp for a while, it would test his men's abilities in an urban terrain. Rarely did they get an opportunity like this, since they saw most of their action deep in the Colombian jungles.

"This operation should not only prove the ability of our men to handle a sensitive operation, but it will also demonstrate they can be as effective in both urban and jungle warfare," he'd told Hurtado.

Hurtado's main directive called for Aguilera and his men to investigate Inez Fuego's claims that Havana Five may have learned of their plans. That kind of thing wasn't unusual, and it bore witness to another good reason why Aguilera hadn't been overly interested in doing business with these types. The National Liberation Army had enough problems without allying themselves to criminal organizations, irrespective of how valuable those alliances may be.

Aguilera didn't consider this an operation requiring a lot of thought. They would form up at the designated rendezvous point, get their final orders and then scout the various locations. They had an order of operations—what Aguilera felt amounted to little more than a hit list—and the estimated resistance they could expect at each location. Aguilera had suggested they hit each location simultaneously but Hurtado disagreed, arguing they might have to call up reinforcements if all didn't go as planned.

While he utterly dismissed such a preposterous notion, Aguilera opted not to argue with his friend. Hurtado was in charge and Aguilera contented himself to follow orders. Yes, he had only duty to consider here, and the sooner they got this job done the sooner they could return to Colombia where the real struggle continued. Aguilera considered that his ultimate duty lay not with Inez Fuego's petty squabbles but the continued fight for freedom by his own people.

Aguilera looked away from his paper and locked eyes with one of his men. They had entered the country easily enough, split their ten-man detail into pairs and blended in with the locals. The sun now dipped slowly and steadily and in that twilight, with the cooling of the day, the streets would soon be filled with people: people in the clubs and local eateries; people returning from work; people involved in family outings. All of this would give his men the opportunity to blend in, avoid attention. Once they were together again, they could begin their operation in earnest.

Aguilera nodded to his man as the bus they rode slowed to a halt. The man got up first and the captain followed a moment later, careful to keep a couple of people between him and one of his operatives who had boarded the bus two stops earlier. They disembarked and went in opposite directions but met two minutes later on a minor side street where they had rented a cheap room.

The operative, a young soldier named Julio Lima who doubled as Aguilera's aide, went first and procured the room key. The captain met him upstairs a few minutes later. The two men searched the entire room, swept it for bugs with special handheld equipment Aguilera brought in a bag, and then physically searched every appliance and piece of furniture to ensure there were no listening devices.

Their duties complete, Aguilera produced the satellite phone from his bag and contacted Hurtado by the allegedly secure line arranged by Inez Fuego. Aguilera had strict orders to make contact once to let the colonel know of their safe arrival, but following that they were to maintain communications silence until Hurtado contacted him to advise the main force arrived. He expected that to be some time early the following morning.

"Yes?" Hurtado said.

"We've arrived safely," Aguilera stated in a very nonchalant fashion.

"Did you have any trouble getting there?"·

"None."

"Excellent."

"We've scheduled the meetings as originally planned," Aguilera continued, meaning they were still on schedule and he awaited the arrival of the rest of his team.

"That's fine. Do not be late. This merger is very important."

"Understood. Will that be all?"

"For now," Hurtado said. "Enjoy your evening."

Aguilera waited for a click to sound in his ear before disconnecting the call. Anybody listening, even someone trained to detect deception, would have believed their conversation sounded like nothing more than a standard business call. Aguilera had done considerable research into the psychological tactics employed by the very best covert operations units around the world. The satellite feed hook-up that powered their phones also permitted them to access online computer resources all over the world, as well, and Aguilera had made great use of those resources.

Hurtado had assigned Aguilera one other mission. They would need weapons before their reconnaissance, and since bringing a weapons cache onto the island ran significant risks it seemed better they procure those weapons once inside Havana. Fuego had made those arrangements, as well. Aguilera would go and inspect the weapons to make sure they satisfied the needs of the unit as a whole. From that cache he could take what he needed to proceed with his own operations.

With luck, the remainder of his team would arrive over the next few hours. Once they were together, they would proceed to the docks where the weapons awaited them. Aguilera understood they were actually being held inside a customs storage facility. That seemed humorous that their suppliers would store the weapons right under the noses of Cuban officials. As far as the Cubans were concerned, of course, the crates had already been inspected and cleared, and were simply awaiting pickup by their proper owners.

Aguilera wondered for just a moment exactly what kind of political connections that would take. Whoever had pulled off that one probably spent a lot of money in bribes and profit-sharing to get certain high-ranking officials to look the other way. He refused to believe they could do something like that without feeding off the cooperation of those inside the government. Either way, that this suited Aguilera's purposes. In just a few hours, the operation would commence.

DOMINIC STEIN HUNKERED OVER the chess board and studied his opponent's pieces intently. This was now his seventh game running with Crosse, and while his partner had won the previous six, Stein had him on the run this time. So far, Crosse was down three pawns, a bishop and a rook. The move was to Crosse who had been watching the board intently for at least the past fifteen minutes. Stein couldn't figure it. He considered every angle before taking this particular offensive position and he'd sacrificed both his knights to get here. In truth, Crosse really had only one logical move and then after that it was two moves until Stein had him in checkmate.

"Not a damn thing you can do about it this time, buddy," Stein said.

Crosse's eyes never left the board as he replied evenly, "Never count your chickens before they hatch."

"We're not talking about a hatchery here, we're talking about chess."

As Crosse finally made his move he said, "And like I say…"

Stein's jaw hit the ground when he saw Crosse's move. The man had used his queen to neatly take Stein's bishop. To make matters worse, his move simultaneously put Stein's king in check. Stein studied the board. A minute went by, then two…

He swept his hand across the chessboard and cursed. He jumped from the chair and, forgetting about the low ceiling, whacked the top of his head against a low-hanging rafter. That caused a flurry of additional expletives as Stein rubbed at his head. He kicked the brick wall near his bunk and tried to calm his rapid breathing. Stein felt a stabbing pain in his chest, as if someone had just put an ice-pick through his heart, but it quickly subsided. Could it be a heart attack? No, he was too goddamn young for that, and beside the fact he had always been in pretty good health. Probably more like a brief anxiety attack.

"Well, what in the hell did you do that for?" Crosse said, getting on his feet but careful not to hit his own head.

NO POSTAGE
NECESSARY
IF MAILED
IN THE
UNITED STATES

BUSINESS REPLY MAIL
FIRST-CLASS MAIL   PERMIT NO. 717   BUFFALO, NY

POSTAGE WILL BE PAID BY ADDRESSEE

GOLD EAGLE READER SERVICE
3010 WALDEN AVE
PO BOX 1867
BUFFALO NY 14240-9952

Get FREE BOOKS and a FREE GIFT when you play the...

LAS VEGAS
GAME

Just scratch off
the gold box with a coin.
Then check below to see
the gifts you get!

YES! I have scratched off the gold box. Please send
me my **2 FREE BOOKS** and **gift for which I qualify.** I understand
that I am under no obligation to purchase any books as
explained on the back of this card.

366 ADL ENWS

166 ADL ENX4
(GE-LV-08)

FIRST NAME	LAST NAME

ADDRESS

APT.#	CITY

STATE/PROV.	ZIP/POSTAL CODE

7	7	7	Worth TWO FREE BOOKS plus a BONUS Mystery Gift!
🍒	🍒	🍒	Worth TWO FREE BOOKS!
♣	♣	♣	TRY AGAIN!

Offer limited to one per household and not
valid to current subscribers of Gold Eagle®
books. All orders subject to approval.
Please allow 4 to 6 weeks for delivery.

"Because I felt like it!" Stein shouted.

"Sore loser," Crosse muttered, and he took his seat.

"More like claustrophobic."

"You aren't claustrophobic. If you had been, they wouldn't have ever let you pass your last psych exam."

"I didn't mean literally," Stein said. "I'm just sick and tired of being cooped up in this shit hole. Why the hell did Stone leave us here, anyway? Why not send someone to get us out of Cuba? I'd take a federal holding cell to this place any day of the week."

"Well, it's kind of like he already said. We aren't exactly in a position to be asking for too much consideration."

"Yeah," Stein said, now finally content enough to tell his partner the truth. He whirled and fixed Crosse with an angry stare. "I don't imagine with you deciding to kill Colonel Waterston."

Crosse scowled. "Aw, shit! Come down off your high horse, Dom. You're just as guilty as I am in that. You could have bowed out any goddamn time you wanted to, but you didn't."

"I was sticking beside my partner."

"You were covering your ass!" Crosse followed that with a laugh of disbelief and shake of his head. "So was I. And the sooner we both admit it, the sooner we'll own up to it. They'll probably send us to prison for life. Maybe even string us up by our necks as war criminals."

"I'm going to get hung," Stein said. "That's the way Saddam went out. I'd rather they cut my head off or something. I don't want to die by hanging."

"We don't hang anybody anymore, Dom."

Stein nodded his head with enthusiasm. "They do in Texas, Les. You can still get hung in Texas."

Crosse looked at his friend with astonishment. "Are we in Texas, Dominic? Are we?" He swept the room with his hand and said, "Does this look like Texas to you?"

"Hey!" a woman's voice shouted.

Both men turned with surprise to see Isidora standing in the doorway, hands on her hips. "Why don't you two shut up! I can hear you almost up front. People come in are going to hear you, too, if you don't shut your mouths!"

She disappeared behind the slammed door as quickly as she had appeared. The sound of her heavy footfalls faded and Stein finally took a seat on his bunk. He rubbed his head again where it still smarted from smacking it on the ceiling. He never thought his career would have taken such a horrific turn as this. And now they stood a chance of never seeing their home country again.

"I wonder," he said quietly to Crosse, who had turned his attention to a game of solitaire, "how did we ever get roped into this thing to begin with, Les?"

Crosse didn't say anything for a time. Finally he held up an ace of spades from one of his three-card draws and said, "I guess that's just the hand fate dealt us. You know?"

"You think we're paying for all of our past sins?"

Crosse snorted. "What are you talking about? You going religious on me or something?"

"No." Stein leaned his back against the wall, "I'm just wondering if maybe we're simply getting recompensed for the all the shit we've done in our careers."

Crosse stopped paying attention to his game and looked Stein square in the eyes. "Hey, we done a lot of good stuff, too, Dom. I figure that's got to count for something somewhere. Don't you?"

"I suppose."

For a long time the men didn't speak, each lost in his own thoughts. Images of his childhood ran through Stein's mind, pictures of his father and mother. He remembered watching two older sisters graduate from college. One went on to become a successful doctor and the other had her life snuffed out by an overdose of booze and drugs, the product of an unhappy marriage and two successive miscarries.

Despite his own hardships and those of his family, Stein could remember a time where things hadn't all gone to shit. The first ten years of his own marriage had been blissful. While he never had kids, Stein didn't count his experiences as loss. He was a decorated member of the DIA, at least he had been at one time, and he'd managed to spend the better part of his prime a free man in the service of his country. Those were things for which he could be thankful.

But as Stein faced the upcoming road he found his courage starting to falter. Certainly he and Crosse would be held up to public ridicule. The trial would go public, more than likely, and his counsel would most likely recommend separate trials since it was Crosse who actually pulled the trigger. The partners would split up, probably never talk to each other again—if they were permitted by the government to see each other at all—and they might even ask him to make an evidentiary turn against his partner!

"You know something, Les," Stein said, "they may want me to turn on you in court. They'll be looking to hang one of us for Waterston. I just want you to know up front, I won't do it. I won't tell them what I saw. Not ever."

"Uh-huh," Crosse said, not really seeming to pay much attention.

"You believe me. Don't you?"

"Yeah, of course."

Stein relaxed. He knew that while Crosse acted like he wasn't paying attention, the guy really heard and processed every word. He knew Stein would never turn on him. That didn't mean the federal prosecutors wouldn't put the thumbscrews to him. They would come after him with everything they had. Stein knew it because it's what he would have done in a reverse situation. They would be looking to squeeze the lifeblood from the traitorous bastards who had taken the life of one of their own.

Worse, they would probably be subject to stand trial in a military court-martial. Things didn't go nearly as well in these as in a civilian criminal trial. First, they would be judged by military officers; these people would consider themselves comrades-in-arms with a guy like Waterston. They would see him as a brave, Army officer just trying to do his duty, betrayed by the very men he trusted. Yeah, that wouldn't paint either Stein or Crosse in a very good light.

Somehow he had to redeem himself. Somehow he needed to see if he could make up for what he'd done, for the part he'd played in Waterston's death. Stein couldn't live with himself otherwise. He couldn't stand the idea of going down in the public forum as a traitorous criminal, a murderer with the blood of an unarmed Army officer on his hands.

"Hey, Les?"

"What is it *now,* Dominic?"

"I need to get out of here, man," Stein replied. He sat forward on the cot and pinned Crosse with a serious gaze. "The only reason we're in this mess is because Fuego betrayed us. I've got to change that."

Crosse finally dropped his draw pile on the table and sat back in his chair with a sigh. He folded his hands behind his head. "What are you going on about now?"

"Something Stone said to us before," Stein replied. "It really got me. We have to take responsibility for our own actions. Andres betrayed us and that's the only reason we had to go on the run. I think we ought to find this bitch and get the information she owes us."

"You heard those guys," Crosse replied, gesturing at nothing in particular. "We're supposed to wait here until someone comes for us."

"I don't think so."

"Now, Dom, I'm telling you, don't get any funny ideas. We've done enough damage."

"No, I don't think we have," Stein said. The wheels were turning as he began to formulate a plan. "We know Andres has connections to Fuego. We also think we have a pretty good idea where to find her."

"And what if we're wrong. Huh? Then what?"

"Then we find Andres and we literally squeeze his nuts in a vise until he tells us where the fuck to find her! Okay?"

Stein felt the agitation and stabbing pains come on again and realized he'd started to hyperventilate. He tried to pretend he didn't notice the stunned look on Crosse's face, but something there didn't look right. Crosse's expression seemed almost accusatory in some way, as if he could hardly believe he was looking at the same person. Well, maybe he wasn't—maybe Stein had changed with this turn of events.

"We need to do this, Les," he pressed. "We need to make this right. Okay? We just do."

Crosse studied his friend a little more and finally nodded. "Okay, Dominic, okay. Let's make it right."

CHAPTER FIFTEEN

It didn't take much effort on Mack Bolan's part to get Pirro to talk.

The Executioner learned the location of Inez Fuego's massive estate along Havana Bay, and that the man Pirro worked for was named Lazaro San Lujan. The name didn't ring any bells for Bolan, but he contacted Stony Man and asked Aaron Kurtzman to get everything he could on the guy. "Know thine enemy" was a mainstay rule in the soldier's arsenal; the more he knew, the better he could plan the operation.

The more troubling piece of information came when Bolan learned of the young girl's identity. Her name was Marisol Melendez, the younger sister Basilio Melendez had told him about and made Bolan swear to protect. Well, she wouldn't be safe in the hands of a guy like Pirro. Despite her protests, Bolan watched as she collected her few meager possessions and then he escorted her out of the house. He also confiscated Pirro's cellular phone and cut the line to the receiver on the public phone in the hall on his way out. It wouldn't stop Pirro from contacting San Lujan, but it would certainly slow him down long enough to facilitate a clean escape.

Bolan also learned the men he'd taken down in the corner market store had been working for San Lujan. Why the guy hadn't decided to confront Bolan remained a mystery. The soldier figured San Lujan had been alone and observed the Executioner chasing Pirro, which led him to conclude the enforcer had probably gone for reinforcements. In all likelihood, San Lujan realized he would likely lose a one-on-one confrontation with Bolan. This told him that San Lujan was neither stupid nor an amateur. He'd return soon enough, and with a large team of men who would be toting plenty of firepower.

Bolan escorted Melendez for about six blocks before finding a shop from which he could place a call to his friends. Encizo answered on the first ring, got his location, and within ten minutes they arrived. Automobile ownership pretty much remained confined to the upper class, so getting around in the city didn't take long. They soon reached a trendy, higher class hotel right on the shores of the bay.

Once secure in the hotel room, Bolan confined his new charge to the room without a phone. Melendez studied him from the chair to which he gestured, the purest expression of venom in her lovely features.

"I have to tell you something," Bolan told her as he sat on the corner of the bed directly across from her. "Your brother's dead."

Tears immediately welled in her eyes at the news. Bolan wanted desperately to recant his statement, deliver it with a bit more empathy, but time didn't permit him to coddle her. She seemed older than her age, which Bolan guessed couldn't be more than seventeen.

"I know that's hard to hear," he added.

"You kill him?" she asked.

Well, at least she hadn't assumed Bolan was responsible. That demonstrated she had some brains. "No. In fact, I tried to save his life."

She grabbed a pillow off the nearby love seat and wrapped her arms around it as she opened up the water works. "Then who kill him, mister?"

"I'm not sure," Bolan said. "But I'd guess it's the same people your friend Pirro there is working for."

Melendez's face instantly flushed. "You lie!"

"I have no reason to lie to you," Bolan said. "Your brother made me promise to get someone to look after you. I intend to keep that promise. You want to leave Cuba? Maybe go to America where you can care for your baby in peace?"

"I care for baby here fine."

"Don't kid yourself. The same people who killed your brother will likely consider you a liability, in which case you're in for a short lifespan. I can't protect you here. You have a chance to escape from Cuba now. Your choice. But I plan to keep my promise to your brother, and you'll decide how easy or hard you want to make my job."

"Pirro no kill me." She spit, although something in her expression told Bolan she didn't really believe it.

"Pirro isn't who you have to worry about, Marisol. You need to worry about San Lujan. Maybe even Havana Five. They killed your brother for basically no reason, and they'll do the same to you, baby or not. Is that how you want to raise your child, looking over your shoulder for the rest of your life?"

Melendez didn't answer him but Bolan could see the wheels turn. He didn't really have any hard evidence that Havana Five would come after her, but the possibility existed, especially once Pirro told San Lujan about Bolan taking her along. Pirro knew about her brother and that meant he probably knew Havana Five killed him. Bolan didn't have proof San Lujan would have been the one who actually ordered the hit, but it seemed more likely given his interest in Stein and Crosse.

Bolan stood, folded his arms and stared hard at her. "I'm going to leave you here with my friends to think about it. When you make up your mind, you can tell them what you want to do."

He turned and left the room, closing the door behind him. Let her sit in there and chew on it for a while. He couldn't make up her mind for her; well, he could have but it wouldn't have helped his cause any. Bolan had always been a man of his word, and if he promised Basilio Melendez to keep an eye out for Marisol, then he would do it. Still, he never guaranteed he'd force Melendez's sister to accept his help.

Grimaldi looked up when Bolan emerged and nodded toward the door. "What did she say?"

"Still being stubborn," Bolan said.

"Great."

"She needs to come to this decision on her own," Bolan said. "Just give her some time. I told her when she's ready to tell you what's up. Stay or go, make sure you drop her someplace safe. At least give her a fighting chance."

Grimaldi nodded his understanding. "Will do, Sarge."

Bolan gave Encizo his undivided attention as he dropped into a chair beside the Phoenix Force warrior. "You get anywhere with Andres?"

"Anywhere would be an understatement," Encizo replied with a knowing grin and a wink. "He took me right to the top man. Guy by the name of Santiago Famosa."

Bolan nodded. "I studied his file briefly. What's his angle?"

"Well, it wasn't too difficult convincing him he had an associate waiting in the wings to make a move."

"He already suspected somebody," Bolan concluded.

"Yeah, and I didn't get the impression it was Inez Fuego. I didn't get the opportunity to find out who it was, but ruling out Fuego leaves only three other candidates."

The Executioner considered that. "Macario Lombardi's a ladies' man, and I doubt he has the intestinal fortitude to openly challenge Famosa for the power seat."

"I'd say you're right about that," Encizo replied. "So that leaves either Armanteros or Valdese."

Nicanor Armanteros certainly had the resources but he hardly possessed the chicanery needed to stage a full-scale coup. According to Stony Man's intelligence, Armanteros also preferred to leave the more gruesome activities to his colleagues. He'd funneled most of his monies into the holdings of legitimate business ventures—if any member of Havana Five could make such ridiculous claims of legitimacy— and he wouldn't have so willingly parted with the money it would take to butt heads with the likes of Famosa and crew.

"I don't think Armanteros has the liquid cash," Bolan said.

"That leaves Eduardo Valdese, then, and I'd say he's the likeliest candidate of all. Guy has his fingers into every dirty racket known to organized crime." Encizo began to read from his PDA. "He's got known actions in prostitution, gun-running, drugs, smuggling and money laundering."

"Just to name a few, eh?" Grimaldi interjected. The pilot came from the refrigerator with a beer for himself and bottled waters for his comrades. "Sounds like he's setting himself up to run for public office in the next regime."

"Not too far from the truth," Encizo replied. "Valdese is also particularly brutal in his business dealings."

The Executioner nodded. "He has a reputation for being ruthless, that much is clear. I think Famosa suspects Valdese is the one who's up to something."

"So that just leaves us with one question," Encizo replied. "How do you want to play this?"

"Where's this meeting supposed to take place?"

Encizo gave him the address of the warehouse supposedly located in a small wharf on the western side of the Havana Bay inlet. "Maybe a three-mile drive from here. I didn't know anything about it. Andres is the one who told me."

"You think you can trust him?"

"That's what I asked," Grimaldi said.

"I think we can trust him about as much as anyone in this business," Encizo said with a shrug.

Bolan nodded and then quickly ran down for Encizo and Grimaldi his conversation with Pirro. "If Pirro's telling the truth about Fuego's estate, she's located about a mile away," Bolan said. "I think if an American makes contact with her she'll be too suspicious. This is better left to your unique touch, Rafe."

"Okay, sure. What do you want me to do?"

"This San Lujan obviously went for help," Bolan said. "I think he saw me. But neither him nor his men will know you at all. I'd wager Fuego's got something cooking and since the rest of the group is obviously close to figuring it out, she'll be desperate for any allies she can find."

"You want me to go in friendly," Encizo said.

"Yeah, but as a freelancer," he said. "Tell her you heard

she had troubles. The kind that you can help her solve. Tell her what's going down at this warehouse tonight. Drop names if you have to, but get her on the defensive."

Encizo nodded. "I get it. Then we reel her in with bait and hope she bites."

The Executioner nodded. "Just don't come off too cocky. She'll be mistrustful of everyone. Keep it as plain and simple as possible."

"Simple I can do," the Cuban warrior replied. "And I know just what to say."

"What about me?" Grimaldi asked Bolan.

"You, ace, need to find us a chopper. Any ideas?"

Grimaldi showed his long-time friend a wicked grin. "You know me, Sarge. I got connections in every port on Earth."

"That's good," Bolan said. "Because I plan to make this little meeting tonight."

The time had come for the first blitz play of the game. Judgment had come to Cuba with the good guys on defense long enough. Mack Bolan planned to go on the offensive and put the ball smack dab in the middle of enemy territory. By the time he finished, their end zone would be transformed into a war zone.

STEIN AND CROSSE FORMULATED their plan.

They couldn't risk taking out Isidora in front of possible witnesses, so they had to wait until she closed up her salon. If anyone could call it that. The run-down building where Isidora did business might have been the perfect front, but that's about all it was. How she'd managed to fool anyone this long working as a citizen spy for the American government surpassed all understanding.

Well, it didn't make a bit of difference because Stein and

Crosse would be out of her hair very soon. They made their play at what they reasoned would be about the time she brought their dinner.

Crosse sat in his same position playing a new game of solitaire while Stein kept one ear to the heavy door. He couldn't make out a sound but insisted on reporting he hadn't heard anything every five minutes. Crosse began to wonder if his friend and partner hadn't completely lost his mind. Maybe that bump on the head had affected him in some negative way.

"I hear her coming, Les."

"Well, get ready then."

Stein could hear the sound of the mock door with brick covering slide aside and then the wooden door swung in. And that's when he went into action. He grabbed Isidora's arms, both of which were extended with a tray carrying two steaming plates of something that looked awful and smelled worse. The rancid odor of seafood struck Crosse's nostrils as Stein hurled Isidora across the room and drove her into the opposite wall.

Stein was on Isidora in a second. Crosse started to opened his mouth to shout in protest, but he was a moment too late to stop what happened next. Stein, holding a large chunk of masonry brick, brought both hands crashing into Isidora's skull. The woman's head split open like a cantaloupe and blood splattered the dusty weapon Stein held. The DIA agent struck her a second time and her body twitched only a moment before going deathly still.

"What the fuck are you doing?" Crosse seemed only to hear the echo of his scream in the small, dungeonlike room, never having remembered the words actually coming out of his mouth.

Crosse stared with complete horror at Isidora's motionless form. He shoved his partner aside as Stein got on his feet. He bent at the waist and felt for a pulse at her neck and wrist. Nothing. He then put a hand over her mouth and held it there a long moment before realizing she wasn't breathing. Crosse stood and whirled on his partner, fists clenched.

"Why did you kill her, Dom? What the hell did she ever do to you?"

"If we'd just knocked her out, she would have called Colonel Stone," Stein replied. "I have no desire to spend the rest of my life in prison. As long as he doesn't hear from her, we've got time to find Fuego. It might be a good long time even."

"And what about the people they were sending to smuggle us out of this little hellhole, huh? You ever think about *that* for a second? What do you think's going to happen when they get here and figure out we're gone and she's dead?" Crosse jabbed a finger at Isidora's corpse, scolding Stein like a puppy who had just done his business on the carpet.

Stein looked apologetic. "Sorry, Les, I didn't think about what I was doing. I was desperate, man."

"Yeah, well if they didn't plan to give both of us the needle before, they sure as hell will now. Come on."

Crosse led Stein to the front of the store. He went to the door and examined it only to discover Isidora had locked the bolt from the inside. Crosse ordered Stein to help him start searching for a key. After nearly five minutes of ransacking shelves and drawers, Crosse smacked himself on the side of the head and returned to the body. Sure as hell, he found a ring of keys in the partially torn pocket of Isidora's smock.

For a moment he studied her face, now serene with death. Hell, she probably hadn't seen anything like that coming. He felt sorry in a way, sorry for this whole damn mess. Crosse hadn't meant for anyone to get killed. He'd shot Waterston point-blank, sure, but out of sheer necessity. He'd done it because he'd felt the security of his country was at risk. But Dominic, well, he'd done this out of pure fear and adrenaline. Yeah, guy was definitely starting to crack up.

Crosse returned to the front and unlocked the door. He opened it slightly, looked both ways, then stepped out and gestured for Stein to follow. Clearly and necessarily, Crosse would have take charge of this little expedition while keeping onc eye on his friend. And when Stone found Isidora, he'd go absolutely ape-shit. There wouldn't be any place they could hide.

For God's sake, Dom, he thought. You just signed our own death warrants.

CHAPTER SIXTEEN

Rafael Encizo decided to visit the finest haberdashery in Havana, possibly even all of Cuba.

Encizo knew the place because of the family who owned it. The grandfather had started it the business as just a small shop maybe ten or twelve years prior to the installment of the Castro regime. His son kept the place open with nothing more than reputation and the sweat off his brow, and now it operated under the third generation of the family, Heriberto Benitez, known as Berto. Encizo had known him as a youth.

Berto hadn't seen the Cuban warrior since they were kids, so he didn't recognize the man who walked in and requested the finest tailored suit available. Of course, such art could not be rushed and if he wanted it special made he would have to come back in a week. Encizo spent quite a bit of money to reinforce how important it was he look his best and quickly. Like his father and grandfather before him, cash spoke volumes to Berto.

Ninety minutes later, Encizo left the shop wrapped in a fine silk suit in ecru, a sort of pale taupe, inlaid with a silvery mesh pattern. Patent-leather shoes completed Encizo's ensemble, which he knew would come off as neither loud nor sleazy. Even to Fuego's practiced eye, Encizo would likely appear to be everything he claimed. Of course she would check his references, which he already had Stony Man working on even as he climbed behind the wheel of his rented BMW—a quick swap of some local plates would give her the impression he was an in-country source—and pointed his car in the direction of her bayside home.

Encizo liked playing this part in some ways, but in others he chomped at the bit, ready for some action. Still, this was Striker's show and he had to follow orders. He didn't worry about Bolan's faith in his abilities. Any opportunity to work next to the Executioner was a good one, and Encizo wouldn't have traded places with one of his Phoenix Force comrades right now for anything.

The drive from the haberdashery to Fuego's estate took less than ten minutes. He didn't receive much of a challenge at the automatic gate; in fact, the security team buzzed him right in. This surprised Encizo, to be sure; he'd expected security to turn him away, particularly since he didn't have an appointment. Encizo drove purposefully slow up the winding drive that led to the estate. He studied every angle of the property, watchful for any egresses that might come in handy later. If they were to conduct any operations against the estate, Bolan would want a clear picture of the layout. Encizo noted the absence of any electronic security, cameras, proximity sensors, or otherwise, which only told him they were probably well hidden.

Four men in slacks and shirts greeted him at the door. They frisked him quickly and professionally for weapons, found the Glock Model 21. A tall, muscular man emerged and looked at the weapon one of the men showed him, then gazed in Encizo's direction with mild interest. They stood there for a long time, then the guy nodded and turned with orders for the other to escort Encizo inside. The men showed him to a wing off the grand foyer and disappeared, leaving only the apparent leader to watch him.

"You are taking a risk coming onto Mrs. Fuego's property with a gun, friend," the man said. Encizo remained standing and didn't say a word. Finally the man extended his hand. "The name is Bustos. I'm second in command of Mrs. Fuego's security detail. I understand you don't have an appointment."

"No, I don't," Encizo said, taking the overstuffed chair Bustos offered with a gesture. "But I'm here on a very important matter."

"And what business do you have with Ms. Fuego?"

"Her business."

"No, I'm afraid it's my business, too. Especially when you come onto her property armed."

"I'm here as a friend."

"Fine. I won't dispute that," Bustos said with a warning smile. "But I'm afraid I can't let you talk to Ms. Fuego unless you tell me what it's regarding first."

Encizo looked around, made a show of puffing air through his cheeks like he was indecisive, and then nodded. "I suppose it's okay, assuming you'll be discreet with the information."

"That depends on what exactly what we're talking about. But if you're worried about me running off at the mouth, you have no reason to be concerned. I've worked many years for Mrs. Fuego, and we never discuss her business outside these walls."

"Fine. I'm here at Lazaro San Lujan's request."

"Really," Bustos said, sliding his hands in his pockets and studying Encizo. He was looking for deception but Encizo had plenty of practice in this game. "And what exactly is your relationship with Mr. San Lujan?"

Encizo shrugged and looked at his fingers. "He's an…associate." Encizo looked Bustos in the eye then. "A friend, actually. Or rather, he was."

Bustos looked shaken now. "What are you saying? You aren't friends anymore or—"

"He's dead, Mr. Bustos," Encizo cut in. "I was notified a half hour ago and as soon as I heard I came right away. Just as he asked me to."

Encizo couldn't be sure if the pained expression on Bustos's face was the result of remorse or shock—maybe a mix of the two. The story had been Bolan's idea and the more he considered it, the more Encizo figured how brilliant it was. Bolan's confiscation of Pirro's mobile phone revealed the last two numbers dialed were the same. A quick source check by Aaron Kurtzman's team using the Stony Man satellite pinpointed the GPS signal given off by San Lujan's phone, and that revealed his exact location.

Bolan then crafted the idea of keeping tabs on San Lujan and having Stony Man spoof the phone with a no signal message to prevent him from calling Fuego. Meanwhile, Encizo would drop in with the "tragic news" of San Lujan's demise and an offer of his services for the sake of friendship. That would give Bolan and Grimaldi time to locate and actually neutralize San Lujan and friends before he could get to Stein and Crosse. Then they could make the wharf and rendezvous with Famosa's people by 2300 hours while narrowing the odds.

Through it all, Encizo would have the hardest part. Keeping San Lujan at bay wasn't going to be any trouble as long as they knew where he was. Convincing Fuego her trusted enforcer was dead would take a bit more doing. Rafael Encizo felt up to the task.

Bustos reached into his coat, causing Encizo to tense, but he only withdrew his cell phone. He hit a single button and pressed it to his ear. Encizo watched as Bustos became increasingly agitated when he got no answer. Bustos disconnected the call and went to a nearby landline. He dialed in a six-digit number and put the receiver to his ear while he kept one eye steadily on Encizo. After waiting for a time he gently dropped the receiver into the cradle.

"He's not answering, is he?" Encizo taunted.

"That doesn't mean anything!"

Encizo remained calm. "Maybe it doesn't to you, but I triple-checked my sources as soon as I heard. Trust me, he's dead. If he wasn't, I wouldn't have had any reason to make myself known. Now, I've told you all I'm going to. You don't want me to give the rest to Mrs. Fuego, fine. I'll get my gun back and leave peaceably. Otherwise…"

"You're not going anywhere yet, friend. Wait here."

Bustos spun on his heel and exited the room. Encizo noticed the full bar. He rose, poured himself a single malt Scotch whiskey over ice. He took a few sips, nodded with satisfaction and returned to his seat. He considered risking a quick call to Bolan but quickly dismissed the thought; someone would be watching him on closed-circuit monitors and probably eavesdropping on any conversation he had. Better to wait here solemnly and not do anything to arouse suspicions.

Nearly ten minutes passed before Bustos returned with Inez Fuego. Encizo rose quickly as she entered, acknowledging that she was a beauty, and that newspaper photos and press clippings didn't do her a bit of justice.

"Welcome, Mr....?" she began as she extended her hand, palm down.

Encizo took her hand and gave it a gentle shake, replying, "Marquez, Cipriano Marquez."

"Mr. Marquez, I wish we could have met on different circumstances." She gestured to the chair he'd sat in and Encizo complied even though she hadn't seated herself yet. This was her turf and an act of nobility on his part would have been an insult. "Mr. Bustos has told me of your news."

"Has he?"

"Yes." Now she took a seat across from him and crossed her legs. "Would it surprise you to know that I spoke with Lazaro San Lujan just a few minutes ago?"

"No disrespect intended, ma'am, but I would say that was quite impossible," Encizo replied.

The Phoenix Force warrior couldn't be sure but he figured she was bluffing. Stony Man wouldn't have allowed him to stick his neck out like this only to get it chopped off. Sure, there were risks in his job but they didn't send him on suicide missions willy-nilly. Many years had gone into Encizo's conditioning and training, too expensive and valuable to give up without a fight. If he'd been compromised, they would have found a way to tell him even if they couldn't do anything about it, leave him a fighting chance. Besides, he had more than an employer watching his back; they were his friends.

Bustos stepped closer to Feugo's seat. "Did you just call Mrs. Fuego a liar, Mr. Marquez?"

"Wait, Jeronimo," Fuego said, raising her hand. "I'd like to hear what Mr. Marquez has to say."

"I won't mince words, ma'am," Encizo continued. "Just

as I told Mr. Bustos, I wouldn't be here if Lazaro were still alive. I was told to deliver this message in the event of his death and I have done that. But I also guaranteed him that if something like this happened, I was to offer my services to you unconditionally."

"I see," Fuego said. She shifted in her seat, clasped her hands and cocked one elbow on the low backrest. "And exactly what services are those?"

"The kind Lazaro provided you," he said. "Of course, I would maintain my autonomy as a freelancer, and I would require no compensation."

"What?" Bustos interjected. "That's absurd! Nobody offers anything for free anymore."

Encizo looked Bustos in the eye with an unimpassioned and inoffensive expression. "I do."

"Why?" Fuego challenged.

Now Encizo knew he just about had her. She was asking him the questions, which meant he'd piqued her interest. He'd drawn her in and now he had one shot to make it sound as good as possible. The next few minutes would make the decision for her where it regarded Encizo. He'd either convince her of his sincerity or she'd order Bustos to take him somewhere remote and put a bullet in his head.

"I owe Lazaro my life," he replied. "It's a debt I've never been able to repay. Fortunately, he wasn't the kind of man to hold that over my head. He was a true gentleman and a good friend, and I intend to keep my promise. If you don't wish to take me in his stead, then I beg your permission to leave. Otherwise, I'm here at your service and willing to do whatever you ask of me."

"I can read people quite well, Mr. Marquez," Fuego replied after a long silence. "And there's no doubt in my mind that you speak genuinely. Anyone outside of these walls would have never spoken so highly and truthfully of Lazaro San Lujan. But clearly…yes, clearly you knew him well. I accept your offer."

Encizo bowed his head in reverent fashion. "I'm eager to be in your service."

"What do you know of our most recent operations?" she asked.

"Very little, I'm afraid," he said. "You speak as another one who knew Lazaro intimately, so you would also know he wouldn't speak loosely of your affairs. I know the basics, and the rest I've gleaned from rumors on the street. I'm afraid my intelligence network doesn't include the very tight circle that is Havana Five."

"So you know of my affiliation with the Five."

Encizo favored her with a wan smile. "As I said, I've heard rumors. Nothing more."

"And what else have you heard?"

"I know that they're planning something against you. Lazaro called me earlier tonight, told me that he had encountered trouble from some Americans. He didn't have time to give me details but he said he was taking care of it, and if I didn't hear from him at an exact time that he was dead. Naturally, I checked my sources before making such an assumption."

"How did he die?" Bustos inquired.

Careful, Rafe, this is where it could get out of hand. Play it just like Bolan told you. "I don't know. I only know that he died at the order of someone high inside the Five."

Fuego and Bustos immediately shared a panicked look. Bingo! The plan had worked. Encizo had played his part, kept his cool, and things had gone exactly like the Executioner predicted. Now all he had to do was to get them fired up and convince them that trouble was brewing. Whatever they had planned, they would lead him to the source of it and maybe even disclose the location of the ELN terrorist camp. For now, he would pretend not to know a thing about that. Yeah, Encizo had offered the bait and Fuego took it hook, line and sinker.

And the pinch was set.

MACK BOLAN KEPT ONE hand on the steering wheel of the car they had procured in Guijarro the morning after their narrow escape from the Cuban police in Matanzas, his other on the tracking signal being pinged through Stony Man's satellite. The Executioner kept his speed down, not enough to attract suspicion from authorities but adequate to react to any situation he might encounter. Thus far, things were going as planned, although Bolan never put too much stock in such affairs. The minute a soldier assumed things going well in any operation would continue in perpetuity was buying himself a potential load of trouble.

The next twenty-four hours would be intense, of that much Bolan was sure. He decided too many players were involved, and the only way to be certain he could put this thing down once and for all would be to eliminate anyone who wasn't playing for Uncle Sam on this one. In a way, the Executioner didn't see anyone could get in the way. He had his work cut out for him. The members of Havana Five, Inez Fuego included, were only out for their own slice of the pie. The ELN soldiers were nothing more than a convenient tool of terrorism being wielded to suit the whims of a vengeful widow. Finally, the lives of hundreds of innocent students, a large number of them American, were potentially at stake.

It wouldn't be hard to draw the battle lines on this one.

Bolan had a clear sight picture of the enemy and he intended to take the fight to them before this thing spiraled completely out of control.

Bolan figured the jumping off point started with Lazaro San Lujan. If all had gone well, and so far he'd heard nothing to dispute the assumption, Inez Fuego had probably gotten the news of San Lujan's death. In actuality, San Lujan had an appointment with Bolan and that probably wasn't too far from the truth. The Executioner had chosen his target carefully. There were no lingering questions in his mind that Lazaro San Lujan posed too much of a danger to their operations, not to mention the guy wouldn't relent until he'd eliminated Crosse and Stein. He'd already demonstrated that much.

Bolan swung a left on the road that led out of the city. San Lujan had been holding the same position for the past three hours, which made it doubly easy for a whiz like Bear to pinpoint his location. Bolan didn't know what he would come up against when he reached the location, but all of Stony Man's intelligence said it was a massive estate. Bolan guessed it was home to one of the leaders in Havana Five. They had already identified the estates of Famosa and Fuego, which left only three. But which one? Who would San Lujan had gone to for help, and why not pull reinforcements from his own backyard first?

It didn't make sense to Bolan, but then he didn't really need it to. The Executioner had a plan either way. He would strike fast and hard, and he would push at the enemy relentlessly until his message got through. In the trunk of the car he certainly packed the right tools. He had the FN FNC carbine along with one of the silenced MP-5s, and plenty of spare ammunition for both. He'd even managed to lay his hands on two M-67 fragmentation grenades procured by one of Encizo's military black market contacts. Now Mack Bolan simply needed a target.

CHAPTER SEVENTEEN

Bolan parked his vehicle about a mile from San Lujan's location and went EVA. He made the rest of the trip on foot, attired in his blacksuit with all the usual riggings of war. The streets here were broader, less developed and maintained, with large spans of open land between properties. Bolan past one estate then another under cover of darkness and foliage. Eventually, the signal strength from San Lujan's mobile phone convinced Bolan he'd found the right house.

The Executioner observed a mansion from atop a nine-foot brick wall that ran the length of the property line on the north. He studied every vantage point he could make out through the cheap, monocular NVD. Oddly enough, he saw neither movement nor sentries. The place seemed almost too quiet, and Bolan was betting whichever one of the Havana Five lived here relied heavily upon electronic security.

For a brief moment Bolan had hoped to run a soft probe on the place first but it appeared he'd run out of options before he got started. Okay, then, a full-frontal assault it was. Bolan replaced the NVDs in a soft case, then dropped quietly inside the perimeter. He immediately went into motion, rushing the house proper as fast as his legs would carry him. The throbbing in the lump on his head began once more with the exertion but Bolan ignored it. Letting a little pain distract him now might result in experiencing a lot of pain later.

Bolan got within about fifty yards of the house when his trouble appeared. Four men toting assault rifles burst from what looked like a servant's entrance and fanned out. Bolan had the advantage since they'd come from a well-lit interior and their eyes hadn't adjusted yet. He knelt and leveled the muzzle of the FN FNC. First produced in 1978, the FNC—often confused in its condensed state as an SMG rather than a full AR—packed a significant punch. Bolan demonstrated that fact quite effectively as he squeezed the trigger on the gunman that poured from the house. The first pair fell under a volley of 5.56 mm M-855 slugs and the Executioner's unerring accuracy.

The remaining pair was obviously caught off guard by Bolan's sudden assault, and they dived for cover with impressive speed and agility. Bolan rolled from his initial position and went prone. The angry buzz of rounds whizzed the air where he'd been a millisecond earlier. He sighted on a fresh target and squeezed the trigger. A triplet triburst punched through another gunman's face and split his head down the middle.

The last man broke from the cover of a fountain and headed back for the house, realizing that seventy-five percent of his team had just been neutralized. Bolan triggered a sustained burst that cut a bloody figure eight across the runner's upper torso. The impact flipped the man off his feet and dumped his corpse on the lawn.

The Executioner got on the move again and made it to the

servant's entrance unmolested. He peered around the corner, assault rifle held at the ready, but nobody arrived to challenge him. He slipped inside and closed the door tightly behind him. He stood in a narrow hallway that looked like it opened onto a kitchen. Bolan advanced with caution into the kitchen. The lights were dim in that part of the house, not surprising since suppertime had come and gone.

Bolan wound his way through the massive kitchen toward a door on the opposite wall. He stopped short of it when he heard the slap of feet on wood coming from just the other side of the door. Bolan slapped the light switch, bathing the kitchen in complete darkness, and then crouched against the wall near the door. It swung inward violently a moment later and another quartet of armed men burst through it. Bolan heard curses in Spanish as the group ran into the kitchen fixtures and knocked dangling pots off their racks.

The noise and confusion provided the distraction Bolan needed. He opened up full-bore with FNC, spitting a fusillade of lead in a sweeping pattern. The Havana Five gunners twisted and danced as Bolan cut them down in a single, full-on assault of hot lead. The force of the rounds propelled one man into a large stove hard enough to push the heavy appliance several inches. The head of another man exploded under the heavy-caliber slugs. The remaining gunners slammed into each other by the force of the bullets pounding their tender flesh.

Bolan's ears rang as the echo of the FNC's reports died. The Executioner didn't flip on the lights—he had neither the time nor inclination to actually see the result of his handiwork. The stench of spent cordite and blood that filled his nostrils provided enough information on that scene of carnage.

The soldier pushed through the swinging door, which

opened onto a massive formal dining room. A double-door entryway at the opposite end of the room led to a well-lit foyer. Bolan crossed the dining room and peered around the corner of the doorway. A wide, spiral stairwell wound upward. A massive, crystal chandelier dangled from a high ceiling, bathing the whole foyer in bright lights. Bolan looked for a switch to dim or kill the light emanating from the massive fixture but didn't see any visible way to cut the power. Hairs stood on the back of his neck as he risked stepping into the foyer.

Only Bolan's superb reflexes saved him from certain death as he dived to avoid the maelstrom of bullets that burned the air around him. Directly across he saw a trio of gunmen using the door frame into another room for cover. Bolan rolled onto his back and yanked one of the fragmentation grenades from his load-bearing harness. Bolan primed the grenade with a yank of the pin, rolled to avoid a fresh volley of rounds as his aggressors tried to finish him, and tossed the bomb into their midst. He went flat once more as the shooting stopped and the threesome watched the rather innocent-looking device roll to a stop between them. It took about three seconds for them to realize what it was they were staring at, and another to exchange petrified looks.

The heat of the high explosive nearly seared the flesh on Bolan's hands, which he had wrapped over his head and ears to protect. As the explosion died into secondary ones, Bolan looked up to assess damage and look for further threats. None came to him. He scrambled to his feet, switched out magazines in the FNC and continued his search for San Lujan.

LAZARO SAN LUJAN COULD hardly believe what he saw over the camera monitors in the security room of Macario Lombardi's home.

The American who had so effectively and permanently eliminated his men in Matanzas and Havana had somehow managed to track him here. San Lujan watched with a pang of fear and shock as the scene unfolded over the monitors. Within a few seconds the American cut down four of Lombardi's house guards, and this time it looked as though he'd brought enough hardware to start a small war. Moreover, he was dressed in what looked to be black fatigues, and he fought with a practiced efficiency. San Lujan had never seen a single man do what this American had, and he'd certainly never gone up against such a man.

The thin curtain that filtered the light from the outside swished aside. Macario Lombardi entered the room, stone-faced, and studied the monitors just as the American moved inside the house. For a moment Lombardi expressed obvious disturbance at the gall of this intruder. His home had been invaded and four of his very well-trained men hadn't been able to stop him.

"What the hell is going on?" he demanded of San Lujan. "Is this some trick, Lazaro? Because if your mistress has betrayed me—"

"This is no trick, sir," San Lujan replied quickly. "This is one of the Americans I told you about."

"One?" Lombardi emitted a scoffing laugh. "They send one paltry American after me? He is not capable of—"

"Excuse me, Don Lombardi, but I think you have no idea what this man is capable of. He just neutralized four of your men without so much as a flinch."

"He's inside the house now, sir," the security monitor announced.

Lombardi ran his fingers through his hair with a very indecisive expression. San Lujan wanted to order a full response, but this wasn't his call and not his house. If Lombardi hadn't spent so much time puffing out his chest and reminiscing about old times between him and Natalio, this wouldn't be happening right now, here, on his own turf.

Lombardi looked at San Lujan as if he'd just noticed him standing there for the first time. "What should we do?"

San Lujan found it a little odd that a guy of Lombardi's experience would be asking him what to do. But he sure as hell didn't plan to pass up the opportunity. "I think you'd better send everything you have up against this man. Otherwise you might—"

More gunfire resounded below their feet from what sounded like the kitchen area. Lombardi stood there another moment and then ordered the controller to alert all of the house guards. Lombardi turned and San Lujan immediately followed him. As they walked hastily along the main, second-floor hallway, San Lujan started to wonder where Lombardi's personal protection detail had gone off to.

"Don Lombardi, where are your bodyguards?"

"I sent them on an errand," he said. "I didn't think I'd need them with house detail here."

"Well, then, I would prefer to stay by your side until this is over."

Lombardi stopped, turned and placed a hand on Lombardi's shoulder. "I accept the offer. You're a good man, Lazaro, just like Natalio. I wish I'd been stronger with the rest of the Five when it came to his demise."

"What's done is done," San Lujan replied, although what he really wanted to do was to reach out and throttle the little coward. While he remained the only one to agree to help Inez Fuego, he'd been just as responsible for letting San

Lujan's master and friend go to his grave. "We must focus on now."

Lombardi nodded and then turned and headed down the hallway.

MACK BOLAN EXTENDED THE stock of the FNC as he ascended the steps, knowing he wasn't close to having cleared the opposition.

It did surprise him a bit that he hadn't seen more resistance than this, which meant either they were waiting to trap him in the upper levels or they had been completely unprepared for an assault. Bolan was betting the latter as the most plausible explanation. Hired guns would be swarming the place soon enough, though, which left the Executioner very little time to locate and destroy San Lujan. Like most of his operations, sense of duty drove Bolan to his near obsession with San Lujan. Rafael Encizo had risked his neck walking into Fuego's proverbial den of butchers, and it was entirely up to Bolan to make sure the story of San Lujan's death transitioned from fable to reality. Not to mention the world would be a better place without San Lujan corrupting or murdering innocents like Marisol and Basilio Melendez.

A pair of defenders emerged from a door at the far end of the hallway as Bolan reached the top of the stairs. The warrior knelt and rounds from their SMGs zinged overhead. He steadied the stock of the FNC against his shoulder, acquired his targets and squeezed the trigger. Bolan felt the bare kick of the stock against his pectoral as he neutralized the pair. A few rounds took the first hood in the guts, shredding his stomach and intestines like they were paper. The other gunman took four rounds square in the center of the chest with enough force to drive him into the door at his rear.

Bolan got to his feet and moved forward, the FNC held at hip level. A noise to his rear caused him to turn and crouch. Neither of the armed gunners who emerged from another room looked like they had expected to encounter Bolan. In fact, it looked as though someone had rousted them from a sound sleep because neither was completely dressed. One wore rumpled slacks, T-shirt and loafers. Bolan cut them down with short, controlled bursts. Their corpses fell into each other awkwardly before hitting the ground.

The Executioner continued sweeping the second floor, watchful for threats. He eventually reached a door and kicked it down to find he faced some type of curtain. Bolan pushed it aside with the muzzle of the FNC. Inside the room, illuminated with only a single red light bulb, he saw a number of monitors that appeared to span a good amount of the grounds. One had a detached garage and Bolan watched as a two men, accompanied by three others with pistols, stepped into view of the camera and engaged the garage door.

Bolan immediately recognized two of them: one was San Lujan and the other one a leader in Havana Five, Macario Lombardi. Suddenly, Bolan spotted men on several other cameras making entry to multiple points in the house. So, Lombardi had called in reinforcements to deal with Bolan while he made his escape. Well, he'd made a critical flaw in assuming Bolan hadn't come without backup.

The Executioner always had a Plan B.

Bolan reached up to the microphone hidden beneath the high-neck color of his blacksuit and flipped the tiny switch that sent out a high-pitched signal. That signal could be obtained just about anywhere by a similar receiving device carried by Jack Grimaldi. About ten seconds elapsed before the pilot's strong voice broke through the high-pitched whine and bursts of static.

"Eagle One to Striker," Grimaldi said. "Signal received and I'm en route."

"Eagle, be advised you're coming down in a hot LZ."

"Roger, Striker. You have three minutes."

The Executioner acknowledged, then whirled and left the control room. He sprinted down the hallway and descended the stairs. About two-thirds of the way down the first crew emerged from a parlor on the right. Bolan triggered a sustained burst from the FNC, taking out three of the six gunmen before they had time to react. Heads imploded under the force of the heavy-caliber slugs at close range. The others tried to find cover, but Bolan had surprise and picked them off one by one.

The first man hit the floor and rolled. As Bolan continued down the steps, he led the guy and squeezed a short burst. The gunner rolled right into the rounds and took hits in both his spine and stomach. Another gunman managed to grab cover behind a freestanding marble display beneath a rare ceramic piece. Bolan reached the bottom step and slid onto his buttocks and back. The smooth material of his blacksuit slid easily across the dazzling, polished floor of the foyer. He squeezed another sustained burst from his weapon while still sliding and cut the man's cover to ribbons, followed by his target a few seconds later.

The last gunner managed to get enough time and position to lean back on the trigger and spray the area Bolan occupied. One round zipped off the floor and grazed the soldier's left thigh. He bit back the pain through clenched teeth as he rolled out of the slide, gained one knee and whipped the Beretta from its shoulder holster. At that close range the gunner would have beaten Bolan had he tried to use the FNC. The man's eyes went wide milliseconds before Bolan squeezed the trigger. The 93-R coughed as a 125-grain subsonic round entered through the man's mouth opened in surprise and blew out the back of his skull. His body flipped backward and landed in a sprawl. A torrent of blood began to pour from his head.

Bolan gritted his teeth as he climbed to his feet and headed into the parlor, knowing he stood less chance of meeting further resistance going that way. Bolan found a window, opened it and went through head-first. He shoulder rolled outside and onto his feet. The sound of chopper blades thundered in his ears. As he jumped into the copilot seat, he couldn't remember the last time it sounded so good to him.

Grimaldi had the chopper airborne and pulling away from the ground with lightning speed as the remnant of guards emerged from the house in search of Bolan. The Executioner held one of the headset earphones against the side of his face and spoke into the microphone.

"Look for a vehicle," Bolan ordered. "Should be moving away from the house."

Grimaldi spotted it almost immediately and rapped on the Executioner's knee. He pointed to a silver BMW just as it streaked out of the driveway and sped from the estate. Bolan gestured for his friend to come down on top of it. The road the car traveled left the swanky, upper-class neighborhood and merged onto a four-mile stretch of bayside highway.

The Stony Man pilot came down over the vehicle until the skid on Bolan's side came parallel with the cross frame of the roof. Bolan swung the Beretta into open air and triggered three rounds that shattered the back window. A pair of petrified faces stared back at him. The Executioner yanked the final grenade from his load-bearing harness, armed it and hurled it through the opening. The car skidded and swerved to the side of the road, attempting to stop so the occupants could bail. Even as the chopper lifted high into the night sky, a fiery explosion lit the darkness below.

"Score another one for the good guys!" Grimaldi hollered.

"Score two," Bolan replied.

CHAPTER EIGHTEEN

Ciro Aguilera studied the nine men arrayed before him, and could not contain the swell of pride that beat in his chest like a second heart.

These were the finest soldiers he'd ever trained. More than just covert operations specialists, way more than just hired guns, these men were some of the most elite freedom fighters ever produced for the ELN. Aguilera had trained them in counterintelligence, weapons, bare-handed fighting, military tactics, urban warfare and escape and evasion. Each possessed individual specialties that ranged from linguistics to crypto-analysis to information technology.

While Aguilera didn't like working under Inez Fuego, he had to admit she'd supplied them with the very best training equipment and facilities money could by. The men who sat in front of him now had all managed to penetrate Cuba with relative ease and not engaged in a single encounter with customs or police authorities. That was nothing short of remarkable, considering their numbers. Now all they had to do was to procure and inspect the weapons Fuego had arranged for them to complete their mission.

Aguilera's force would serve much like an advance team. They had begun immediate work to secure temporary quarters for the fifty-some men Hurtado would send by the morning. From there, Aguilera would break them into their designated teams and they would execute their missions of destruction on schedule. Their intelligence to this point led Aguilera to believe none of the leaders within the criminal organization suspected a thing.

"Fighters of the people," Aguilera began ceremoniously. "We have been brought here for a high purpose, much higher than the mere execution of common criminals." He paused to look over them for the purposes of dramatic effect, then said, "Before we can return to our homeland and carry on with the cause, our mettle and resolve must be tested. Colonel Hurtado has told me that we must prove ourselves ready and worthy of the fight ahead, and I concur with him on this point. We must be sure that all of your training will pay off, because once we are back in the field there will be no second chances. Do all of you understand?"

There were nods and mutters of acknowledgment. Aguilera continued, "Our mission is to secure the weapons for our operation. We are to meet with our connection tonight. Six of you will take the perimeter of the building where we are to meet. You will act as contingency in the event something goes wrong, and double as security during the transaction. I will accompany the remaining three to ensure we receive everything as agreed. Are there any questions?"

Aguilera nodded to a soldier who raised his hand. "What if they try to take our money without providing the merchandise, sir?"

Aguilera couldn't repress a smile. Already his men were acting like seasoned professionals by thinking ahead. "There is no reason for us to worry about this. Our sponsor has already consummated the transaction on our behalf. No money shall change hands. We will merely receive what already belongs to us."

Another soldier raised his hand. "And what if they do not want to give us the merchandise?"

Aguilera smiled again, although this time it lacked any warmth. "Then we will take it. Are there any other questions? Good. Let's prepare to move out."

ANDRES TRIED NOT TO SHOW his nervousness as he sat wedged between two large thugs in the back of Santiago Famosa's limousine. Well, one of Famosa's limousines anyway. He could be grateful for the darkness because it hid the trickles of sweat that ran down his back and forehead. It felt like a sauna to him despite the air-conditioning that hummed beneath the purr of the vehicle engine.

Most of the heat came from the stares of the fat, dark-eyed man seated across from him. Many might have viewed Famosa as nothing more than a fat slob, but Andres knew the danger that lurked beneath that slovenly exterior. His nostrils burned with stink of Famosa's cigar. He wanted to scream at the oaf, tell him to put it out before they all died of asphyxiation, but he knew such an outburst would probably cost him a finger or two.

Earlier in the evening, Andres had considered coming clean about the entire setup, spill his guts about the man he knew as Rafael Pascal and his former affiliations, but he quickly chalked it up to nothing more than impulse. To betray a man like this already fell into the realm of a capital offense in Cuba, but to then actually admit his betrayal came under the heading of suicide. While he wasn't afraid to die, he saw no reason to accelerate the process. If he did fall, he definitely did *not* want it to be at the hands of some low-life, criminal pig who wore delusions of grandeur like a tailored coat. No, Andres figured it better he take his chances with the Americans. At least he could predict how they would think and act under a given situation.

Andres was pretty certain of one thing: Rafael Pascal wasn't acting alone. A guy like him would have backup. Andres had dealt with him a couple of times before, in other locations while he still worked for the CIA, and he remembered at least four other guys besides Pascal on that detail. He didn't know anything else at the time, but he did remember how much of a commotion they stirred up. Those guys had plain scared the living shit out of him. Pascal worked with a very dangerous crew indeed, and Andres really didn't want to have any part of whatever they were up to this time around. He'd already allowed himself to be more involved in this mission than he ever planned.

And then there were the two American DIA agents he betrayed. Certainly that's what had brought Pascal and his entourage to Cuba. Andres had told him how he didn't agree with Inez Fuego's plan to betray the two men, using them as scapegoats to cover up her plans to assassinate the other leaders of Havana Five, neither had he been particularly interested in arranging the murder of Basilio Melendez.

Fuego simply hadn't given him a choice!

Yes, that was it…she and her cronies had coerced him into betraying Stein and Crosse. And he certainly hadn't liked the fact he couldn't deal with Fuego directly. She always sent her goon, that…what was his name? Oh, yeah, Bustos, who as Andres's contacts told him wasn't even top dog within Fuego's hierarchy. Well, none of that mattered now. Pascal had promised the Americans would intervene in this little meeting and Andres wouldn't be implicated in any of it. Somehow, that didn't make him feel any better.

"What's the matter with you?" Famosa finally asked. "Why don't you sit still?"

"I'm sorry," Andres replied with an apologetic smile. "I didn't realize I was restless, Chago."

Famosa studied him suspiciously for a time and then offered him a drink, which Andres accepted immediately. Yes, maybe a little nip would quiet his nerves. Famosa spared no expense, even for those he viewed as little more than lackeys, and poured Andres a tumbler half filled with very fine brandy. Andres accepted the drink gratefully although he noticed how Famosa passed it to one of his thugs to give him rather than handing him a glass directly.

Andres wanted to down the whole thing in one good shot but he refrained and sipped gingerly from the tumbler. He knew a guy like Famosa could smell fear on him like a wolf on wounded prey. If he showed his nervousness any more, Famosa would become suspicious and that could blow the entire operation. And then after he dealt with the Americans he'd figured out Andres had been part of the treachery, and Andres would wind up with his throat cut and his body dumped in some remote grave along the bay.

After another ten minutes of uncomfortable silence, and culmination to the point where Andres thought he might spill his guts, a rap at the window provided the diversion he longed for. One of the bodyguards cracked the window and spoke to their outside man. They talked of the arrival of four men, just as agreed, and that the men were searched and found to be armed. Andres didn't catch all of the conversation but he managed to get bits and pieces.

"They are refusing to surrender their weapons," the man outside told one of the guards. The guard turned to Famosa and awaited instructions.

"Why?" Famosa asked. "I've been told they've already paid us for the weapons. Don't they trust us?"

"It would appear not," Andres ventured.

"You shut up," he said.

He turned to the man standing outside and said, "Just give them whatever they want and let's be done with this. It doesn't sound like there's anything at all to what Mr. Marquez told us. He didn't even bother to show up. Give them the merchandise as agreed and let's get this done."

"Yes, Mr. Famosa," the man outside said quickly, and then he was gone.

As the bodyguard rolled up the window, Famosa said to Andres, "I don't know what's going here, but Marquez is obviously a liar."

Before Andres could conjure a reply, the sound of a helicopter buzzed past and few moments later there were shouts followed by a cacophony of automatic weapons fire. Andres tried to squeeze past the bodyguard and get the door open to escape, but the man easily pinned his smaller frame into the seat.

"What the hell is going on?" Famosa asked.

"I don't know," Andres said. "But it looks like maybe there *is* something to what Mr. Marquez told you after all."

"That is good…very good, because we are more than ready for trouble." Famosa looked at the bodyguard and nodded. "Give our men the signal."

ONCE LESLIE CROSSE AND Dominic Stein had traveled a distance from Isidora's shop—not without the puzzled stares of nearly every man, woman and child who passed them on the street—they decided it would be better to find someplace to hide out until evening fell and they could move under cover of darkness. They chose a spot beneath the rickety stairwell that led to a pad-locked closet in the basement of a run-down motel.

When darkness finally came, the two made their way toward the club where they'd first encountered Andres. They couldn't be sure he'd be there, but it wasn't unusual for North Americans and Europeans to frequent such establishments and they would look much less conspicuous there than in a fancy hotel. Besides, they had expended all of their cash in bribing the Cuban police commandant back in Matanzas, which left them only what they could find at Isidora's. She had hidden about two hundred Cuban Convertible pesos in an old cigar box. Fortunately they were of smaller denominations, fives and tens mostly, and on average the CUC equaled U.S. currency dollar for dollar so it wasn't difficult to figure out how much they really had.

As they entered the club, Stein raised his voice to be heard above the blare of the music. "I don't see him."

Crosse merely nodded and made a slow and careful inspection of the club. They were barely inside the door, and Stein had already assumed Andres wasn't here. This worried him a bit. Stein had been acting strange ever since they'd dumped Waterston's body. The first time they'd met Andres he'd thought his partner might actually lose it because of how jittery he was acting. As time went on it seemed like Stein had grown perpetually worse in his anxious behavior.

"What are you doing?" he asked, leaning close to Crosse's ear.

Crosse expressed irritation. "I'm looking for Andres."

"I said I didn't see him. I don't think he's here."

"Well, then, we might have to wait for him."

Crosse noticed Stein's eyes lock on a corner booth, the one where they had first met Andres and they knew the information broker favored. Crosse immediately recognized one man as Andres's bodyguard, the same guy who had taken care of their boat. If he couldn't tell them where Andres was off to, maybe he could tell them where they might find their boat. If nothing else, they could use what money they had to bribe the police to look the other way while they escaped from Cuba and headed to Mexico.

Crosse came back to reality when he saw Stein halfway across the club and headed straight for the bodyguard with purpose. Crosse started to rush after his partner but he didn't get there in time. Stein managed to get one hand around the bigger man's throat, taking him completely by surprise. As Crosse drew nearer, he noticed the bodyguard had white tape across his nose and the shadow of a dark bruise across his jaw. Crosse was betting someone had beat them to Andres, but he'd never find out the truth if he let Stein get to the guy first.

The bodyguard reached up and tried to deflect Stein's choke hold but that only exposed his left side, into which Stein fired a hard right jab. The guy squealed something unintelligible as Stein dragged him into an alcove. Crosse looked around to see if anyone noticed but the party was in full swing and everybody's attention was on the live band performing on stage.

"Your buddy Andres!" Stein demanded. "Where is he?"

"I... I do—"

"Don't tell me you don't fucking know, asshole! Don't lie to me or I swear on my mother's grave I'll cut your heart out with a dull knife!"

Crosse could see the apoplectic hue to Stein's skin even in the dim lights. The guy was definitely close to completely losing control. Crosse thought about interfering, but he decided to act with discretion for the time being. Yeah, better to let Stein scare the hell out of him and get the information they needed faster than spend the next two to three hours dicking around with one of Andres's lackeys.

"Try again," Stein said, his knuckles whitening. In a dark, even tone he asked, "Where is Andres?"

Stein released his grip enough that the bodyguard could sputter out a response. "He left. He left with… someone."

"When?"

"Maybe six, seven hours ago."

"An American?" Crosse asked,

"No, no, a local. He looked Cuban, spoke Spanish."

Alarms went off in Crosse's head like a fire bell. So it hadn't been the American, but there was no doubt they were talking about one of Stone's companions. He could definitely have passed himself off as Cuban, which is probably a damn good reason why he was inside the country helping Stone and the other American.

"Did you get a name?" Stein demanded.

"I thought I heard Señor Andres call him Pascal, but I'm not sure."

"And all of this," Crosse said, gesturing at the man's face. "He did all this to you?"

The bodyguard nodded but the only sound he emitted was a wheeze. Crosse realized it only because he could see all color had left Stein's hand. His partner's wrist had begun to shake as the bodyguard's knees started to fold. Crosse grabbed Stein's arm, tugging as hard as he could manage, shouting at Stein to stop but the guy was simply immoveable.

A moment later something popped and blood appeared at the corner of the bodyguard's mouth as his eyes rolled into his head. His body slumped to the ground.

Crosse looked furiously in all directions but it seemed they were far enough back in the alcove that nobody noticed them. Crosse looked at his friend with horror as Stein released the bodyguard's corpse and watched him slump to the ground with murderous satisfaction. Stein turned to look Crosse in the face. Something purely wicked had surfaced in those eyes and Crosse couldn't be sure what it was. He knew one thing: it scared the holy shit out of him.

"Let's go, buddy," Crosse said quietly. "Come on, let's go find Andres."

The look in Stein's eyes dissipated to something less crazed, and Crosse led the way out. He made the decision right there: it would be the last time he turned his back on Stein. He couldn't trust his friend anymore, a man who had been his partner for more than ten years. At least not if he wanted to get out of this alive. He hated to admit it, but he almost felt trapped in their current situation, and he couldn't help but wonder if either of them stood any chance of getting out of this alive.

Once they were on the street, Crosse said, "That wasn't a real good idea, Dom."

Stein didn't say much for a time, then out of the blue he asked, "Why not?"

"Huh?" Crosse replied.

"Why wasn't that a good idea?"

"Because you killed him before we could ask him where our boat is."

"Our boat?"

"Yeah. Didn't you notice he was one of the guys with Andres who took over after we dumped Waterston overboard? He took our boat. We might have been able to get away with it."

"Kill him?"

"Yeah," Crosse said. He stopped now and faced his friend. "You killed that guy, Dom."

"Nah… No, I didn't."

Crosse looked into Stein's eyes, trying to find any trace of joking or humor there. He didn't see it. Stein actually believed he hadn't just choked the life out of a man less than five minutes earlier. Okay, this was just getting too weird for him. One more stunt like that and he was going to unload Stein, but quick.

Crosse got serious and tapped his friend's chest. "Don't play with me, Dom."

"I'm not playing with you," Stein replied. "I'm telling you, I only choked that guy unconscious."

"Okay, fine, let's say you did."

"No, let's not *say* I did. I did."

"Okay, so you did." Crosse didn't see any reason to agitate Stein in his present state. "What about that Isidora? I suppose you didn't kill her?"

"No, I killed her," he said with a quiet chuckle. "But that was more of an accident, you know? I didn't mean to kill her. But she was a bitch. You said the 'dragon lady' to Stone. You were right. Heh… Dragon lady, yeah. That was funny, Les."

Crosse turned and sighed. "Come on, Dom. Let's get out of here."

CHAPTER NINETEEN

Eduardo Valdese listened to the mundane reports from his advisers until he could hardly take any more, then sent all of them out of his office with their tails between their legs.

Valdese was a pure businessman. He didn't like it when people tried to pump him with a lot of bullshit and especially not the ones on his own payroll. He'd listened to these windbags long enough. Through the latter part of the afternoon and well into evening, he listened to them drone on and make one stupid suggestion after another. Nothing he heard even remotely appealed to him, so finally he kicked them out with orders to go home and think about it until they bled from their ears.

Valdese lacked two things: intelligence and leverage. Oftentimes those elements went hand in hand. He could use the right information at the right time to leverage his position inside Havana Five. Recently, however, he'd found that everyone was becoming increasingly dissatisfied until they reached a point that they didn't trust one another. Not that Valdese had ever trusted any of his equals...no, his *associates,* and he recently found better reasons to trust them even less than before.

First of all, he felt they were allowing Inez Fuego to manipulate them. He tried to tell the others but that fat, ignorant Santiago Famosa had slapped him down like a little kid, and he'd done it in front of the others. Valdese didn't give a damn if the guy was chairman of the Five or not; he would never tolerate being treated like that for long. And if the great Santiago Famosa didn't think Valdese had what it took to stand on his own two feet, he had another think coming. Next time they met it might not be under such official circumstances.

It surprised him more that Nicanor Armanteros, his alleged friend, hadn't come quickly to his defense. All of them had seemed to forget that it was Valdese who had warned the rest of them about Natalio Fuego's indiscretions; how he'd run drugs along the coastline using information obtained from high-ranking officials inside the government while refusing to disclose his activities to the rest of them, and his failing to funnel part of those contributions to the general funds. Of course, what Valdese failed to tell them was that he had confronted Fuego alone. For a piece of the action, he'd offered to overlook Fuego's little operation and promised not to tell the others. A mere fifteen percent was all he'd asked.

No, that wasn't going to happen. Even when Valdese threatened to tell the rest of the Five, Fuego wouldn't budge, besides his adamant denial that anything like that was going on at all. It was then that Valdese realized he couldn't trust the guy any longer and he renounced their friendship. He told the others immediately but they didn't want to act without proof. So Valdese brought it to them by way of a couple informants inside the Cuban police command. Only then would Famosa and the others vote to eliminate Fuego, and because it was Valdese who stood as his initial accuser would he be so kind as to take care of it?

After that, something happened in the dynamics of the Five that had never happened in all their years of operation. They began to mistrust one another. And Famosa, whether he realized it or not, began to treat Valdese more like a hired gun than an equal player in their arrangement. Valdese had suggested wiping the entire slate clean of the Fuegos but the others voted him down and said they had to bring Natalio's widow into the fold because they had no proof she knew anything of his wrongdoing.

Valdese had to wonder, but he kept his silence. Now, after all of these years, he'd finally gained bona fide proof of her deception and intent to wipe them out, and instead of thanking him they called her onto the carpet like a naughty schoolgirl being summoned to the principal's office. Well, that's not the way Valdese did business, and it sure as hell wasn't how he preferred to deal with traitors. All that little debacle had proved was how Havana Five was no longer an effective and viable business partnership.

Valdese planned to officially sever those ties, but he needed a plan to get away with most of his holdings intact. He considered an amicable split—specifically he would agree to continue his contributions to their emergency fund as well as a small piece of all his action in Havana—but he would be permitted to operate as a completely autonomous entity. Almost unanimously his people told him it wasn't a good idea and that in all likelihood the others would consider it an insult and have him run out of the country.

Well, they were welcome to try. With nobody to back his play, then—his underbosses were obviously so afraid of the organization that he couldn't rely on their support—Valdese decided the best way to split would be through the spectacular use of force. But his force of men, while impressive, would not suffice in such an effort. All Five leaders were equally matched when it came to that; they had kept it that way to ensure nobody got bold enough to try a grab for power. No, this would require a different kind of demonstration.

And then the idea hit him. Fuego's private army would work perfectly to his advantage. All he'd have to do was convince them that Fuego planned to betray them, just as she had the Five.

The jangling of the desk phone interrupted his train of thought. He considered ignoring it, but few had this number and if it rang there was a pretty good chance it was important. Valdese stared at it for a long moment as it rang twice, three times, and finally he picked up midway through the fourth ring.

"Yes?"

"Boss, it's Manuel," replied the voice of one of his lieutenants. Manuel Garza ran most of Valdese's numbers and gambling operations in central Havana. The guy was pretty much a weasel, but he brought a lot of revenue into Valdese's coffers.

"Yes, what is it, Manuel?"

"You're not going to like it."

"What do you mean, I'm not going to like it? You call me up with bad news and now you want to play guessing games with me? What is it, Manuel?"

"Someone has made a move against us. All of us." Garza paused a moment, then added, "I've been advised that Don Lombardi is dead, and rumors are that there may be others. I called because it worried me. I thought maybe…"

Garza didn't finish the thought, but he didn't have to. Valdese could feel his heart begin to beat quickly in his chest. He thought maybe he should be happy, but he couldn't believe what he was being told. Fuego couldn't possibly have acted so soon. Valdese had it on good authority that she wasn't anywhere near ready to move against them. In fact, the majority of the ELN force were still on Juventud. If they had begun their operations on the island in force, his contacts surely would have notified him.

"Your loyalty's commendable," Valdese said, although he actually thought it pathetic.

Garza had always been one of those who nipped at his heels like a whiny dog looking for any way to please its master. Valdese's ex-wife had insisted on keeping three miniature poodles in the house and he couldn't remember being happier to see all three of those yappy mutts go when their divorce was finalized. It almost made the settlement he paid worth it.

"What of the others? Have you heard any word?"

"No, although I understand there may be trouble at Don Famosa's deal on the wharf."

"Deal? What deal?"

The silence on the other end of the line got so heavy that Valdese thought the call had been disconnected. Garza's voice cracked when he finally replied, "I apologize, Don Valdese, but I just… Well, you see—I thought… I just assumed—"

"Mother of God!" Valdese screamed. "Spit it out, Manuel!"

"Don Famosa, he had an arms deal tonight."

Valdese could feel the blood rush to his face as he considered that. The light was beginning to dawn on him. He remembered how Nicanor Armanteros had said his sources spoke of Fuego buying arms outside their little circle. Valdese recalled how strange this was, and even made a point about the fact she hadn't gone through Chago to do it. Now he saw what was really going on. Chago was in on it with her! They planned to split the profits and cut the rest of the bosses out on the action. First they took out Lombardi. Not a terrible surprise when he considered he was Fuego's staunchest support. She gained his trust and then knifed him in the back.

"Are you there, boss?" Garza inquired.

"Yes, I knew about that." There was no point in letting Garza think he'd been duped so easily. "I just forgot."

"So, what do you want me to do?"

"Do? You don't *do* anything except keep making my money. I'll take care of this."

Valdese hung up without even thanking Garza. Yeah, the guy had probably just saved his life but he didn't intend to let Garza in on the indebtedness, even if he was right. Guys like Valdese didn't get far if they showed their underlings any weakness. Sure, Havana Five was a powerful group and most people thought twice before crossing them, but they had never been immune from infighting. They had just been spared because they were too busy feeding their greed. Now, the tide had changed. This would be the moment where Valdese could really assess if he still had allies or if he would be in this alone.

Valdese dialed the number of Nicanor Armanteros. He answered on the first ring.

"Nicanor, this is Eduardo. Have you heard?"

"I have," Armanteros replied. "Just now."

"What do you think?"

"I think we need to pull together and end this thing. Alone

neither of us can stand against this. We can only hold on to what we have if we agree to forge an alliance."

"You trust me, then?" Valdese asked.

"No," Armanteros said. "But then neither of us would be where we are now if we were the trusting types."

Valdese had to admit he couldn't argue with the guy's logic, whatever else he might think of him. "A truce then," he said. "We will stand together as one."

"Together as one," Armanteros replied.

JACK GRIMALDI CIRCLED THE wharf several times before Bolan gave him clearance to make his run.

With the green light from the Executioner, Stony Man's ace pilot brought the MD 900 into a straight-on, low-altitude buzz. All eyes on the ground expected police or military insignia on the glistening aluminum body of the craft, but instead they saw only an unmarked chopper painted steel blue. Some brought weapons to bear but they were merely pistols and Grimaldi was moving too fast for them to land an accurate shot. The pilot swung the chopper around, made a second pass, then did a second one-eighty and touched down smoothly on the center of the wharf building roof within seconds.

Bolan was out and moving. Grimaldi's position on the roof would offer him cover, at least enough until Bolan could get to them via the roof ladder mounted to an exterior wall. The Executioner descended hand over hand and reached ground zero quickly enough. He rounded the corner and nearly ran straight into a pair of gunmen armed with assault rifles. Bolan reacted by sending the stock of the FNC crashing into the face of one of the men. He sidestepped as his first opponent fell and the second man charged him. Bolan unsheathed his Ka-Bar combat knife and jammed it under the man's rib cage as he passed. The attacker led out a howl of pain that choked off as the knife puncture his lung and nicked his descending aorta. Bolan withdrew the knife and the guy collapsed, twitching as he bled out from the internal wounds.

Bolan sheathed the knife, double-checked the action of the FNC and then moved to the opposite end of the building. He peered around the corner and noticed gunners trading shots with some of Famosa's thugs. Well, it looked like Encizo had pulled it off, after all—they weren't really focusing on Bolan as an enemy right now. Good. Maybe he could get inside the warehouse and figure out just what they were up to.

Backtracking, the Executioner found a back door that he tried to open. No luck. He reached into his small satchel of tricks provided by Stony Man, formed a pancake-size amount of C-4 against the door, and primed it with a remote-activated blasting cap. Bolan stood down a respectable distance and engaged the small switch on the remote. The high explosive did the job intended, blowing a massive hole in the door where the lock had been.

The soldier moved carefully past the smoking door and crouched just inside. He could hear the echoes of shouting and gunfire but none appeared directed at him. Bolan maneuvered through the rows of crates and containers, careful to stay in the shadows they cast under the dim overhead lighting. As he moved closer to the front of the warehouse it got brighter and Bolan proceeded with increasing caution.

The battle raged on and it sounded as if the intensity was increasing. Bolan steeled himself for trouble. The amount of activity suggested more combatants had joined the fray. Well, he couldn't allow that to concern him right at the moment. He had a more important goal. Andres had told Encizo about this rendezvous and that Famosa planned to sell weapons to someone, although he didn't know to whom. Given Crosse and Stein's theory about the education conference, Bolan chalked that bit of intelligence up to more than mere coincidence. Especially when he considered the penalties for gunrunning in Cuba. It was considered an especially serious crime because Fidel Castro considered himself the ultimate protector, and therefore if someone was funneling guns through his country, then he assumed they were intended to overthrow the government. While such a view clearly demonstrated the dictator's pathological paranoia, it spoke volumes to the criminal outfits and made them think twice before selling arms, especially to domestic buyers.

Bolan continued to wind his way toward the front of the warehouse. He stopped short when two men rounded the corner at the far end of a row of goods. They were dressed like the previous crew but only toting pistols. Blood ran down the arm of one of them and they approached Bolan's position at a breakneck pace. The Executioner dropped to one knee and leveled the FNC but before he could get off a single shot both men fell under a storm of autofire. The slugs riddled their backs and they pitched onto the cold, unyielding stone of the warehouse floor.

Four of Famosa's gunmen with SMGs stood at the end of the row, smoke curling from the muzzles of their weapons. The two men who fell revealed a sight to their killers they obviously hadn't expected to see—the Executioner, his raven black attire stark against the overhead lighting, with his weapon now trained directly on them. Their reactions, while impressive, were just a moment too late. Bolan depressed the trigger of his FNC and sent a fusillade of rounds downrange. The slugs perforated the stomach of one man and the chest of two more. The remaining survivor turned and tried to escape the assault even as his buddies fell but Bolan found his mark with a single round to the side of the man's head. The heavy-caliber bullet punched through his skull and washed the wall behind him with brain matter, blood and bone fragments.

Bolan pressed onward and took a narrow opening created by crates stacked several high on either side. He crouch-walked the few remaining steps to his final target. Peering carefully over the top of one of the crates, he saw the battle had begun to dwindle. It appeared Famosa's crew was winning, although for the several dozen or so gunmen he'd sent into the fray, the unknown defenders were doing a fair job of holding their own.

Bolan used his combat knife to pry up part of the wood and look inside. He pulled away some grease paper enough to make out the familiar shape of a brand-new AKSU. That confirmed his own suspicions; there was a hell of a lot more going on here than a simple case of retribution. Maybe Crosse and Stein really *had* stumbled onto a larger conspiracy. It didn't justify what they had done in Bolan's mind, but he could certainly understand their volatile reactions. Well, these guns wouldn't be killing any college kids or any other innocent people.

Bolan retrieved a few quarter-pound sticks of C-4 and placed them at strategic locations on the crate, as well as a few of its neighbors. He then rolled some between his hands, wrapped it around the fuses and attached those to the full blocks. He double checked the work and then moved away from the crates as quickly as possible. He couldn't be sure he'd gotten all the weapons, but he'd left enough plastique there to easily cut through several eight-inch steel I-beams stacked end to end. It was enough to do the job.

CHAPTER TWENTY

The deal hadn't gone as planned, and neither had his contingency.

The first thing Captain Ciro Aguilera hadn't figured on was that he'd be dealing with a bunch of second-class thugs. Hurtado had told him these would be professionals—it was foolish that he'd believed this based solely on assurances from the Fuego woman—and immediately they were told to surrender their weapons. Well, Aguilera didn't know how things were done in Cuba but a soldier never surrendered his weapon. To anyone.

The sudden appearance of an unmarked chopper was the second thing to happen, an event that appeared to surprise the Cubans as much as his own men. Surely the Cuban police or military would have operated in marked aircraft, and they would definitely have made a show of force. No, this had to be a private operation, maybe the product of a double-cross.

Then the chopper disappeared from view, landing on the rooftop of the warehouse, and that's when the shooting started. Aguilera and his men immediately produced their sidearms in their defense. This triggered a chain reaction, and suddenly they found themselves surrounded by a virtual army of well-armed enemies. However, the enemy's superior numbers and firepower lacked the cohesion of a crack unit like Aguilera's team, and they were sorely outmatched by the sheer skill and experience of the ELN freedom fighters.

Aguilera's team rendered six of their attackers impotent within seconds following the initial engagement, breaking into a fire-and-maneuver pattern that got them inside the warehouse and allowed them to find cover among the relative safety of thick, wooden crates. From those defensive positions it was simply a matter of taking down the opposition as it entered the warehouse. The bodies stacked up quickly, and Aguilera thought that would have served as a warning to newer arrivals. Again, the enemy demonstrated its lack of expertise and it ultimately turned into little more than target practice for him and his men.

Aguilera could hear another battle raging outdoors. His three two-man teams on the perimeter were expertly concealed, and from their positions they would have little trouble neutralizing any external resistance. One way or another, he planned to complete his mission and walk away with the weapons intact. This had become of paramount importance. Colonel Hurtado could not be expected to succeed in his own mission if Aguilera failed in his.

The gun battle intensified inside the warehouse, but Aguilera's men persevered and the opposition's numbers dwindled steadily. Soon, the only sounds of battle seemed to be on the outside. Only one oddity attracted Aguilera's attention—the sound of an explosion coming from the rear of the warehouse during the most intense part of the battle. Aguilera focused on the enemy he could see. He would deal with any flanking maneuver soon enough.

A few of the enemy gunmen managed to slip past their blockade at the door, driving two of his men from cover. The pair remained together rather than split apart, which Aguilera found commendable but also knew might cost them their lives. He wouldn't be able to help them—to leave cover now would spell his own doom. Within a minute after they broke cover, Aguilera heard the reports of the SMGs the enemy gunners had carried, then a moment of silence, followed by controlled bursts from a singular and distinctly different weapon. This one sounded more like an assault rifle.

Aguilera and his aide dropped the last two gunmen entering the door and the interior of the warehouse fell into an instant, deathly quiet. The firefight outside had also dimmed to sporadic shots here and there. Aguilera held position another minute and then moved deeper between the labyrinth of varied shipping containers stacked three and more high. As the ringing subsided in his ears, Aguilera heard the rustle of clothing and movements. Someone was near the weapons stash.

The captain looked down and checked the action on his weapon. He hadn't realized he'd fired his last round. The slide had locked rearward on the bolt. Aguilera thumbed the released, eased it forward and holstered the weapon. He looked around, spotted a crate with its lid ajar and crouch-walked forward to look inside. Light gleamed off the blade of a brand-new machete—maybe fate had finally decided to smile rather than to defecate on him. He eased the weapon from the crate and continued in the direction of the noise. It took him only a minute to trace the source of those sounds.

A man dressed in black had just finished priming the weapons crates with plastique. As he turned to make his exit, Aguilera stepped into his path and immediately sized him up.

The guy wore a holstered pistol beneath his left arm and toted an assault rifle—the one Aguilera had probably heard going off earlier—but he wouldn't have time to use them in this proximity.

Aguilera stepped in and raised his machete.

THE EXECUTIONER GOT A FEW feet down the aisle before a shadow loomed in his path. He didn't recognize the big man but he knew the murderous intent behind that expression. The man's dark eyes looked like twin obsidian inlays of a bronze terror mask. He wore civilian clothes, jeans and a short-sleeved polo shirt, but Bolan recognized the poise of significant training and physical conditioning when he saw it. The soldier then noticed the man holding something low behind his thigh. He tensed his muscles like a cat ready to spring and that single action saved his neck. The man brought his hand around in a horizontal swing, and Bolan ducked in time to avoid the machete blade that looked sharp enough to sever his head from his body.

Bolan stepped back into a ready position and prepared for the fight of his life. His attacker lunged again, this time thrusting the machete at him, but Bolan saw the attempted feint and ducked rather than sidestepped. His foresight prevented decapitation for a second time. The man swung the machete and the blade whistled past millimeters above Bolan's head. He saw that the maneuver left the man off balance and he made his move. The warrior took his weight low to maintain his center of gravity, and wrapped muscular forearms around the man's waist. His powerful legs boosted him enough to take the guy off his feet. Then it remained simply a matter of gravity doing the rest for him.

Bolan body-slammed his opponent into one of the crates.

The man grunted with pain but on the outset it didn't seem to have much effect. The warrior estimated the man probably had three inches and a better forty pounds on him. Bolan stepped back as the man regained his balance and charged. Bolan delivered a front kick that his opponent trapped in a forearm lock, but it was enough to deflect the man's impetus. Before he could take the second half of the move, a leg sweep, the Executioner delivered an elbow to the man's jaw.

The blow stunned his opponent and Bolan seized the advantage. The grip on his leg loosened, the warrior brought his foot down with his weight behind it and stomped the enemy's instep. Bolan twisted out and drove his elbow into the protruding bone where the cervical spine met the thoracic one. Then he stepped back and finished with fight with a kick that drove the man's skull into a nearby crate. The wood splintered and cracked under the impact and Bolan's opponent slumped to the floor unconscious.

Bolan turned and retrieved the FNC that had torn from the cheap, vinyl strap. He took a step in the direction of his escape route once more and a second man appeared, this one also dressed in civilian clothes but nowhere near the size or maturity of the first. The man started to raise his pistol but Bolan beat him to the draw with the FNC. He triggered a short burst that drove the man off his feet and dumped him on the cement floor.

The Executioner broke from the area into a trot, anxious to get away before anyone else showed up to challenge him. When he was a safe distance he triggered the remote detonator. The crates of weaponry went up in a fireball explosion, superheating the grease paper and producing a dark, searing cloud of wreckage. Secondary explosions ensued as the magazines caught and fresh balls of red-orange flame accompanied the sensational first blast.

Bolan cleared his six, climbed to the roof and rushed for the chopper. All gunfire on the exterior battlefield had died, and the Executioner saw the flare of headlights as several vehicles swung out of the waterfront lot and sped from the scene. With any luck, Bolan figured he'd planted enough of the C-4 to nullify the weapons cache. Once more the enemy thought they could outsmart him, and once more they had been schooled in the flaw of their thinking.

And they hadn't yet even begun to feel the Bolan blitz.

"MR. MARQUEZ," INEZ FEUGO greeted Encizo upon entering the room where he'd sat the past three hours in limbo. "I'm sorry to keep you waiting."

Fuego had changed into a stunning outfit clearly tailored for a night on the town. She wore a black silk blouse glittering with tiny sequins that was cut low enough to give him a peek at the ample cleavage beneath. White stretch pants hugged her legs all the way to midcalf where they were met by high-heeled boots of gray suede. For a moment, Encizo had a little trouble concentrating although if his enamor showed Fuego didn't appear to notice. Maybe she'd become accustomed to men going dumb-faced when they saw her.

"Your credentials check out," she continued. "And you have quite a reputation for a man who seems to have just fallen out of utter obscurity."

Encizo couldn't resist a boyish smile. "I'll assume that's a compliment."

"Assume as you like," Fuego said, obviously not humored by his attempt to be coy. "But I still don't trust you."

"You wouldn't be as Lazaro described you if you didn't."

"Yes, that is one thing that still remains unverified," she

said. "I cannot seem to confirm or deny your story about Lazaro. I therefore must assume he's still alive. You understand, of course."

"Of course."

"Where is it you said you first met?"

"You'll forgive my bluntness, but I didn't say."

She folded her arms as she crossed a leg beneath her and sat on the edge of an ottoman. She cocked her head and for the first time since they met, the clip of a smile played at the edges of her mouth. "Not at all. Candor is not something for which I expect one to apologize."

Encizo only nodded in acknowledgment.

"But since I have no way of contacting Lazaro, and since I've sent Mr. Bustos and a team to look for him, I suppose it's only fair that I at least invite you to attend a social engagement with me this evening."

"I hope you won't think me too forward here, but I'm a bit surprised you are considering going out at a time like this."

"Like what?" She shrugged, stood and put her fists on her hips. "I don't make it a habit of babysitting my security teams, Mr. Marquez. And particularly not where it concerns Lazaro. I would think that he's old enough to take care of himself. I've trusted him with my most sensitive business dealings and he's never failed me before. I would hate to think I must now start second-guessing his every move."

Encizo rose and gestured at himself. "Very well. I trust I'm dressed adequately for this event?"

"More than so," she said. "In fact, I'd suggest you lose the tie. A dressier but more casual approach is desired in such circles as this one."

"And what circle is that?"

Six large men entered the room and after looking at them

in turn, she replied, "The kind where people become very closemouthed if they see an unfamiliar face."

"So you want me to be seen but not heard," Encizo replied.

"Not exactly."

"That's what I thought I just heard, in which case I think I'd like to pass."

Fuego grinned now and let out a laugh. She had a cute little laugh, and Encizo became a bit concerned because he found himself becoming attracted to her. There was something about this woman that primed the manhood. It wasn't the physical part of her—although he had no difficulty believing Inez Fuego was likely quite a little pistol between the sheets—rather Encizo found her an intoxicating mix of guts and brains wrapped in one heck of a figure.

"I'm sorry, but it seems you're mistaken on a point here. I'm not giving you a choice. You will accompany me to this little get-together while I await confirmation that Lazaro San Lujan is dead or alive. Once that's known, we will finally settle your rather abrupt and sudden appearance as an innocent bearer of bad news. If it turns out you've told me the truth, then I will weigh the options to either retain your services or have Mr. Bustos feed you to the wild and varied species in our beautiful Havana Bay. But if you are, hmm…well, let us just say mistaken about Lazaro, then I'm sure he will be happy to confirm your relationship. Until that time, you will do exactly as I tell you and you will do so without question. Am I being clear?"

In a moment Encizo recanted everything he'd thought about her. There was no mistake. Fuego was a dangerous and sadistic woman, a Cleopatra-meets-Pandora wrapped in a smoldering package of lies and manipulation. Encizo had no trouble believing the story Crosse and Stein had told them.

This one was without promise or hope, a figure of moral ambiguity who had obviously passed revenge long ago and now bordered on obsession. This was not the Inez Fuego of either media fame or legend. He could see now why she had reached a point in her life where she could run in the social circles of the mucky-mucks within the Castro regime.

"I see," Encizo replied. "Well, then, I guess we shouldn't be late."

Encizo stepped forward and offered his arm, rewarded with an increased tenseness in all six guards. She favored them with a warning look and then put her arm in his. The pair walked out of the room surrounded by their entourage of brutes. Encizo took note of the fact that all six of the men carried themselves like armed men. Well, at least he could count on that much going for him. If it came down to it, he could probably find an opportunity to disarm at least one of them. In the meantime, he'd remain cool and buy the Executioner all the time he could.

WHEN MOISES HURTADO HEARD of the defeat of Aguilera's men, he mobilized his entire force and ordered them to prepare for departure. It might have seemed extreme, but Hurtado considered this an extreme circumstance. In some queer and enigmatic turn of events, Fuego's contacts had betrayed them and murdered his men. Such an atrocity could not, and would not, go unpunished. He couldn't have it known that the ELN would tolerate this betrayal. Hurtado cursed himself because he hadn't heeded Fuego's warnings. What burned his gut even more was the fact he'd ever trusted her to begin with. Aguilera had tried to warn him of the dangers in this alliance and he'd refused to listen, unable to see past his own blinding ambitions.

Well, he wouldn't stand for it. He couldn't stand by idly while a brood of common criminals chewed up everything for which he had fought and trained. The innocent blood of his finest warriors had been spilled for nothing. There hadn't been any warnings, any chance to step back and find a peaceable solution. No, Fuego and her lackeys were mongrels, feeding their greed like ravenous wolves on a fresh kill. There wouldn't be any reasoning with them. Common criminals like Fuego understood only one thing, and Colonel Moises Hurtado planned to speak to them on their level. He would talk to them in the only language they understood.

The report had been vague, the ramblings of a lone survivor. According to his man, Aguilera and the group had made the rendezvous according to plan. Then something had happened, some type of verbal exchange, and suddenly a chopper buzzed overhead and that's when the shooting started. The soldier reported he couldn't really tell friend from foe, that maybe there were multiple parties involved, and so he'd started to shoot at anyone not on his team.

The soldier's words began to fall on ears that became increasingly numb until Hurtado couldn't stand to hear any more. All he knew at this point was that his friend, the wisest and most faithful friend he'd ever known, was dead. This would no longer be a mission of revenge for Inez Fuego's purposes. Hurtado had his own connections. He would ensure that those responsible for murdering his men would pay. They wouldn't tolerate such brutality from the armed forces of the Colombian government, and he sure as hell didn't plan to let such an atrocity pass—especially not when it was committed by nothing more than a rogue band of petty thieves. Yes, he would teach her *never* to cross the National Liberation Army, the people's army. Hurtado had spent the majority of his life fighting for the lives and liberty of his own. That included the men under his command.

And at first light tomorrow morning, he would set out to strike a blow for them that would surely make the whole world sit up and take notice.

CHAPTER TWENTY-ONE

The deeper Mack Bolan got into his mission, the more complex it became.

All of Inez Fuego's skullduggery had culminated to this moment, and the Executioner now realized just how dangerous she was. At first, Bolan had to admit he didn't consider her the greater threat. But as he peeled back the layers of the onion, the stench of treachery and blood became worse, and he now had cause for great concern regarding Rafael Encizo.

The other disturbing element came with the call from Stony Man Farm. Brognola had arranged for assistance from CIA operatives to retrieve Stein and Crosse and smuggle them out of the country. Unfortunately, Isidora never made her regularly scheduled check-in, and Bolan became disturbed when Brognola told him what they found.

"They caved her skull in," Brognola said.

"No sign of a struggle?" the Executioner asked.

"None."

"Then I'd have to guess it was Stein and Crosse who did it."

"Agreed," Brognola replied. "Otherwise we would have found their bodies next to hers."

Bolan couldn't argue with that. Not only did he have a sixth sense about these things, but it remained the only plausible theory. With San Lujan out of the picture, the only other person who knew their location was the street prostitute, Pirro, and if he didn't have San Lujan to tell then he had nobody. That left Inez Fuego being the only one who would know about them, outside of Andres, and Encizo had her occupied for the time being.

"Maybe Andres turned on you," Brognola suggested.

"No dice," Bolan said. "Like you say, there was no sign of struggle and neither Stein nor Crosse posed any threat to the other members of Havana Five."

"True."

"I'm betting they're out there and looking for trouble," Bolan said.

"Let's hope they don't go looking in the wrong place."

"Is there a right place for those two?"

"I don't suppose."

"This will complicate things, Hal. Let me see what I can do to get a line on them. I'll get back to you."

Bolan disconnected the call and considered his next option. Marisol Melendez had decided to take him up on his offer and seek refuge in the United States. Encizo had made the arrangements with some connections inside the tourism office. The upcoming First Annual Congress for Diversity in Education would make the perfect venue to get her out of the country. If she could get to the U.S. before her child was born and start the immigration naturalization process, her son would legally be considered a U.S. citizen, which would afford her all the rights and privileges that came with that as the child's mother.

"What was that about?" Grimaldi asked the Executioner.

The ace pilot had dropped Bolan in a remote field a quarter mile from his car, then returned the chopper to his contact and grabbed a cab back to the hotel where the Executioner met him. Reports were going out on all wires of the action at both Lombardi's estate as well as the wharf, and Bolan figured it was time to lay low until the excitement died down. The Cuban police would be throwing a dragnet over the city and surrounding area right about now, and the last thing he could afford was an encounter with law enforcement.

"Stein and Crosse killed the woman who protected them and then split," Bolan said quietly.

"Holy guacamole," Grimaldi replied slowly. "Not good."

"No, especially since I don't know why or what they're planning."

"You think they'll try to go after Fuego?"

"Anything's possible," Bolan said. "Neither of them struck me as cowards."

"If they were smart, they'd find a quiet way out of here and never show their faces in public again."

"You're right, but I don't think escape's on the agenda. They made no secret how they felt about getting stiffed by Fuego and friends. I think they'll be looking for payback. I'm betting they'll start with tracking down Andres."

"Well, if they find anyone who saw Andres just prior to Rafe making contact, they're going to know we're already onto it. Especially if they get wind of the noise you've already made."

"And they have some inkling of our plans and how we operate," Bolan said. "That information could prove invaluable if those two fall into the wrong hands. Like I told Hal, it's not like they won't draw attention to themselves. They're on foot, they don't have money, and they aren't strongly connected with inside sources."

"Not to mention they've killed a CIA operative, which will definitely put them at the top of the Company's hit list."

Bolan nodded. "They'll have to take their chances. I don't have time to go looking for them. We have to go as planned before this gets out of control."

"I'm game," Grimaldi said. "What's next on the agenda?"

"Whoever we went up against back at the warehouse wasn't Havana Five. At least not all of them. Those were two separate groups and some of them had extensive military training."

"You think they were ELN," Grimaldi said. It was more of a statement than a question.

"It's a good possibility," Bolan replied. "I'm betting they were an advance team. I hit a whole weapons cache while I was inside that warehouse. Enough to supply an army."

"So I don't get this. We know Rafe used Andres to get to Famosa. He's the head of Havana Five, right?"

Bolan nodded.

"Then if the weapons you destroyed were being supplied by Famosa to the ELN, that would mean he didn't have a clue who they were for. Either that or…" Grimaldi trailed off in midsentence, chewing on his upper lip, one eyebrow furrowed in contemplation.

"I know what you're driving at," Bolan said. "Why would Famosa be selling weapons to a terrorist army who were supposedly contracted to kill him and the rest of Havana Five's leadership?"

"Yeah! That doesn't make sense. I mean, I don't believe for a second that a guy with Famosa's reputation would risk selling arms to an outfit he didn't know anything about. And

I sure the hell don't buy the theory he thought they were some other outfit."

"Right," Bolan said. "Which means that whoever's really pulling the strings here knew the ELN would ditch Fuego's mission."

"What the hell is going on?" Grimaldi asked.

"It stunk from the beginning," Bolan said. "But now I see how it all fits together. And if I'm right, it's one of the most ingenious schemes I've ever encountered."

That much was sure.

Bolan realized that up until now, they had always assumed Fuego's motives for building her little private army were solely for the purposes of revenge. But using the ELN terrorists for such purposes seemed to be overkill. The numbers didn't add up, either. Stein and Crosse had told him they had photographic evidence that there were at least a hundred troops or more at the ELN training camp. It would have drawn much less attention and been less complicated for Fuego to hire a small team of elite assassins to get the job done.

When it came right down to brass tacks, the common denominator here wasn't Fuego or any other member of Havana Five. The only one who had known about all the operations of the various players had been Andres. It was Andres who'd provided San Lujan the information he'd needed to kill Melendez, and it was Andres who'd led Encizo to the head of the organization. It was Andres who'd known about Plan Colombia from his previous ties with the CIA, and only Andres had possessed intimate knowledge of Fuego's plans.

It all made perfect sense to the Executioner now. Andres had played all of them from the beginning. He had probably been the one to convince Fuego to fund the ELN operations, not disclosing his real intent. Then he drops a bug in the ears of the other members of Havana Five. Naturally, they would shore up one another against Fuego. Then Andres arranged the deal to buy weapons but told Famosa who he was really selling to. He then used Bolan's plan of making Famosa think that he'd been betrayed, but then after Encizo left he told Famosa the truth about who the real buyers were.

The only thing Bolan hadn't figured out was why. What did Andres have up his sleeve? How did sowing all of this mistrust and dissension among the leaders of the Cuban underworld benefit him? Was it about money and, if so, from whom? A breakdown in order among the crime trade would force the hand of the Castro dictatorship into action. Andres would lose his ability to move about freely in Cuba, bartering information. Unless it would buy him an inside track with some internal faction, or a seat of power in the highest echelons of the regime.

If he could demonstrate the inability of Castro's people to maintain order by arranging a major terrorist attack, it would engender enough support for a coup, in which case the stage for a civil war would be set. And the more Bolan thought about it, the more he realized how much Inez Fuego would actually contribute to such a devious plot.

Bolan recalled Encizo's words less than twenty-four hours earlier. "She's a socialite, and very influential both politically and financially."

"We need to go," Bolan said, jumping from his seat.

"Where?"

"To pull Rafe out of the frying pan."

As soon as they walked through the front door of the massive entryway, Encizo knew what Inez Fuego had meant about the people who clammed up when among unfamiliar company. Encizo recognized half of those faces by their extensive dossiers in Stony Man's data archives. Moving casually among the private art collection being shown were at least a dozen political players in the highest parts of the regime.

Most of them moved in pairs, and while they weren't dressed for a black tie affair he noted that they certainly had on their Sunday best. Most carried drinks, as well, and Encizo immediately noted the private bar. He started to ask if Fuego wanted a drink and detached her hand from him, but she grabbed his forearm tightly.

"Don't leave my side," she said in a tight whisper through clenched teeth.

A few people nodded toward her in recognition and she favored them with a smile, a muttered hello, and even that dainty laugh on occasion. Encizo wanted to vomit, her act disgusted him so much. Beneath that facade he knew churned the mind of the devil's spawn.

It seemed to Encizo she hadn't so much as shed one tear upon hearing of Lazaro San Lujan's death. Of course, he knew that part of her didn't believe he *was* dead, but he doubted when Bustos confirmed it that her reaction would be much different. Fuego was a user who bent people to her will, and particularly the men in her life. In most cases she had bankrolled the success by playing the part of the wilted flower with a broken heart. Men would fall for that, but although Encizo saw her as a beautiful woman, he also saw through her like a sheet of glass.

Since Inez Fuego had decided to treat him like a prisoner, Encizo figured one good turn deserved another. The first obligation of any prisoner was to escape by any means necessary, and Encizo had already taken an inventory. This private art gallery sported some pretty impressive pieces, and some had probably been acquired through less than legal means. That meant the owner would have protection around and plenty of it· the kind of protection that was armed.

Encizo hadn't even considered the fact Fuego's security on tourage wouldn't accompany them inside the house, and the fact they waited outside after dropping them off at the front door had taken him by surprise. The interior was another story entirely. Encizo immediately started to scan the premises and picked out at least a few possible candidates acting as armed security for the gallery, plus a couple of definite ones.

They continued through the collection, and Encizo could only peruse the various paintings and sculptures with vague interest. What he sought most was an opportunity, an opening that would allow him to escape his invisible bonds. The "gallery" was actually split into several large rooms along the front of the mansion estate, each connected by a grand oval foyer off the main entrance. Their little tour through the rooms afforded Encizo the opportunity to get a better lay of the land, mark any egress points.

Yeah, he was pretty confident he could escape but he'd have to take the high ground to do it. That wouldn't be easy as long as Fuego insisted he not leave her side even for a second. If he did, though, what could she do about it? It's not as if she could start a riot of any kind, or convince anyone he was doing anything wrong. What he needed was what his Phoenix Force comrades would have termed a reverse diversion. Rather than draw attention away from him, he needed to draw it toward them.

And what better way to do that than get the focus on one of the most influential people there.

Encizo waited until they were the only ones present in a secluded part of the gallery and then ripped his arm from Fuego's grip. The Cuban stepped inward and wrapped the muscular part of his forearm around her neck. He pulled back and immediately pinched off both carotid arteries, severing the flow of oxygenated blood to her brain. The constriction of muscles against her throat prevented her from crying out. If he increased pressure he would have most probably snapped her neck, and the Phoenix Force warrior had no desire to murder a defenseless woman in cold blood.

Fuego lapsed into unconsciousness in under thirty seconds.

Encizo eased her to the floor and immediately began to yell for help. The clatter of footfalls on the polished floor signaled the approach of at least half a dozen people, mostly men, who appeared a moment later. They ran to his aid and he began to explain how they had been standing there, admiring a fine piece, and then suddenly she collapsed. One man said he had medical training and put his ear to her nose, his eyes roving over her chest.

"She's breathing," the man said. "But very shallowly."

That would make perfect sense. Encizo asked for directions to a phone and as soon as he got them he dashed away as if going to call for help. He had nearly reached the phone when one of the security detail Encizo identified earlier appeared. The Phoenix Force commando picked up the heavy brass handset, began to explain to the guard what was going on and then cold-cocked the guy when he turned his back. Encizo patted him down and ultimately came away with a 9 mm Makarov. It was a bit surprising to find such a piece, but it was a weapon and he could hardly complain.

Encizo left the telephone room, moved past the crowd

now totally fixed on Fuego, and ascended a wide stairwell. He couldn't guess what he'd encounter above but he figured it was better than waiting for Fuego's men to shoot him dead. As soon as they were alerted to what was happening, they would definitely spread out to search for him, inside and out, and once the security detail figured out they had been duped he'd have a whole bunch of angry people hunting him with weapons.

He reached the second floor and began a room-by-room search for an easy way down. He finally found it in the fourth room he checked, a bedroom with a balcony. The thing was styled with a pair of columns that raised it to the level of the exterior door. Encizo opened the doors, looked over and estimated no more than four-meter drop. He could do that with his eyes closed.

The sound of shouts reached his ears, and he could hear frantic movement and the start of engines at the front of the house. This was his chance to get clear, and he had to do it right since he probably wouldn't get a second opportunity. Encizo leaped over the balcony, landed and shoulder rolled to absorb the impact. When he came out of the roll, his foot caught in a rut on the lawn and he twisted his ankle. The force brought him down onto the sod. Hard. Encizo bit back the pain and got to his feet. He started down the lawn, hobbling along like one-half of a three-legged race team.

And behind him the sounds of pursuit grew in volume.

Encizo knew it was going to take nothing short of a miracle to get him out of this one.

CHAPTER TWENTY-TWO

Encizo got his miracle in the form of Mack Bolan who, behind the wheel of the car bought in Matanzas, seemed to come out of nowhere along the south end of the property line.

The wood posts and crosspieces splintered under the impact of the car's hood as Bolan smashed through the ranch-style fence. He brought the car to a skidding stop across the slick grass and Grimaldi jumped from the passenger seat to help Encizo.

Bolan quickly scanned his friend as Grimaldi got him into the back. He'd noticed the limp but he didn't see any blood. This wasn't the time or place to play twenty questions. He'd find out later what went down. Bolan put the vehicle in Reverse and eased down on the accelerator so as not to dig themselves into massive ruts. As he focused on driving, Grimaldi leaned out the side window and let fly with a volley from an MP-5 he'd commandeered. The reports were like high-speed whip cracks inside the confines of the car. The ace pilot eased off the trigger and Bolan saw the opportunity to put the vehicle into a J-turn and get the hell out of there. He maneuvered the car along the backside of another vast yard and then got them onto a paved road within a minute.

"Thanks, Striker," Encizo said breathlessly.

"Don't mention it," Bolan said.

"How did you find me?"

"You owe Bear for that one."

"That's for sure," Grimaldi added. "Apparently, he decided to download a memory database from the SIM card in San Lujan's cell phone. It was only a matter of cross-referencing numbers dialed and received before he was able to get Fuego's mobile number."

"And once he had that, he was able to track her via GPS the same way he did San Lujan," Encizo concluded.

"Bingo."

"What did you find out?" Bolan asked.

"Not much, unfortunately," Encizo said. "She's got another heavy, guy she calls Mr. Bustos, who was supposed to be checking out my story about how San Lujan biffed it. I'd venture it's safe to assume he'll confirm my story?"

Through the rearview mirror Bolan locked eyes with Encizo. "Yeah."

"You get any closer to the location of the training camp?" Grimaldi asked.

Encizo shook his head. "I don't think she would have trusted me too soon with the information anyway. But I take it you guys must have learned something, or you wouldn't have shown up in time to save my tail."

"Would you buy ESP?"

"Not likely."

"Your buddy Andres," Bolan cut in. "How well you know him?"

Encizo leaned forward in his seat to get a better look

through the front windshield. "Phoenix Force worked with him a few times. Why?"

Bolan kept his eyes on the road as he replied. "I've concluded he's our missing link."

"In what way?"

Bolan ran it down for him in condensed version. He explained how Andres was connected to every member in Havana Five, his ties to the death of Basilio Melendez, and then theorized how his success against Lombardi and San Lujan—plus the meet between Famosa and the ELN force—had all been a little too tidy.

"Sounds like a pretty logical explanation," Encizo replied. "And it makes sense, because what this really comes down to is simple numbers."

"Right."

They could all agree on that point. What concerned Bolan most now was the inevitable conflagration between the ELN and Havana Five, not to mention the other impacts it might have if a war got started in Havana. According to what Stony Man had told him, Bolan now felt the President's fears had merit. The very idea of a war breaking out—whether between the ELN and criminal underworld in Cuba or otherwise—in the middle of a multinational event could have disastrous consequences for everyone.

"We have that other matter, too," Grimaldi reminded Bolan.

"What other matter?" Encizo asked with trepidation.

"Stein and Crosse escaped," Bolan said. "They killed Isidora and split. Nobody has seen or heard from them, but Hal thinks the CIA will go on a manhunt."

"Apparently, Isidora was quite a valuable asset inside the country," Grimaldi added. "She was one of the few strong links they had here who managed to stay under the radar of the regime's counterintelligence people."

"The Company will definitely be looking for blood," Encizo said.

"Right," the Executioner replied. "Barb's doing what she can to put their controllers on hold but I don't think it'll wash."

"Well, I can't say I'd shed any tears," Encizo replied. "I know it complicates things, Striker, but what else can we do? They made their bed and... You know the rest."

Bolan nodded. "Yeah, I know. I think we're going to have to step it up. Can you work through that injury?"

"Try and stop me." Encizo showed him a wicked grin. "It's only a mild sprain. Nothing some tight bandaging won't fix for now."

"Good enough because we've got plenty of work to go around. Any ideas where we can resupply?"

"I've got a few resources I haven't tapped into yet."

Bolan produced a half smile of his own as he replied, "I figured you might."

AARON KURTZMAN HUNKERED OVER his keyboard, studying the computer terminal in front of him.

After staring at the blue screen with white lettering a few minutes more, he looked up at the massive global map rendered in the latest 3D engine technology and zoomed onto Cuba and surrounding areas with the tap of a key. For the past twelve hours he'd barely left his terminal. He needed sleep, sure, but in some situations it just wouldn't come. If he'd tried to sleep he knew what would happen: he would toss and turn, unable to tune out the sounds around him.

"You look lost in thought," Barbara Price said as she entered the Computer Room.

"Wish I was lost in answers," Kurtzman replied.

"What are you up to?" Price asked. She knew full well, but sometimes it helped guys like Kurtzman to talk about it.

"I'm cross-referencing all of the information I dumped off Inez Fuego's cellular phone in the hope I can find something useful."

"Like what?"

Kurtzman didn't stop typing or look away from the screen, but he grinned as he said, "Like maybe what methods she might have used to contact the ELN terrorist group."

"Okay," Price said. Now interested, she pulled a chair over next to his. "But we can't even be sure there's anything legitimate to that theory. We only really know what Striker's told us up until now."

"I think there's plenty of merit to the theory," Kurtzman said. He sat back and pointed to a set of squiggly red, blue and green lines framed inside some type of graph. "See those? They're microwave transmissions, much like you would see from a SEAL magnaphone or, in this particular case, a civilian satellite phone."

"Inez Fuego?" Price inquired.

Kurtzman nodded. "I think so. She was using a very advanced encryption algorithm to cover them, but that's only good for garbling whatever's being sent over the microwaves, whether voice or data. It doesn't do anything to hide the actual waves themselves."

"Is it something you can use?"

Kurtzman looked at her in mild surprise, then leaned forward in his seat and made a show of cracking his knuckles. He muttered in a cocky tone, "'Is it something I can use.' Oh, sister."

The cyberwizard began by breaking the various micro-

wave transmissions into their subphase variances. He then
used these to triangulate their vertical direction, the times and
dates they were recorded, and communications licensing
handle of the company that had telnet shares for the particular satellite used. Eventually he backtracked that to a small
company in Cuba, which was actually an international sub-
sidiary of a North Korean firm. Kurtzman spent the next
forty-five minutes hacking into that company's communications network and database while Price looked on in satisfaction. Eventually, he was able to cross-reference the records
in that database and trace those back to the termination point
of each signal.

The majority of the work done, it then became a simple
matter of using communications modeling software developed by Akira Tokaido, the resident brainchild of a dozen
software and assembly languages and chief architect of
nearly all the proprietary software programs used by Stony
Man. Mostly they used in-house applications to do their work
because of the inherent risks that came using commercialized
programs. If they did utilize any commercial code, it had essentially been reverse compiled and modified by the Farm's
cybernetics team to work exactly as they needed it to while
removing any chance of that software penetrating Stony Man
systems and reporting back to its creators. To see the secrets
of a nation end up in the databases of a major software vendor probably wouldn't win them any awards with the brass
in Wonderland.

The work took more than two hours in total, some delays
inherent while Kurtzman stopped to explain one bit or another to Price. Normally he would have probably asked her
to leave him be but he actually enjoyed her company and her
astute insights had helped him work through problems on

more than one occasion. While nobody would have called Barb Price a technology expert, she knew her way around computers well enough, especially after her stint with the National Security Agency and its SIGINT Group.

"There," Kurtzman said, jabbing his finger at the result. "The signals correlate back to a location—Isla de la Juventud." He rattled off the latitudinal and longitudinal coordinates flashing on the screen.

"We'd better call Striker," Price replied.

"ISLA DE LA JUVENTUD?" Mack Bolan repeated.

"Literally translated, the Isle of Youth," Encizo replied.

Bolan nodded and then gave his attention to Kurtzman. "You're sure about that Bear?"

"As the fact I was born nude," Kurtzman quipped. "There's no question, Striker. I've triple-checked the calculations. I even ran them by an outside contact."

"Makes sense," Bolan said. "It would be the perfect place to hide an army until you were ready to use them. Barb, any way we can get onto the island easily?"

"Depends," she said. "It's just before 2300 there now, yes?"

"Right."

"Your best bet would be to go in under cover of darkness," she said. "There are no public boats running between the mainland and there at this time of night. But I'm sure we can find something."

"Do it," Bolan said. "See if Hal can pull strings at Gitmo. If we *are* dealing with a large terrorist cell, I want to go in with all the military-grade equipment and supplies we can get our hands on."

"That won't be easy," Price replied. "Most of what they'll

have is officially marked. Everything we supply you will have to be untraceable. If the Cuban government has any inkling the U.S. military was involved, especially on a non-military target, it might consider operations conducted against the island as an act of war."

"I understand your concerns," Bolan said. "But I don't think the Cubans want that kind of publicity, especially not if it goes public that an ELN terrorist training camp got hit. I'll leave handling of political ramifications to the diplomats. For now, it sounds like you know what I'm asking for. We had a couple more things that need tidying up here, but I think they'll wait."

"Understood. We'll get right on the supplies you need."

"Also, touch base with Hal. Have him pass a little message on to our Company friends. Let them know their former buddy Umberto Andres-Ituarte is the one responsible for many of their problems here. Maybe they'll call off the dogs on Stein and Crosse if we throw them a bigger bone."

"You think he had a hand in some of this?"

"I think he had a hand in a lot of this," the soldier replied. "And I'm going to chop it off. Out here."

Bolan broke the connection and recounted the details in abridged form for Encizo and Grimaldi. Taking down the remaining members of Havana Five wouldn't be the troublesome part. If they could hit the ELN terrorists before they got off the island, that would negate a lot of the activities happening here and diffuse a potential war between the ELN and Havana Five, or even actions against innocent bystanders.

Bolan asked Encizo to tell him more about the island.

"It'll be a challenge," Encizo replied, "and it'll take us at least three hours to get their by boat. Quietest means will probably be hydrofoil."

"Best point of entry?" Bolan asked.

"The least populated areas are around the black sand beaches," Encizo replied.

Grimaldi furrowed his eyebrows. "Black sand?"

"It's the literal truth," Bolan explained to the pilot. "It's a natural phenomenon caused by volcanic activity. Tourism tends to congregate on the south side where the white sand beaches are located."

"We'll also have to consider this point of entry at night from the aspect of cliffs. Another reason that region isn't popular is due to the ridges and cliffs along some of the coastline."

Bolan nodded. "Definitely a good place to conceal their operations."

"Sounds like it'll be tough to get to them," Grimaldi said.

"It will."

"What about a plane?"

Bolan shook his head. "It'll draw too much attention. And there's not time to get all the clearances we'll need. We'll skip Rafe's contact for now and wait for Stony Man to put something together."

The plan seemed sound enough but something bothered Bolan. Somewhere in the back of his mind, something tickled that sixth sense. He'd learned to listen to those instincts, and they told him this would hardly be a walk in the park. If he had his choice, he would have preferred to do as Grimaldi suggested. A low-altitude plane would permit them to fly below radar and make a night jump. But that also presented some risks, not to mention it would most likely alert the Cuban government to a foreign insurgence in their airspace and might get them shot down. No, they would have to do this one quietly.

At least until they engaged the enemy.

CHAPTER TWENTY-THREE

Jeronimo Bustos couldn't tell if the flush to Inez Fuego's face or the heat generated from her fierce anger was melting the ice applied to her bruised neck. Not that it really mattered, since the gravelly tone to her voice hid none of the fury behind it. Her words dripped with the venom of a thousand cobras when she spoke to anyone, and at one point she shouted for all but Bustos and their private doctor to "get the fuck out of here and find that crazy bastard." She had gone on to say something about the man's testicles and some condition she envisioned for them, but Bustos was too busy shooing them from the room to hear the entirety of her tirade. The doctor finished his work and then told her to rest and not speak too much. Apparently, the man who called himself Marquez had nearly fractured her larynx.

"A couple more centimeters and he might have," the attendee said. He looked at Bustos. "That was not by accident."

"By design then?" Bustos demanded. "You're telling me that he was a professional?"

"I don't know what exactly that means," the man said.

"But I will say that he knew how much pressure it required to get results. If he wanted to kill her, he would have."

Once they dismissed the doctor, Bustos sat and studied Fuego for a time. He felt a bit helpless in that he should have been there for her, but he couldn't also help remember she had ordered him to investigate Marquez's story. He had done exactly as she instructed, but as a result he wasn't there to protect her when she needed him. He didn't trust Marquez, so why had she decided she could take him alone?

"Spare me the lectures, Jeronimo," she said as she stared through his concern.

"I wasn't going to say anything," he replied.

"I could see it in your eyes," she said. "It was stupid. I got that. What did you find out?"

He lowered his eyes, unable how to tell her.

She had the grace to keep him from having to. "He's dead, isn't he? I can sense it now. You saw him?"

"There wasn't much left to see," he replied. "I'm sorry, Inez. Truly sorry."

Fuego looked like she might cry but then the hardened edge returned to her expression. This would probably push her over the edge, and at minimum it would send her right to it. She had lost Natalio to violent means and now her most trusted aide and protector. Bustos knew he could never fill San Lujan's shoes, but then he wouldn't have tried. He had a different kind of philosophy when it came to security. He *never* left his client's side. He kept his eye on the principal and that's how he did things. As next in line to succeed San Lujan—assuming he got Inez Fuego's blessing and support from the remaining lieutenants—he could do things differently.

"I told you it wasn't a good idea to go without me," Bustos said.

"You're feeling guilty," she said, scrutinizing his face. "You were following orders. And that's what I'll need in my new head of security."

"Thank you," he said simply.

She nodded once, then continued, "So how did it happen? The Americans he told me about?"

Bustos nodded. "One American, in particular. He used military-style weapons and tactics. He had high explosives, I'd venture grenades of some kind from the descriptions I got, along with assault rifles. He also had air support. He chased Lazaro and Don Lombardi along Highway—"

"Wait a minute! He killed Macario, too? You're telling me Macario Lombardi's dead?"

"Yes, ma'am."

Bustos couldn't tell from Fuego's expression if she were going to cry or burst into laughter. While it might have come as a surprise to her, to hear news of the Lombardi's death would hardly have broken her heart. She had noted he seemed the least accusatory in the meeting to which Bustos accompanied her early that morning, but it certainly didn't mean she felt disinclined to pardon the actions that contributed to the death of her husband.

"So, this American has apparently decided to embark on a vendetta of his own," she said. "Who is this man? Do we know?"

"Not yet," Bustos replied, "although I've already started a search on him. We do know he was seen talking to a prisoner at Guantánamo Bay."

Fuego nodded. "Basilio Melendez. The one Andres arranged to assassinate."

"You think the Americans somehow connected Andres to us?"

"Why not?" Fuego asked in a matter-of-fact tone. "They managed to find Stein and Crosse before Lazaro did. I'm sure they were told about him. Don't assume these men are stupid and never underestimate them. They'll figure it out soon enough and then they'll come after us."

"They already have, obviously," Bustos said, gesturing at her neck to illustrate the point. "And I haven't underestimated them at all. I know what I'm doing, Inez. And I think it's about time we stop waiting for them to come to us. There's another thing I have learned."

"And what's that?"

"Famosa knows about your hand in arranging to sell weapons to Colonel Hurtado. My contacts tell me it's all over the streets now. And…" Bustos paused, uncertain how to proceed, then decided the best way with her was simply to say it. "And it would seem that Armanteros and Valdese have forged a partnership against the rest of the group."

"What kind of partnership?"

"The kind that involves lots of men and guns."

"They wouldn't dare start a war with the others!" Fuego declared.

Bustos shook his head with a cautionary gesture. "Don't be too certain. They are solely profit-driven, given to act without pause or conscience. They would stop at nothing to protect their assets, Inez."

Fuego appeared to give this some thought. Of course, she knew he spoke the truth. It wouldn't take much convincing of that. The walls she had built around herself over the years were crumbling, trampled underfoot by the real world, and Fuego didn't know how to handle it. She never really did know, probably. She had played a role in a man's game but nobody agreed to change the rules of that game. Natalio had always handled the business arrangements and after his death Lazaro San Lujan had taken over. Now it was Bustos's turn get into the act and he planned to make the most of it.

"So we can no longer trust those who once called themselves friends and allies," Fuego concluded. She stood, the ice pack forgotten, and put her hands on Bustos's arms. "You're the only one left I can trust. I need you to handle this for me. I don't know what to do."

"We can start by getting as many men as possible to help us. We're going to need support and plenty of it."

"What do you suggest?"

"Valdese and Armanteros won't risk a street war. If we chose to go up against their combined strength alone, we would certainly lose. Especially since I don't think we'll have an easy time of convincing Famosa to come to our aid."

"I don't want his help anyway," she said. "I'd lose everything I had before I'd crawl back on my knees to that slug."

"You won't have to," he said.

She cocked her head. "What do you mean?"

"I managed to convince Lombardi's men that we were pretty sure one of the others hired the little American hit team to make it look like someone else was behind it. I've told them you'll offer your support and fold them into our organization out of respect for Don Lombardi. They bought every word. They're anxious to make someone pay, and that makes them vulnerable."

"Clever," Fuego stated. "That's so good it's almost frightening. You have quite the devious mind there, Jeronimo."

"I do try, ma'am."

"So that gives us some manpower. But I don't see how it will be enough to hold off the combined strength of the other three."

"And again, you won't have to," he said. "Their sole purpose will be to keep us secure here. Colonel Hurtado's army will do the rest. He'll be seeking vengeance against those responsible for the death of his men. And remember, he'll be bringing nearly a hundred well-armed and well-trained soldiers. Not even combined could their people hope to repel a force like that."

"Well, it sounds as if you've thought of everything," Fuego said with a smile. She sat on a nearby sofa and crossed her sensuous legs.

Bustos tried not to notice the additional flesh exposed by the ride-up of shorts into which she'd changed. He swallowed hard as he averted his eyes and said, "It's an acquired art. You simply have to learn to read people."

"And what of the Americans?" she asked. "How do you intend to take care of them?"

"If they're here for the reasons I think they are, they'll remain plenty busy with full-scale war going on relative to the others. That leaves us only having to locate Stein and Crosse."

"And how do you propose to do that?"

Bustos replied. "Oh, let's say we're going to dangle a carrot they won't refuse."

"Well, it's going to be difficult to find them," she said. "If they're even in the country."

"Oh, they're still here. And I know exactly where to find them."

"I have to admit," Fuego said, "I'm impressed. You have obviously given this quite a bit of thought. And now I want to know something else."

"What's that?"

"I can see you looking at my legs. Why do you pretend not to? Am I not beautiful to you?"

"Mrs. Fuego, I—"

"Oh, *Mrs.* Fuego is it now? Well…*Mr.* Bustos—" she rose and slinked onto the armchair next to him "—I don't see any reason to tease you. There are certain, oh, let's call them 'advantages' to being the boss. There are also advantages to being the boss's right-hand man. Wouldn't you agree?"

Bustos swallowed hard again but this time it felt like something got stuck in his throat. In all his years working under San Lujan, he'd never known of a time the two of them were intimately involved, neither had he ever heard of Fuego throwing herself at a man. Not that she had to, of course; the beauty dripped off her like saliva off the teeth of a starved mountain lion. Only Fuego was twice as dangerous as a hungry wildcat. Bustos felt a little suspicious at first but then he saw the erectness of her nipples through the almost sheen material of her button-down shirt as she gently curled her hands around his head and brought him to her chest.

Funny, he'd never noticed the translucence of that material before now. What the hell was his problem? Here was a beautiful woman, drawing him to her like she would an infant, and he was acting like a virgin schoolboy. He couldn't help but feel some hesitancy—sleeping with the boss tended to get complex. Well, it had been a while for him, and he could already feel his response press against the crotch of his tailored slacks. He would worry about the ramifications later.

Much later.

FOR THE SECOND TIME IN less than a day, the gods rained favor upon Pirro.

After trying to reach San Lujan without success, Pirro began to ask questions on the street. Havana was hardly a small town but word spread fast about the battle between Santiago Famosa, rumored to be head of the Five, as well as rumors of violence against some of Don Macario Lombardi's men. Some were calling it just the beginning of full-scale war between the various factions, which would be the first of its kind in the history of Cuba.

Pirro didn't really want to attract attention, so he stuck to asking simple questions and awed reactions. Still, the news he heard did nothing to allay his fears. There seemed no question about it now. Havana Five was breaking up, and with it would mean an end to the status and protection he had enjoyed to this point.

"Lazaro San Lujan's dead," Manuel Garza told him.

Garza was a street-level boss for Don Eduardo Valdese. Pirro neither liked him nor the Valdese family. He saw Garza as nothing more than a hood. It was Garza's people—Pirro discovered this but he'd never let on that he knew—that had tried to squeeze him for a piece of his action on the streets. Garza backed down only when Mr. San Lujan intervened and warned Garza and his people to keep their hands off. So Garza made this announcement with some sense of victory in his voice.

Not that Garza was quite ready to exploit the situation. Whoever took the place of Lazaro San Lujan would make the decisions about who and what territories fell under the protection of Inez Fuego, and until those decisions were made official Garza didn't risk stepping on toes and attempting a takeover. That was a pretty fast way to get the throat laid wide open with a razor.

In any case, the thought of war on the streets between the Five meant Pirro's days of protection were coming to a close. He had lost his meal ticket and before long he would probably lose the support of the Fuego family. Then again, maybe they would be too busy fighting with one another to worry about the measly amounts he made. Or better yet, he might even be able to step up his status a notch or two by financing the war effort. Either way, he had to gain something of value if he wanted to stay alive.

And that's when his good luck turned up again when, while walking his street and looking for a customer, he spotted the two Americans leave Isidora's store and look around furtively. Although San Lujan might be dead, he'd stressed the significant importance of these two men to the organization at large. Maybe this would work to Pirro's advantage. He already had the goods on Isidora, but that probably wouldn't buy him much. He could barter that with her one-on-one later. No, better to follow these men for now; he would deal with Isidora all in good time.

Pirro hadn't prepared himself for the kind of journey he'd undertaken. For a few hours the two men got out of the rain and ended up in the basement of some apartment building in an area well off Pirro's map. He stood in the entry of an alleyway, shivering in the rain despite the warmth of the night, and observed the entrance. He couldn't let them out of his sight no matter how much misery he might have to endure. A couple of times some men who knew his kind by sight approached him, even one woman who looked very pretty, but he warned them off. They moved on without argument.

After a few hours the men came out. By this time it had stopped raining and the streets were starting to fill again with the night crowd. Eventually, Pirro followed the Americans to the nicer part of downtown. The men entered a clothing shop and emerged sometime later wearing new clothing. Pirro tracked them again, but this time they ended up at a

club. He decided to give it no more than thirty minutes before he tried to call Mr. San Lujan again. He'd have to find
some way of reaching him. He didn't have the cell phone anymore, although he knew the number by heart, but San Lujan
hadn't answered. He refused to believe Garza was right.

Damn that American, anyway, who had not only destroyed
his phone but also stolen Marisol off to who knew where.
He'd probably rape her or sell her, maybe even take what he
wanted and then simply kill her. Well, maybe not. She was
pregnant and the guy didn't strike him as that kind of sadistic bastard.

The fact he'd told the American the truth, though, bothered Pirro most. He could have lied—he had to protect the
Fuego family since he owed them that much—but instead
he'd decided to tell the man everything he knew. He lied at
first, or he tried to lie, but the American saw right through it
and while he never threatened Pirro's life, he didn't really
have to. Something about that man had almost commanded
him to answer the questions, as if under the power of some
invisible force.

Either way, it didn't matter now because if he didn't figure out what the Americans were up to he wouldn't be of
much value to the Fuego family. When they left the club, he
followed them to a run-down motel. Guns were sold there,
along with information. The outfit itself was run by a man
Pirro knew only as Andres, a name he'd heard Mr. San Lujan
speak only one time before.

The young man settled in to wait once more. It wouldn't
be long now. Whatever they were planning would happen
very soon, Pirro was certain. The Americans were up to
something and by the way they acted, the way they looked
around furtively and tried to keep to the shadows wherever

they walked, told Pirro they were doing something they weren't supposed to be doing. Maybe they weren't acting on behalf of that big American after all.

Well, time would tell.

CHAPTER TWENTY-FOUR

Barbara Price and Stony Man paid off in a big way.

Within an hour of their arrival, Bolan met with their contact at an arranged location: some private docks on the northwest coastline of the Cuban mainland. The man neither offered nor asked for a name, so Bolan didn't bring it up. They gave each other the passwords and then the contact set right to work in showing Bolan the merchandise. Somehow, this wisp of a fellow had managed to procure about everything they would need for their mission to the Isle of Youth.

"I see you recognize the Higgins Boat, no?" the man asked in an accent Bolan couldn't identify. "We have converted it with some modern equipment, of course."

We? Who was "we"?

The man continued, "We replaced old engine with new one. You now can do about thirty-five knots, maybe little less, no? You will also run silent—" he put his finger to his lips to emphasize the point "—so no have to worry someone hear you."

The man tugged on Bolan's arm, pulled him down the

dock a bit to the front area. He reached down and flipped a tarp aside to expose a massive strongbox. He grabbed a rope on the box and used it to yank open the lid. Inside was a vast arsenal of just about everything the Executioner could have hoped to have for a run like this one. Beside a pair of MP-5s with what looked like at least a thousand rounds of ammunition, the waterproof case also contained combat knives, including a Cold Steel Tanto. Bolan looked back to see if Encizo noticed and the Cuban grinned at him with a wink. The Executioner returned his attention to the cache. The case also sported a brand-new .50-caliber Desert Eagle Action Express. But Price definitely thought ahead. The .44 Magnum version would have been sufficient under normal circumstances, but the Executioner would need the more stopping power in this package. Since they would probably have to climb and scramble among the ridges and cliffs of the beach to reach the training camp, Bolan would have to travel light.

There were also Diehl DM51 grenades. The DM51 could function as either an offensive or defensive grenade, depending on whether the user chose to keep in place the fragmentation sleeve, a hollow plastic shell packed with more than six thousand 2 mm steel balls. The grenade was packed with PETN high explosive, and if the user removed the sleeve the DM51 served the perfect offensive role.

Completing the list was the choicest of the small arms lot, an HK 21-E machine gun. Presently in service with the Mexican army, the German-made export version of the HK 21 included an extended receiver and bidirectional, dual-feed mechanism based on bolt stroke. The weapon chambered 7.62 mm NATO ammunition and boasted a cyclic rate of 800 rounds per minute at muzzle velocity of greater than 2,500 feet per second.

With a nod of approval from the Executioner, the little man closed the lid and replaced the tarp. He studied each one of the trio in turn and then, without a twist of his fingers in a sort of lazy salute and a wan smile, he walked off the dock and disappeared into the darkness. The total encounter had lapsed less than two minutes. Just the way Mack Bolan liked it—no complications.

Bolan looked at Encizo as Grimaldi jumped into the boat and prepared to cast off. "Thirty knots…about forty miles per hour?"

Encizo nodded. "Sounds about right.

"How long will it take us to get to where we're going at that speed?"

"Assuming the wind's at our backs and we don't run into any trouble, I'd say that'll put us on the beach in less than three hours."

Bolan looked at his watch: they'd hit ground zero about 0300. It wouldn't give them much time to get onto the island and find the training camp. He hoped the coordinates Kurtzman provided were dead-on because they'd only get one shot at this. If their intelligence proved correct, they had to advance about half a mile inland to reach their target.

In a way, Bolan had to admit he was glad to have some company along for this mission. He'd never been keen on bringing members of the team into his own missions, even the sanctioned ones, but part of him didn't really mind, either. It had once been a strict rule of his to work solo but over the years he realized the value of allies in particular situations, and if he had to work with others he preferred they be the men of Stony Man because he knew he could trust them with his life.

After all, he'd handpicked most of them.

"We're ready to go, Sarge," Grimaldi said as he stowed their gear. The pilot looked hesitantly at the wheel propped high in the back and said, "Um, at least I think we are. You ever captain one of these things?"

Bolan shook his head and gestured toward Encizo. "No, but I assume Rafe has."

Encizo took the cue with a mischievous grin and slid easily from the dock into the rear cockpit. The original Higgins Boats used during World War II had consisted of a coxswain, engineer and two crewman minimum. Obviously their contacts had managed to modify the boat some so that it worked in a self-sufficient matter. Encizo turned the key and for a moment he thought the engine hadn't started until he heard the almost imperceptible churn of water and felt the steady vibrations in his feet.

He let out a wolf whistle. "Wow, that guy wasn't kidding."

Grimaldi cracked a grin. "Definitely purrs like a kitten, doesn't she?"

"Let's get moving," the Executioner said. "We've still got a full night ahead of us."

To HIS COMPLETE SURPRISE, THE password Crosse had used when he and Stein had arranged their initial meeting with Andres managed to get them past the pair of huge guards and into the basement of the hotel. Andres apparently had plenty of resources, because in addition to his significant information-brokering network, the man kept an impressive stash of knives and firearms.

The two hundred dollars they had, however—minus the thirty they'd used to buy fresh clothes—wouldn't have bought them a popgun. Not that Andres's salesman knew that, or the pair of human guard dogs posted at the sound-proof door leading to the basement armory and lounge. This would make things significantly easier.

The man who met them was a greasy, unwashed type with missing teeth and BO that spoke volumes about the man's habits in the area of personal hygiene. He was portly, stood about a half-head shorter than Crosse, and his flabby arms were covered in tattoos only an Egyptologist specializing in hieroglyphs could decipher. He went only by Fresco, but Crosse doubted it was his real name. That was fine; they wouldn't be there any longer than necessary to get what they needed.

Fresco looked at the pair as they emerged onto the open basement. He sat perched on a high stool behind a low counter, arms crossed, and lit cigar stuck in his mouth and a girlie magazine shoved between his pudgy mitts. Only the gun oil and scent of burned powder worked to cover the obvious odors wafting off Fresco. After their first encounter, Stein had crowned Fresco with the moniker *pocilga,* the Spanish noun for "pigpen."

Fresco made a face that Crosse couldn't differentiate as a scowl or a smile. In a heavy accent he said, "*Señores!* Andres no tell me you coming back."

"We told him we might be back for some additional things," Stein replied casually before Crosse could say a word.

Crosse wanted to slap his partner but cooled off. He'd told Stein to keep his mouth shut and speak only if Crosse spoke to him. He couldn't risk Stein blowing this deal. Dominic Stein was a lot of things, including Crosse's best friend, but his partner had never been that good in playing a role. More than one time they had nearly had their covers blown during an undercover operation because of Stein's ineptitude toward those things that required a bit more stealth and subtlety.

"Yeah, we told him we would be back," Crosse said. He cleared his throat and asked casually, "You haven't seen him around, have you? We weren't able to reach him at the club."

Fresco shrugged and dropped his magazine on the counter. "He no keep me told on where he go and what he do. I just do what he say, sell to who he say. What Fresco do for you?"

"We need some guns," Crosse said.

"Yeah," Stein added. "What kind you got?"

"Oh, Fresco have whatever you need," the big man said as he slid off the stool. He scratched under his armpits and ambled over to a locked rack on the opposite side of the room. Directly ahead were a few shooting lanes just beyond a long counter. The lanes weren't separate by anything more than faded orange paint on the floor and targets at the opposite end. One lane seemed a bit longer than the other two; probably the one they used to test rifles and such.

Crosse followed Fresco to the massive wall cabinet with Stein in tow. The Cuban opened the cabinet and lifted the door handles. The doors were slatted, and they slid upward and over the cabinet like garage doors to disappear into the brick basement wall. The recessed lights gleamed off the tempered glass that was sealed by steel lock at the bottom, which prevented the glass from being slid aside.

"What you like see?" Fresco asked.

"How about that Glock right there?" Crosse asked, pointing to a Glock Model 17. He would have preferred something in .45-caliber but he knew beggars couldn't be choosers, and he was very particular about the guns he liked.

Fresco nodded and disengaged the window lock. He slid the door aside at which point Stein stepped forward, raised a small pistol to the back of Fresco's head and pulled the trigger. The gun salesman's head slammed against the glass with the force of the bullet, leaving a small spatter of blood and brain matter before his body slumped to the ground.

Crosse turned to look at Stein with complete shock. "Where the fuck did you get *that?*"

Stein stopped and looked at Crosse as if completely taken by surprise with his question. He held up a little .22-caliber pistol and said, "What…this? Oh, I lifted it from that bodyguard's jacket back at the club."

So now Stein was an experienced pickpocket in addition to being a half-crazed killing machine. That's it! The guy had gone completely off his rocker, and Crosse didn't want anything else to do with it. He'd go along with Stein for now, but as soon as the opportunity came around he planned to get as far from his partner as possible. He didn't need this kind of shit right now.

"That's great, Dom," Crosse said. "Just great. Any second now those two ogres upstairs are going to come down here and fill us both with holes."

Stein chuckled as he reached into the cabinet and took the Model 17 off the shelf. He weighted it in his hand and then handed it to Crosse, butt first. "It's loaded already."

Crosse took the weapon and after a quick pop of the clip confirmed his partner was correct.

"Shows you *pocilga*'s stupidity there," Stein added, "keeping loaded weapons in his inventory and all. It's a wonder somebody hadn't already taken the guy for a ride on that big black train."

"That's probably because nobody wanted to risk crossing Andres."

"Andres has to answer for, Les!" Stein said, carelessly

wavering the muzzle of the smoking pistol at everything in sight. "You got that? He fucked us on this deal and I aim to make sure he pays for that. Guy's a worthless shit."

"Okay…sure, Dom. Whatever you say," Crosse said quietly.

"And don't worry about the lugs upstairs," he said with a confident grin as he pulled a Colt M1911 from the shelf. "That's a soundproof door they're guarding. Besides, they're used to hearing gunfire from down here."

Stein grabbed two boxes of ammunition that were tucked into a recess behind where the Colt had sat and then began riffling cabinets until he found shoulder holsters for both of them.

Crosse shrugged into the leather rig Stein offered without a word. He then procured a couple boxes of soft-nose 9 mm Parabellum bullets. He would have preferred hollowpoints or even hardballs but he couldn't find any, which meant he'd have to settle for the cheaper makes. In addition to the pistol, Crosse selected a backup piece—a Walther P-22 he strapped between his calf and ankle—just in case they found themselves in an encounter with Stone and his crew.

Above all else, that idea unnerved Crosse, although he wouldn't ever have admitted it to Stein or anyone else. Something about Colonel Stone scared the living shit out of him. Crosse considered himself dangerous enough and certainly he possessed the skills of a first-rate combatant, but some guys just wore it as naturally as their own skin. Stone came off as one of those types. Crosse could face an encounter with others of his own kind, the Cuban police, even enemy soldiers on a battlefield. But he wasn't sure he could survive against a guy like Stone; not now that he'd seen the guy up close in flesh and blood.

Crosse shook off the shudder that ran through him and focused his attention on his partner's machinations. Stein had just finished buckling into his own shoulder holster. He pocketed the pistol lifted from the guard and kept the Colt out and ready. Crosse looked at Fresco's motionless body. A massive trail of blood had started to seep across the floor.

"Are you ready?" Stein asked, drawing Crosse back into his nightmare reality.

Crosse nodded and Stein stood, waiting expectantly, until he realized his partner was expecting him to lead the way. Crosse headed for the stairs and then stopped short when he thought better of it. He turned and looked at Stein.

"You know, there isn't much point for us to go anywhere," he told his partner.

"What do you mean?"

"Well think about it, Dom. We don't know where Andres is. We know he's not at the club, which means he could be anywhere. He might have already shacked it up with some broad for the night."

"Doubt it," Stein said with an emphatic shake of his head. "If anything, he'll be with Stone's friend, the Mexican-looking dude."

Yeah, Crosse hadn't thought about that—Stein had a point. Still, it didn't make any sense for them to traipse all over Havana looking for him, calling attention to themselves. They either waited here or they went searching for Andres in any of the hundreds or even thousands of places he might keep himself. The trade-off would be they could wait here an awful long time and the guy might never show up. Still, the chances of finding him had been slim to start with.

"I don't know, something in my gut is telling me we should wait here."

"Fine," Stein said, folding his arms. "Then we wait."

"Okay," Crosse said, nodding and feeling a little better he'd managed to convince his associate to agree with him.

"You know," Stein said in the next beat, "we'll eventually have to take care of those guards."

All of a sudden, Leslie Crosse felt sick to his stomach.

"HIS FULL NAME IS Umberto Andres-Ituarte," Barbara Price announced. A massive picture of his face from his CIA dossier filled the screen.

Brognola grunted. "Handsome fellow. That would make him more dangerous."

"In this case, it's the literal truth," Price replied. "Age forty-seven, place of birth, Mexico. During his adolescent years he and his mother were among several groups caught sneaking across the border repeatedly, deported each time back to Mexico by the INS. Then during the Iran-Contra Affair, the Honduran government learned of his real nationality and put him on their most wanted list as an espionage agent.

"That would have bought him the death penalty, even today, but he managed to escape to Cuba posing as a refugee, and eventually he landed in America. When Miami detectives caught him attempting to fence stolen merchandise, they called in the FBI."

"Seems a little out of place for a petty crime," Brognola interjected. "What gives?"

"Well, that's where it gets interesting. The tapes actually contained highly classified information smuggled out of the country regarding nuclear materials the CIA believed might be located within the Cuban mainland. The tapes later failed authentication, probably put into circulation by the Russians during the cold war."

"But it was enough to get the CIA's attention," the Stony Man chief concluded.

Price nodded emphatically. "Oh, you know it. They swooped into Miami and snatched the tapes and evidence out of the hands of Miami police before the FBI could even get an extradition warrant. The deputy director was hot because the CIA used the U.S. Marshals Service for the pickup."

Naturally. The Central Intelligence Agency was forbidden by legislative and judicial acts to conduct sensitive operations within the United States, or using coercion or other illegitimate practices to act against noncitizens while they were under protection within the legal borders of America or its protectorates.

"So the Marshals turned him over to the CIA without any idea of who they were working for."

"Right. Everyone could claim they got duped and the CIA whisked Andres off to parts unknown. By the time it finally got through all the bureaucratic red tape, so much time had passed nobody cared any longer. Apparently they had decided to move on to bigger and better things not having much to do with noncitizens."

"So he fades into the woodwork," Brognola said, the disgust evident in his tone.

"Exactly," Price replied. "A year later he surfaced in Cuba once more. Legally he was still a political refugee so the Cuban government just renewed his status. Meanwhile, all during the 1990s he brokered information back to the CIA on everything he could dig up. After the Soviet Union fell in 1991, and the cold war dissipated, he lost his usefulness and the CIA basically dropped any official or unofficial relationship they had with him. He knew he wouldn't last long out there without their financial backing, so he gets into the information-brokering business for the underworld. He made powerful friends, including most of the leaders in Havana Five. Somehow he managed to keep his affiliation with each of them a secret from the others."

Brognola expressed disbelief and said, "That's a pretty dangerous game to play. So, we're dealing with a guy who's connected as well as overconfident. Shouldn't be too hard to run him down."

"We've handled worse. Striker thinks it might be in our best interests to locate this guy and turn him on to the agents searching for Stein and Crosse."

"To what end?"

"I think he believes Andres is the greater threat right now," Price replied. "I'd have to agree with him. He's figuring if we give the CIA a whiff of Andres's scent, find some way of connecting him to all of this, they'll back off Stein and Crosse."

"It's worth a try," Brognola said. "What about Striker and crew? Did they make the rendezvous?"

Price nodded and smiled. "About an hour ago. They should be on their way to the Isle of Youth now."

Brognola emitted a heavy sigh—his stomach started to sour and he could feel a headache coming on. "Let's just hope they get there in time."

CHAPTER TWENTY-FIVE

Waves slapped against the boat—they remained the only real noise perceptible to Mack Bolan's ears—as the faint outlines of land glowed in the distance. He looked back at Encizo who caught the Executioner's questioning gaze, glanced at his watch, then held up four fingers.

During their transit, Bolan and Grimaldi had double-checked the weapons and prepared magazines. All three men were now attired in fresh pairs of camouflage fatigues and they were rigged for action. Grenades dangled from their load-bearing harnesses and they wore pistols on their sides in military webbing. With a bit of effort, Bolan had mounted the HK 21-E machine gun.

During their preparations, Bolan took note of some other interesting modifications to the Higgins Boat. If memory served, he remembered the original vessels were thirty-six feet in length while this one couldn't have been more than twenty. Additionally, the vehicle didn't sport the four- to five-foot side walls, but rather this one flared down from the five-foot back to one foot and then back up to about a four-foot-high ramp. As near as he could tell, the ramp was operable. It was still a bit oversize for their crew of three, but the Executioner didn't complain because the thing had performed flawlessly throughout the trip.

With any luck, it would survive intact long enough for them to get out.

Bolan never heard the point where Encizo killed the engine, but he had to have because there was the sudden grating sound of the boat hitting the beach and then the barely perceptible whine as the ramp started to descend before they even got to a halt. Bolan and the rest put it in high gear. He and Grimaldi secured the equipment they would leave behind while Encizo disconnected the battery. At least if someone tried to steal the thing it would slow them.

Not that they planned to still be here at daybreak.

Bolan checked his watch and noted the time: 0143. Good, they were nearly fifteen minutes ahead of Encizo's prediction. That would buy them a little extra time, which could mean the difference between success or failure in a mission of this kind.

With the weapons and boat secure, the trio moved out. Bolan took point with Grimaldi in the center and Encizo on rear guard. They angled up the beach until they reached a line of trees. Pines covered the vast majority of Juventud, which would make their journey through the foliage a bit easier even if at night. Despite the copious rain, the pines still grew high off the ground. A bed of pine needles covered the forest floor, sopped and spongy under the boots of the trekkers.

Bolan considered the task ahead, calculating his options to take his mind from the exertion of their journey. Stein and Crosse had estimated the strength at somewhere between fifty and a hundred. They had lost maybe ten going up against

Famosa, which in a worst-case scenario would leave upward of ninety remaining. The Executioner had gone up against those numbers before, and without assistance, but this would be a bit special. In this case he would be strategizing on the fly and going up against a significantly well-trained force of men.

The only way to take out those kinds of numbers would be to strike first and hard. Once they joined the battle with the ELN there would be no letting up until they were either victorious or dead.

THEIR JOURNEY THROUGH THE forest threw off any sense of time, but Bolan kept his eye on their progress. They were nearly an hour into the hike when they encountered their first obstacle. Encizo snapped on his red-lens flashlight, which despite its filter still cast a powerful illumination while making the light difficult to see.

Encizo leaned close to Bolan's ear. "I'd say maybe a hundred feet high."

Bolan nodded and looked in both directions, then gestured for Encizo to shine his light along the cliff face. It ran for as far as they could see in either direction. Bolan couldn't be sure how far but he knew one thing: they couldn't take the time to go around. According to his calculations they still had almost forty-five minutes before they reached the coordinates of the training camp, and that was assuming they could make the journey solely over flat ground.

The Executioner looked up at the cliff face looming in front of him. "Quite a few small trees growing out of that rock."

"That means it'll be pretty soft," Encizo observed.

None of them had to say that it meant climbing would be

treacherous. There would be loose spots throughout, and that greatly increased the risk of a fall. One miscalculation in judgment, one poorly placed hand or foot, and all three of them could fall to their deaths.

"Well, then," Bolan said as he shucked his gear and removed the climbing apparatus. "I guess we'll just have to do it right the first time."

The others followed suit and extracted their climbing gear. All of them had extensive training and experience in this kind of thing. The trick wouldn't be getting to the top as much as deciding who went first. They finally agreed Bolan had the most experience and so he'd be last, acting as safety and belay man.

"How do you want to do this?" Encizo asked.

Bolan studied the terrain and replied, "We'll use semidirect method. I think we're all pretty comfortable with that."

They nodded. Given their situation this would actually work best. In this case, Bolan would set down some multipoint anchors because they were all close to or exceeded two hundred pounds. Bolan would then attach two ropes to the anchor that would then pass through the tubular belay devices on his harness before connecting with the variable friction devices on theirs.

Encizo had Grimaldi double-check his gear, and then he hooked up to Bolan and started. He told them he hoped to find a shelf halfway up that would allow them to secure a midway anchor point.

"Just in case we have to come down more quickly than we go up," Encizo said with the Cheshire cat grin.

Encizo scaled the cliff like a pro, kicking away loose rock only once during his entire descent. He disappeared from view, probably finding a place to tie off, and then cleared

Grimaldi for his turn. The pilot faired pretty well considering he didn't do this kind of thing as often as Bolan or Encizo. The Executioner watched with concern, but Grimaldi made it without problems.

"Unlock your anchor points, Striker," Encizo called down. "And we'll pull you up manually."

Bolan hesitated, but he saw the value in the time it would save. He kicked out the quick anchors, reattached the carabiner on his harness, and within two minutes he had hauled himself over the edge of the cliff with the assistance of his friends. He nodded a thanks to the pair and then disengaged the harness. They shrugged from the remainder of the equipment and buried it beneath pine needles and brush.

"It would look strange in the daytime," Grimaldi remarked, "but nobody's going to see it at night."

"Come on, guys," Bolan said. "We still have a lot of ground to cover."

WHEN THEY WERE WITHIN a hundred meters of their target, Bolan stopped in his tracks and gestured his friends to do the same.

Bolan thought he'd seen movement. He waited, his ears senses alert for any disturbance or clues of human presence other than their own. It came a minute later. Barely a rustle somewhere ahead, but definitely something. Bolan held up two fingers, pointed at his eyes and then extended his palm to indicate they should wait while he scouted ahead.

They nodded, and Bolan got to his feet and proceeded cautiously, his Ka-Bar fighting knife in hand. He couldn't risk the use of firearms, not this close to the potential training grounds. Whatever they did, subtlety would have to be their guide. Bolan continued closer until additional movement froze him in his tracks. He pressed his back to a tree. The form moved past on his right, the shadow of a rifle barrel protruding from its hands, and Bolan waited another moment before lurching into action.

The Executioner jumped forward and clamped a viselike hand around the target's mouth. He dropped his weight back and pulled the man to the ground, then twisted his body so he came out on top. Bolan drove the knife into the base of his opponent's neck—advancing more than halfway to the hilt—and cut through bone and tissue, finally catching the spinal column. The man's body stopped twitching suddenly as all nerve impulses were severed. A moment later he went totally still.

Hairs stood on Bolan's neck and he turned to see a second shadowy form charging him. The Executioner flipped onto his back and extended his leg, prepared to take the guy with a sharp kick to the midsection. He never connected as a stocky form appeared from nowhere and knocked the man off course. Bolan watched in complete surprise as Rafael Encizo silenced the man in seconds with effective use of the Cold Steel Tanto knife he favored.

Bolan and Encizo worked in concert to strip all weapons from the dead men and toss them into the woods. No point in leaving the enemy something to use if the battle came back this way, which in all likelihood it wouldn't. Still, the Executioner and crew had learned long ago never to take anything for granted on the battlefield. Particularly when it came to handing the enemy any sort of advantage.

That task accomplished, the trio regrouped and discussed their situation in hushed tones.

"That was too close," Grimaldi observed.

"Thanks back there, Rafe," Bolan said. "I don't know where my head was at."

"You're exhausted, just like us," Encizo said. "We've been pushing it hard since yesterday morning."

Bolan shook his head. "Been there before. It shouldn't have happened."

"It didn't," Encizo said, and that put the subject to bed.

"What now, Sarge?" Grimaldi asked.

"I'd say these two prove we're close," Bolan said.

"Looks like," Encizo replied. "But where's there are two sentries…"

Nobody had to finish the sentence. Yeah, they could expect to possibly encounter further resistance, although the Executioner was hoping the cards would fall in their favor and they had opened a hole.

"As long as it's not a roving patrol, we should be good," Bolan said.

"Fair enough," Encizo replied. "How do you want to play this?"

"Let's go straight up the middle," Bolan said. "If they follow standard military training, we'll have some perimeter guards to deal with before we can get inside the camp."

"Then what?"

"Take out the big structures with explosives first," Bolan ordered. "That should create a sufficient amount of confusion. Enough to draw them into the open."

"I'd say," Grimaldi interjected. "Especially when the barrack walls start blowing up around their ears."

The trio conferred another minute and then moved forward, advancing steadily but quietly on the main camp. Bolan hoped there would be some indication they had reached the perimeter instead of them realizing they were well inside after the fact.

Grimaldi spotted the first perimeter guard and Bolan gave

the nod to clear him. The Stony Man pilot performed admirably, waiting in some underbrush until the guy came even with him, then reaching out and yanking him off his feet from the weak point just below the knee. Grimaldi scrambled from the brush and blanketed his opponent before the sentry could move or call an alert. He finished the terrorist soldier with a hand to the mouth and knife to the throat.

Encizo got the next one by taking hold of the man's weapon sling and swinging him into a tree. He pulled the guy's head back and down while simultaneously driving the combat knife into his right kidney. The Cuban eased the terrorist's body to the ground, and together he and Bolan dragged it into the thick brush, then assisted Grimaldi with the other corpse.

The fact they had encountered two sentries this close together indicated the perimeter didn't run a roving patrol, either. This fact surprised Bolan a little, but he considered the thought of the terrorist commander. They certainly wouldn't be expecting a compromise of the security, at least not by trained American commandos, and they had probably figured a two-man sentry team at fixed locations would provide the mesh-style security screen necessary to repel any invaders.

The Executioner planned to exploit that fatal error in judgment.

Bolan crouched at the clearing to the camp and studied the layout, letting his eyes adjust to the surroundings. The sky was clear and the half moon spilled enough light onto the camp that he could make out the structures and their positions. Bolan spotted the observation tower.

He pointed toward it and whispered in Grimaldi's ear. "Think you can get yourself and that HK 21-E up there, Ace?"

Grimaldi looked at the tower a moment. Bolan watched him judge its height, which probably looked much more formidable in the darkness, but eventually a glint formed in the pilot's eyes. He gave Bolan an emphatic thumbs-up; the warrior gestured for him to proceed. The pilot stripped himself of all equipment except the machine gun and three belt clips of rounds. It would make for an interesting climb but Bolan didn't worry. Grimaldi wouldn't have said he felt up to the challenge if he didn't.

Bolan and Encizo conferred on the best place to put their plastique charges, then split off and went about the work.

The Executioner worked with quick, efficient movements. He placed his charges in the agreed places, double-checking the security of each blasting cap before he set the timers in decreasing increments respectively. By the time he finished and got clear, his watch indicated less than a minute remained. The soldier checked the action on his MP-5 and then settled in to wait.

CHAPTER TWENTY-SIX

The earth erupted in a shock wave of explosions so intense it was as if God were raining fire and brimstone on the terrorist camp.

The charges went off nearly simultaneously, the clever timing of Bolan's and Encizo's handiwork. The Executioner counted each one, no mean feat considering some went off almost simultaneously. When he reached number twelve, Bolan burst from his concealment and raided the camp.

The heat of fires and secondary explosions pressed against his skin but the soldier walked between them, a raging specter in his battle dress fatigues, the tools of war dangling from his chest and waist. He was like a machine of war unstoppable amid the havoc and carnage of his own creation.

The first terrorists appeared by crashing through the door of their barracks, which were aflame at every corner. Thick, black smoke poured from the opening they created and the flames inside rose higher, their intense heat cracking the glass as the fresh burst of oxygen fed them. They licked hungrily at the window frames, eager to consume everything in their path.

It was no contest as Bolan opened up on the disoriented men, some wearing only their skivvies and others half dressed, but all armed with their weapons. No amount of discipline could overcome the confusion wrought by a the lung-searing combination of heat and smoke. The Executioner kept his weapon steadied at the hip, triggering short and steady bursts and mowing down targets with the pure selectiveness born from experience.

A moment later he heard the chatter of the HK 21-E as Grimaldi opened up on his own targets.

Bolan pushed all distractions from his mind, intent on keeping the enemy off balance. That would be the only way to defeat them, to pour on the intensity and ferocity and not let up until the battle had been waged to the bitter end. Despite their training, Bolan could tell the vast majority of his enemy had never been in a real combat situation. Their leaders had talked them into a sense of invincibility, maybe by firing a few rounds over their heads here and there, or strapping on some pads and letting them beat the hell out of one another.

The Executioner let his grim and iron determination take hold, intent on visiting a new type of justice on them. He dropped the last man, then changed magazines before continuing on his quest of justice.

WHEN THE CHARGES WENT OFF, Jack Grimaldi thought his teeth might vibrate from his head. The noise and vibrations, however, didn't even begin to compare with the spectacular sight arrayed below him. Everywhere he looked there were bright balls of flame bursting skyward, some so high he could feel the heat against his bare skin and see the night shimmer with the intensity. The fires lit up the camp as though someone had dropped a miniature sign in the middle of it.

The Stony Man pilot yanked on the receiving lever of the HK 21-E, primed the action and began to rain a hail of metal destruction on the enemy troops below. At one point through the thickening smoke, Grimaldi thought he saw Bolan but he couldn't be sure and yet he kept his muzzle clear of that area. The smoke distorted the light and made it difficult to see if he was hitting anything, and the last thing he wanted to do was to cut down his oldest and most trusted friend.

Grimaldi took out his first pair of terrorists as they emerged from the perimeter. He swung the barrel of the Heckler & Koch machine gun in their direction and triggered a sustained burst. The weapon rocked against his shoulder and flame spit from the muzzle. The impact lifted one of the sentries off the ground as the heavy-caliber rounds chopped his chest to bloody shreds. The second one fell and a stray round penetrated the back of his head, nearly blowing it clean off his body.

Grimaldi swept the area and quickly acquired his next targets, a quartet of terrorists who came crashing out of their barracks. The pilot steadied his aim, took a deep breath and let half out before squeezing the trigger. He took these four with a more controlled volley, finding his rhythm and growing accustomed to its recoil and fire rate. Two fell under Grimaldi's nearly perfect marksmanship, and the pilot could only thank David McCarter, Phoenix Force's leader and a champion pistol marksman, for his many hours of tutelage. Despite his success, though, Grimaldi wished he could have a nice compact Uzi for this instead of a massive beast like the HK 21-E. What wouldn't occur to him until later was the fact he remained the safest of the three.

Bolan and Encizo were at ground zero, right in the thick of hell on earth.

RAFAEL ENCIZO BARELY HAD time to congratulate himself for selecting the perfect cover from the perimeter that still afforded him a view of the mast majority of the camp. He'd barely made that position when the first explosions sounded and suddenly the whole thing seemed a lot closer than it had a moment earlier.

The Cuban took his position amid the tall grass, just beyond view of the casual observer, and waited for his first target to present itself. It took nearly a full minute after the explosions died but his first catch of the day staggered into view, weapon held at the ready, hands wiping his eyes being stung by thick, black smoke.

Encizo lowered his eye to the sights of the MP-5, brought the stock closer to his shoulder and squeezed the trigger twice. The double tap of 9 mm Parabellum rounds punched through the man's chest and sent him sprawling to the ground. A second terrorist rounded the corner in time to see him fall. He searched for Encizo but couldn't make him out in the darkness with his eyes drawn to the light of the flames. However, he presented the perfect silhouette and Encizo took him down with a single shot to the head.

Encizo rose and changed positions, convinced that to remain in one place too long would give his enemies the advantage. Part of the strategy relied on the terrorists' belief that they were surrounded by equal or greater numbers, hence the reason for creating so much havoc and confusion in such a short span of time.

He knelt behind a tree and awaited his next targets.

The enemy gunners seemed to materialize through the dissipating smoke and nearly took him off guard. A trio of ELN terrorists crossed along the perimeter of the camp, intent on something ahead of them Encizo couldn't see. They definitely were up to something. The Cuban decided to risk breaking cover and follow on their heels. They rounded a turn in the camp before one looked back and realized they'd been followed. At the same moment Encizo realized they had circled the camp in hope of flanking Bolan who was just visible through the flames and smoke.

Encizo hit the dirt as all three men swung the muzzles of their assault rifles in his direction. A murderous firestorm of lead whizzed overhead, some of it coming very close to him. He rolled as a fresh series of bursts chewed up earth everywhere around him. He got up on one knee behind the cover of the barracks, leaned around the corner and triggered off a sustained burst of 9 mm slugs.

Gunners danced and jerked under the fire, and it was only after he eased off the trigger that Encizo realized he'd bought some support from Jack Grimaldi. The steady chop-chop-chop from the HK 21-E continued well after Encizo stopped firing. He didn't wait to see the results, instead getting his attention back into the game at hand.

Under normal circumstances he would have obeyed orders and stuck to the perimeter, but now he could see the Executioner had his hands full. Encizo wouldn't do his friend any good literally sitting on the sidelines. He needed to get into this fight in a real way, playing his A game.

The Phoenix Force commando stormed the camp interior and began searching for fresh targets.

THE EAR-SHATTERING BLAST outside his window was intense enough to knock Colonel Moises Hurtado from his bed.

Flaming cloth and debris rained onto his head, one piece setting his blanket on fire while the other caught his pant leg. Hurtado beat out the flames and rushed to his wall locker. He ripped a fresh set of fatigues from the locker, dressed, then slid into his boots. He stuck his pistol in the waistband of his pants, then grabbed his rifle from where it lay mounted in a rack beneath his bunk.

Outside he could hear the sounds of heated battle as his men engaged the enemy. He could sense more than one weapon being fired, and even as the explosions continued to sound Hurtado knew his men would repel the invaders. As the battle continued to wage, the colonel considered his options. He could get out there and lead his men into the thick of it—an option that didn't seem overly appealing given he had no idea of the numbers or capabilities of the opposition— or he could gather a quick team, a recon force of sorts, and try to hit the enemy in more strategic locations.

It took Hurtado less than a second to settle on the latter plan.

The ELN colonel moved out of his room, through the kitchen and across the mess hall. The lights from flames outside lit his way just enough that he didn't have to use his miniature flashlight. Good, that would only make him a target. Hurtado reached the end of the mess hall and risked a glance through the door, which dangled from only its top hinge, the other pair victims of an explosion. The entire exterior wall to his left was charred and the wood smoldered red-hot in some places. Only the fire-retardant paint seemed to detract from worse damage.

Hurtado burst from the mess hall and sprinted across a ten-meter opening to the first barracks. This one was fully engulfed, and Hurtado looked through the open window but couldn't see the interior for all the smoke. Whether any of his men had gotten out remained to be seen. Hurtado crawled through the window and immediately began to crawl through the maze of cots. Some men were still in their bunks, almost immediately overwhelmed by smoke.

Eventually, Hurtado practically crawled right into a huddle of four men. Tears filled their terrified eyes, and Hurtado couldn't repress the anger that boiled in his stomach.

"What the hell are you doing?" he demanded. "You're in here cowering while your friends, the real warriors of the people, are out there battling the enemy. Get out of here and go kill those who dare to defy the National Liberation Army! Go! Go now!"

The men looked aghast that the colonel would talk to them like that—he'd always remained calm and level-headed before, leaving such tirades to his enlisted officers—but that had all changed. These men were hardly out of adolescence, he knew, and they hadn't ever experienced a real combat situation in their lives. Well, he didn't give a good damn. They would toe the mark now and they would do so because he was their commanding officer and they were his men.

They got to their feet and rushed the back door. At least they were thinking now, electing to go out the back instead of heading to the front where the enemy would mow them down as soon as they got clear. Hurtado followed them, drilling them with shouts of encouragement.

The first man in line stopped, waved the others to the side, then opened the door and burst into the night. The others followed a moment later in turn, each one with this weapon up and held at the ready. Now that was more like it. These were the crack troops he knew, the ones he'd spent the last four months training. They would perform now. They had finally come into their own and they would be just fine.

GRIMALDI SHOUTED AND whooped with excitement as two more terrorists fell under the onslaught of the machine gun.

As he swung the weapon upward and released the catch so he could lay in a fresh belt, the pilot noticed a red sheen to the barrel. Damn it, he'd have to wait to change out the belts. Placing a fresh belt in the chamber with the weapon that hot was good way to have it blow up or malfunction during use.

Grimaldi released the weapon and unholstered his pistol. He then reached to the harness on his belt and came away with one of the Diehl DM51 grenades. Well, if he couldn't take them out with the machine gun, he'd have to find an alternate means of wreaking havoc and confusion on their heads. Yeah, this baby would do the trick nicely.

The ace pilot yanked the pin and searched for a viable target. It appeared a moment later—several terrorists with weapons skirted from the back of a barracks and took cover behind the next building in line. Grimaldi turned to find Bolan and Encizo and realized the armed squad was headed straight in their direction. Grimaldi let the spoon plunk away from the grenade, counted two seconds and then let fly. The hand bomb sailed in a graceful arc and bounced once on the roof, exploding just as it disappeared over the back side of the roof.

HURTADO WATCHED WITH UTTER horror as his men clustered behind the next barracks. He broke cover and started screaming at them to disperse, but then something hit the roof and bounced into view. Hurtado knew what it was from the sound of it striking the tin roof. He dived to the ground as the grenade exploded in midair. Screams died in the throats of his men, audible only in the echo of the dying explosion. Hurtado lifted his head in time to see the men fall, their bodies shredded by thousands of steel fragments. The explosion had been close enough to the blow off the arm of one man.

The colonel jumped to his feet and rushed their position. He stood amid the mangle of bodies, hopeful he could salvage at least one of his men, but he heard only groans and saw very little movement. The pair that was alive, if anyone could call such misery and agony living, screamed and pleaded at him to end their suffering. Hurtado ended their sufferings with mercy rounds to their heads. Around him the sounds of battle continued to rage but he didn't hear much in the way of resistance.

It was obvious his soldiers had been overrun and suffered a crushing defeat. First the petty criminals of Cuba had murdered his troops in cold blood, and now he'd suffered a vicious and unprovoked attack on his own camp. He couldn't understand it! Who would have the courage to defy his men? Who would launch such a cowardly attack and murder his men in their own beds?

Hurtado didn't know the face or name of his enemy, but he didn't intend to deprive himself of one final chance at retribution. The colonel dropped his rifle, pulled the pistol from his waistband and marched off in search of his enemy.

BOLAN AND ENCIZO MOPPED up with very little effort. The explosive charges had obviously done their work, since they didn't encounter anywhere near the resistance expected. Maybe half of the ELN terrorists had survived the blasts, but before long Grimaldi had opened up with the machine gun once more and cut down about a dozen.

Add another dozen who fell under the marksmanship of Bolan and Encizo, and the rest never joined the battle. Bolan saw a few race into the woods, but he didn't bother pursuing them. A select few wouldn't pose any threat, and if they didn't manage to get off the island and back to Colombia, then they'd get picked up by local authorities or allow themselves to be folded into the communities to avoid prosecution.

In any case, they posed no threat.

The same couldn't be said for the man with soot covering his face and arms who emerged suddenly from the smoke. He raised his pistol and triggered a shot in Bolan's direction before the Executioner could react. The bullet nicked the warrior's ribs, laying a neat furrow through his fatigues and tearing away a good chunk of flesh.

The Executioner gritted his teeth as he hit his knees and rolled to avoid the next four shots the man popped off in a fit of pure rage. Bolan got up on one knee with the .50-caliber AE Desert Eagle unleathered. He snap-aimed and squeezed the trigger. The 280-grain boattail slug slammed through the man's chest with enough force to drive him back. The guy managed to get off two more shots that were high and wide before Bolan finished him with a head shot that split the guy's skull before it exited out the base of his head. The man's body staggered around awkwardly for a moment before hitting the ground. Encizo put another five rounds in the corpse—better safe than sorry—and then rushed to Bolan's side.

Bolan drew his hand from the wound and found it slick with blood.

"How bad?" he asked Encizo.

The Cuban studied his friend's side with professional scrutiny and then squeezed the Executioner's shoulder reassuringly. "Just a bite. You'll live."

"Good," Bolan replied. "Because this mission isn't over yet."

CHAPTER TWENTY-SEVEN

The sun peered over the horizon as Bolan and team arrived at the Cuban mainland. They left the boat and equipment in the designated spot, confident their contact would come soon and remove any evidence they had ever been there. They elected to leave everything behind except the Desert Eagle. They stripped the boat of the weapons, and per their contact's instructions, left them concealed in a copse of trees in a pre-dug hole a few hundred yards off the docks.

Grimaldi had managed to catch a couple hours' shut-eye on the return trip and agreed to take the wheel. Bolan took shotgun and Encizo climbed wearily into the backseat where he could prop his ankle.

"Where to now?" Grimaldi asked.

"The hotel for you two," Bolan said. "It's time you guys got out of here before they lock the entire place down tighter than a drum."

"What about you?"

"One more thing to take care of," the Executioner replied.

"What's that?" Encizo asked.

"Fuego," Bolan said.

"What about Andres?"

The Executioner shook his head. "Something tells me the situation with Andres will rectify itself. Hal put the bloodhounds on him. The CIA will come through on that one, and if they don't, you can be sure Crosse and Stein will."

"Yeah," Grimaldi agreed. "But those two are another loose end entirely."

"Not if they get to Andres the same time as the Company does," Bolan said through a yawn.

"And if they don't?" Encizo asked.

"Then there will be another time and place," Bolan said. "I'll take care of it. Stein and Crosse won't get away with it."

UMBERTO ANDRES-ITUARTE counted it no small fortune that Santiago Famosa permitted him to leave alive, and with his balls intact no less.

Somehow, Andres had convinced Famosa of his loyalty to Havana Five and not to the murderous bastards like Inez Fuego who betrayed him. Unfortunately, it looked as if his original plans were falling apart and that could only mean one thing. It was time to leave Cuba behind forever.

What Andres had never told anyone in Cuba about was the fortune he'd amassed in offshore accounts in the Cayman Islands. Not even his former CIA overlords would be able to trace those funds, and once he disappeared off the map they probably wouldn't consider it worth the time and effort required to hunt him down. Andres had put everything in place the best he knew how, manipulated all the players, and generally he'd managed to maintain his information-brokering network for a hell of a lot longer than most men in his position.

Now the drums had sounded, signaling the coming of an

internal war between the remaining members of Havana Five—those drums also beat a rhythm that spelled hastening to Andres's departure. Beneath a hotel in one of the classier Havana neighborhoods, Andres had established his base of operations that doubled as his point of departure. All he needed to do now that he was free of Famosa would be to have the taxi driver drop him at the club. He'd pick up his bodyguard who he hoped awaited him there, and then they would go to the hotel, pick up his few possessions and be on a plane out of the country before sunrise.

The cabbie dropped him off at the club. Andres searched diligently but couldn't find his man, so he gave up and started to head out.

The manager of the club cornered him at the door, a pair of heavies shadowing him. "Mr. Andres? I am glad you're here."

"What the hell do you want? Isn't my tab paid in full?"

"Yes, sir, yes, of course it is."

"Then what is it, man? I'm in a hurry."

"There has been an accident," the manager replied.

"What kind of accident?"

"Your security man, Mr. Ernesto. He was found dead a little while ago, right behind the curtains around your reserved seating area."

"What?"

"The police were here, asking lots of questions. I told them we didn't notice anything. They asked me to tell you they would like to question you as soon as you arrived. It was very inconvenient."

"You saw nothing?"

The manager smiled, rubbed his fingers, and Andres impatiently stuck his hand in his pocket and brought out a wad of money, which he handed over. The manager smelled the fresh bills and then tucked them away. He tugged on Andres's shirt and steered him to the side where nobody would overhear.

"I told the police we didn't notice anything," the manager said.

"But you did see something?"

"Yes, two men."

When Andres heard the descriptions a cold knot settled in the pit of his stomach and he felt like vomiting. The manager had described the pair of American DIA agents with impressive detail. The last Andres knew the two men were dead, or at least were as good as such; he'd been informed by reliable sources that Lazaro San Lujan planned to find them and kill them. What had happened? How had they escaped? And what of Pascal and his friends? What had become of them? Maybe the Americans had gotten to Crosse and Stein before San Lujan.

Andres thanked the manager, then left the club. The hotel was maybe ten blocks from there—no point in awaiting another cab. As he walked, Andres considered this new bit of information. So Stein and Crosse had killed his bodyguard. But why? Maybe they were looking for him; perhaps they had figured out he was the one who'd betrayed them to Fuego. That meant Pascal would learn of his betrayal eventually, if he didn't already know.

Yes, the time to depart Cuba had definitely arrived.

A VERY LONG TIME SEEMED to pass before the pair of bodyguards descended the stairs. The two men sat passively at stools near the counter, kept their expressions unreadable. The bodyguards looked puzzled until one of them spotted

Fresco's corpse near the open gun rack. They turned toward the pair of DIA agents but the reaction proved completely ineffective because their enemies already had pistols up and tracking.

Crosse took the one closest to him with a double tap to the chest. The Glock jumped in his hand as the pair of 9 mm slugs hit center mass, the first blowing out a lung and the other perforating the lower heart. Blood exploded from the man's wounds. The bodyguard staggered backward, the pistol he'd managed to clear from his holster left numbed fingers, and then he slumped to the ratty, paper-thin runner covering the floor.

Even as the ringing in his ears dispersed, Crosse watched with something bordering between shock and morbid fascination as Stein proceeded to empty his weapon into the other man. It seemed to Crosse like a scene from a movie played in slow motion as round after round struck the man's body. The bodyguard jerked with each impact, and by the time Stein had plugged him with the last trio of rounds the bodyguard lay motionless on the floor.

Stein held up the pistol with exaggerated motions, dropped the magazine while he smiled as his partner. Crosse jumped at the sound of it hitting the floor. He tried to smile back, but he couldn't bring himself to do it. He finally realized that the most remote vestiges of personality he'd known in the man named Dominic Stein were long gone. The man who now stood in front of him with a foolish grin and a few droplets of blood running down his face from the back splatter of a close-range kill was a monster.

"You think he's dead?" Stein asked quietly. Then he burst into a fit of maniacal laughter.

Crosse wanted to pack it in right there, run out of the

basement of that grisly morgue. Run for his life and never look back. He knew plenty of safe places to settle down, find some nice señorita to wash his clothes, cook his dinners, treat him right. Maybe they could even raise a few little ones, carry on the family name. Well, he could worry about that later. Right now he had to remain calm and steady in light of the fact his partner had morphed into a lunatic.

"Hey, Dominic, I don't—"

Stein held up his hand. "Shh! You hear that?"

Crosse clammed up, completely alert, but he didn't hear a thing. He waited another minute and then started to open his mouth when he heard the noise. It was faint, like the sound of a cat scratching at a door, but it was definitely coming from above. Then he heard it clear as a bell: the noise of the heavy soundproof door opening and the clatter of feet on the stairs.

Andres reached the basement and his eyes grew so big that the pupils were nearly indistinguishable from the brilliant whites surrounding them. For a moment, it looked like someone had placed fried eggs over his eyes. Andres wheeled and tried to get up the stairs but Dominic Stein reached him and grabbed hold of the collar. He dragged him down the few steps the man managed to make and, with a mighty heave, slammed the guy into a concrete pier. Andres bounced hard off it but somehow still managed to stay on his feet.

Stein stepped in and Andres executed a perfect back-fist, but the crazed DIA agent saw it coming. He ducked beneath the swing and fired a jab into Andres's gut with the muzzle of his M1911. Air whooshed from the man's lungs and the force drove him into a nearby counter. Stein holstered his pistol, grabbed Andres by his collar and slammed him full-force with a head butt. The blow smashed Andres's nose against his face, split open skin and doused both men with a fair amount of blood.

Andres cried out and crashed to his knees, his hands holding his broken nose. Stein pressed on, relentless, kicking Andres repeatedly in the ribs and then shoving him to the ground with his foot. Andres landed on his left side, barely conscious now. Stein slammed a fresh clip into his pistol, let the slide clang forward, then planted his foot against the side of Andres's neck and aimed the pistol at his head.

"Wait!" Crosse screamed. Stein looked at him in surprise. "Just wait a fucking second, will you?"

Stein looked at Andres, then at Crosse again—almost as if thinking about whether to heed his partner or simply blow the traitorous bastard's brains all over the concrete—but finally something more sane took hold and he took the pistol from Andres's temple but he kept his foot in place.

"What?" he asked Crosse.

The DIA agent stepped forward and looked down at Andres. What a pathetic sight. He knew Stein wanted to kill the guy and in this case he totally agreed. There wasn't any benefit to keeping the asshole alive. Hell, he wanted to see Andres go himself, but he saw an opportunity he just couldn't pass up. Andres remained their only hope in exploiting that chance.

Crosse eyeballed his partner and in a tone of reason he began, "You said you wanted to make all of this right, Dom. You said you wanted to set things straight. Don't you remember?"

"Yeah, I remember. And we should start with him."

"Come on, Dom," Crosse said. He'd holstered his pistol and held up his hands in a nonthreatening fashion. "This guy...well, you see he's just small potatoes, Dom. The real threat here is Inez Fuego. Remember? That's the little bitch who set us up, the one who led us to believe the stories about the terrorist army and the ELN. She's the one we need to kill."

Stein appeared to think about that. "Yeah," he finally replied, "so we'll eventually kill her, too."

"How?" Crosse asked quickly. "How you going to kill her if you don't even know where she is. What, you got ESP or something? You got some sort of special abilities, some remote viewing or something? You just going to call on the all-seeing gods to tell you where she is?"

"All right, shut up!" he said. "I get it already."

"No, I don't think you do, Dom." Crosse pointed at Andres and continued. "Because you were just about to waste our *only* lead. He's our only lead, Dom, the only one who knows how to find Fuego. You kill him, you kill any chance of setting this thing right…fully right. You don't want to do that. Do you, Dom?"

A long silence passed, and it looked at one point as though Stein's eyes had rolled into his head. The guy stood there, his breath coming in closer and closer increments until he was practically gasping. Then the weird breathing abruptly subsided and he came back to reality from wherever he'd spent his last few minutes.

Calmly he said, "No, I don't want to do that."

"Okay, then, let's do it like we planned. We get Andres to lead us to Fuego. Then we deal with her, just like we talked about. And then we can go to Mexico, Dom, and we can finally rest. Nobody's going to look for us there."

"Okay, Les," Stein said, and he let off on Andres.

Crosse nodded and then grabbed Andres low enough to make sure he didn't get the guy's blood on him. He hauled him into a sitting position, then located the cleanest gun rag he could find and tossed it at Andres. Stein went about the task of checking the bodyguards for identification, not because he cared but out of probably nothing more than sheer habit.

From beneath the rag, Andres muttered, "Thank you, Mr. Crosse."

"Don't thank me, you two-timing weasel," Crosse replied through clenched teeth, although he kept his voice low. "If it was up to me, I would have let him put a bullet in your brain."

"I would probably be better off."

"Yeah, why's that?"

"I am now as much an enemy of Inez Fuego's as you are," he said.

"I'm not interested in hearing about how hard you've got it, Andres," Crosse said. "Now if you cooperate and show us where we can find her, I just might be able to convince my partner not to kill you. But if you betray us again, I swear on my mother's grave I'll let him tear you apart one piece at a time, starting with your fingers. You got that?"

"I will show you."

"You better, you little shit," Crosse said. "Don't try to fuck me on this deal. I'm telling you straight."

"They're clean," Stein said.

He looked at Andres. "Get on your feet, asshole. You're going to lead us to Inez Fuego."

WHEN DAWN BROKE, Pirro saw a strange man leave the hotel with the two Americans. He'd watched the man walk in maybe a half hour before, but now all of them were leaving. It looked like the man who arrived earlier was holding something over his face, a towel or handkerchief perhaps, and the three of them headed down the street.

Pirro chased after them, careful to remain far enough back and on the opposite side of the street so they wouldn't notice him shadowing them. Where the hell were they going now, especially this time of the morning? Pirro kept them in sight, passing only a couple of his associates who were calling it a night.

The three men rounded a corner and Pirro had to run to catch up. He couldn't afford to lose them now, especially not after he'd spent this much effort to stake them out instead of getting his tail back to his own neighborhood and making a living.

Pirro rounded the corner and immediate panic clutched his chest. They were gone! Strictly speaking, there wasn't any place for them to go. How the hell could they have disappeared so fast? Pirro ran up the sidewalk, looking wildly in all directions, searching for the trio. They couldn't have gone far. He backtracked a few times, checked the doors of the buildings he passed, but all of them were locked.

Pirro searched diligently but still he couldn't find any sign of them. Finally he turned from the last door and continued up the street. They had to have gone somewhere. He went another half block and finally he spotted them. Two of them were huddled over the hood of an old Chevy parked on the street. Pirro didn't know who owned the car but he knew they didn't.

They were trying to steal it!

Pirro noticed that the two men were one of the Americans and the local, but he couldn't see the other American. He wished he'd been able to reach Mr. San Lujan, but he had to begin to wonder if Garza hadn't spoken the truth. Maybe he was dead. And if that was indeed the case, Pirro knew there was only one way to stay in the good graces of Havana Five.

He'd have to make contact through Garza. He couldn't rely on the fact Garza would vouch for him, tell whoever was in charge now that it was Pirro reporting these activities, but that's a chance he'd have to take. It was better than simply walking away.

Pirro turned and staggered back, losing his balance and landing on his tailbone. He let out a yelp of pain but it squelched in his throat when he saw the second American standing over him. Then Pirro noticed a pistol in the man's hand, which he recognized as a Colt .45.

"Taking a little too much interest in those guys over there," the man said. He kept his voice low and there was the hint of a crazed look in his eyes. "Aren't you?"

Pirro tried the "I no *habla*" routine, but the American didn't appear to buy it. He said, "Well, that's too bad you don't speak any English. I might have let you beg me for your life. Say good night, Gracie."

And even as Pirro saw the man's finger tighten on the trigger, he wondered who Gracie was.

CHAPTER TWENTY-EIGHT

The buzz of the house phone jarred Jeronimo Bustos from his sleep. Inez Fuego turned over and he picked it up, clearing his voice before barking into it. Fortunately, all phones rang when someone picked up the house phone and that meant his men wouldn't know the difference if he were in his room or, in this case, in Fuego's master bedroom. Fuego muttered something and Bustos hoped his man didn't overhear. Then again, who the hell cared if they did? There wasn't any crime against pumping the boss.

"What the hell is it?"

"We have big trouble, Mr. Bustos."

"What are you talking about?"

"Men at the shack just reported a car crashed through the gate. Say there were two Americans in it, and what they say looked like—" the guy's voice faded a second, his attention on someone there with him, and then he came back to the phone "—they said it looked like Mr. Andres."

"Sound the security alarm," Bustos said. "I want every gun in the foyer in one minute!"

Bustos jumped from the bed and into the clothes he'd worn the previous evening. No time for niceties like a fresh change of clothes. Fuego now muttered something a bit more intelligible and Bustos ignored her. Finally, she sat up in bed and eyed him with almost precocious offense.

"Did you hear me?"

"Not right now, Inez," he said, nearly falling down in his haste to don slacks.

"Fuck you, not right now!" she hollered. "I'm still in charge here, Jeronimo."

He stopped, shocked by her tone, but he faced her directly as he buckled his alligator belt. "The Americans from the DIA have just run the gate. They're heading for the house."

"Why the hell for?"

"Probably to kill *you*," he replied. "Get dressed and go to the panic room. I'll let you know when it's safe to come out."

"I'm not going into that thing!" she said, climbing from the bed. "It makes me ill being cooped up in there. You just make damn sure they don't get this far, Jeronimo."

"And what if they do?"

She whirled on him, and he couldn't help but notice how sexy she looked even in nothing but a sheet and a fit of rage. "You're my head of security, deal with it!"

Bustos nodded, grabbed his holster off the bedside table and clipped it onto his belt as he headed for the door. He started to say goodbye but then decided against it. He was pretty pissed at her by this time. How the hell did she expect his protection if she never listened to a word he said? Damn! He knew sleeping with her would be a mistake, and yet he'd let his guard down and she roped him into it. Well, either way he couldn't complain. She was talented in bed.

Bustos took the stairs three at a time and when he hit the bottom there were a dozen armed men waiting for him.

"Cover all possible entries," he ordered them. He turned to his second and said, "Are they armed?"

The guy shrugged. "Could be, Jer. Our guys didn't see any guns, but I'm betting they wouldn't risk something like this if they didn't have a gun or two."

It was suicide! A couple of American whelps and that loser, Andres, blasting through a heavy metal gate like some last great charge. Well, Bustos knew exactly how to deal with their kind. He opened his mouth to give further orders, but the sound of breaking glass cut him short. The pair turned in time to see a bottle crash against the base of the steps. The pungent odor of gasoline assailed their nostrils as the bottle broke and some of it splashed onto the stair runner.

The carpet immediately burst into flames.

"Mother of God, get a fire extinguisher!" Bustos yelled as he drew his pistol and ran to the front door. He opened it in time to see an old Chevy lurch away with a short screech of rubber against pavement. The Cuban security man leveled his pistol and snapped off half a dozen rounds that shattered the back window and ricocheted off the trunk. The vehicle moved away too quickly for him to tell if he'd hit anyone. Bustos turned to look behind him. His eyes followed the flames as they began to leapfrog from one step to the next at furious pace—they had already advanced more than halfway to the second floor.

Bustos thought of Fuego and rushed for the service elevator. There was no way they could get the fire out with mere extinguishers. He'd have to get her to safety first, and she'd accompany him if he had to drag her from the house kicking and screaming.

MACK BOLAN WATCHED THE happenings in Fuego's estate with mild interest. He swept the grounds and marked the location of each hard case before panning back to the action near the front of the house. It hadn't been difficult to slip through the defensive measures. Other than a decorative wall, Fuego had left the place pretty much wide open, apparently confident her security team could handle any threat. In any other situation it probably would have sufficed, but in the case of the Executioner it left a hole so large an amateur could probably walk through unnoticed.

Obviously that thought hadn't occurred to whoever occupied that Chevy. Bolan considered this unexpected turn of events for a moment. He had two options: hang loose and see how it played out or try to complete his mission while confusion abounded. It took him only a minute to decide. Bolan got off his belly, put the Desert Eagle into his hand and sprinted the perimeter of the fence. He'd flank the house, which faced north, on its westward side.

The security teams were completely oblivious to his approach, their efforts solely concentrated on the action with the Chevy. Bolan drew up parallel and continued until out of view of the sentries, then cut a sharp angle in a beeline for the house. He got within thirty yards before encountering a stray challenger. The gunman seemed shocked to see the intruder, and he fumbled with the slide catch on his SMG before finally raising the weapon.

The Executioner triggered his weapon while in motion. The .50-caliber pistol thundered in his grip and a bullet left the muzzle at a velocity exceeding 1600 fps. The bullet caught the gunman in the chest and knocked him off his feet, far enough back that his head struck the side of the house. His body collapsed in a wide flowerbed and went still. Bolan scooped the man's SMG on the run. A quick inspection revealed a round had somehow stove-piped in the unfired weapon and he tossed the useless thing aside.

Bolan reached the back porch just as two men emerged from a sliding-glass door. He took a knee, leveled the Desert Eagle and squeezed the trigger. The first hard case caught a slug in the midsection. His body twisted awkwardly as the muzzle of his pistol aimed skyward. The man's finger coiled reflexively on the trigger and lodged a bullet in the plaster of the round overhang. The second gunner managed to snap off a pair of rounds before Bolan canceled his ticket with a head shot. The 280-grain skull-buster nearly decapitated the gunman and sent his body to crash backward through the sliding-glass door with enough force to fracture the tempered glass. The man's back slid slowly to the flagstone porch, his final resting place.

Bolan advanced through the open door. He immediately sensed some heat and the smell of smoke stung his nostrils. The house interior was on fire. He had thought at first the object the occupants of the Chevy had thrown through the window was a grenade or IED, but when no explosion ensued he assumed it was a brick or rock.

A Molotov cocktail had never occurred to him. Whoever had launched the assault against Fuego wasn't goons sent by a rival head of Havana Five. No, this was turning out to be something more like a personal vendetta, and Mack Bolan was betting he knew exactly who the perpetrators were.

The Executioner pressed onward in his search.

CROSSE TRIED TO KEEP CONTROL of the Chevy but he overcorrected on his turn and fishtailed. The back wheel caught a rut off the drive and yanked the steering wheel from his grip. The car careened out of control and spun out, its back end swinging around until it contacted a brick fish pond. Water gushed from the massive cracks left in the Chevy's wake and flooded the dirt around it, instantaneously converting it to a mud pit.

Andres began to cry out from the backseat, but his protests were cut short when Stein raised his pistol and pulled the trigger twice. Crosse felt the splatter of warm blood wash across his neck and he immediately vomited. Stein looked at his partner with a bit of surprise but Crosse paid him no heed. He risked a look in the rearview mirror and saw Andres's head cocked against the top of the backseat, his eyes propped open in a lifeless stare with a grim look of shock on his face. The image was burned into Crosse's memory.

Stein patted his partner on the shoulder, then got out of the Chevy without a word. Several men with guns were advancing on them now, and Crosse bailed to help his friend. He got behind the open door of the car and started popping off rounds as quickly as he could pull the trigger. The fools continued to advance on them, hosing the area with their SMGs. They didn't even try to find cover, apparently convinced the automatic weapons made them invincible against an enemy armed only with pistols.

They were wrong.

Stein dropped two for every one Crosse managed to cut down, then suddenly the moment came where his partner no longer had Lady Luck on his side. The end came swiftly and suddenly as Crosse watched one of the gunners manage to flank Stein on the right. Stein's body twitched and danced under the assault, taking several rounds in the stomach before Crosse managed to take the gunman with a head shot.

Two men remained and one fired a sustained burst to keep Crosse's head down while the other one changed out mags.

Suddenly the firing ceased and Crosse waited and wondered why they hadn't finished him already. After another minute he risked a glance over the top and saw the entire force rushing toward the house. Someone or something had called them off, maybe related to the thick smoke now belching from several windows on the first floor. Over the dying noise of retreating men, Crosse heard a groan coming from where Stein had fallen. He left cover and sprinted to his friend's side. He could see Stein moving ever so slightly, and he gingerly turned the guy onto his back.

There was so much blood pouring from holes in his friend's belly, he wouldn't have known where to start plugging them. Instead he dropped his pistol, grabbed Stein's hands and used them to cover the belly wounds. He then laid his own hands over that and applied pressure. It did nothing to ease Stein's pain but at least he could staunch the flow of blood. Not that it mattered. The thick droplets continued to ooze from the corners of his mouth.

Stein coughed and said, "We…we s-s-set it right, Les. Didn't we? Huh?"

"No," Crosse said, smiling at his friend the best he knew how. "No, Dom, *you* set it right, man. You did that."

"W-we're partners," he said. "That's what we do for each oth…"

"Yeah, that's what we do," he said. "You take it easy now, Dom. I'm going to get you some help."

"Wh-when we done h-here, we goin' t-to Mexico, eh, Les?"

"Yeah, Dom. You said it. We'll go to Mexico and the Bahamas. Hey, how about Jamaica, Dom? Would you like Jamaica?"

But Dominic Stein wasn't talking anymore, because he wasn't breathing. He had finally found his long-deserved rest. And Leslie Crosse knew he'd found it, as well. So he sat with his partner, his friend, and he waited and hoped some rain would come to wash away all the blood. So much blood.

IT DIDN'T TAKE BOLAN long to find a set of back steps. He'd nearly missed them as they were tucked into a narrow alcove behind a service elevator. He stabbed the elevator call button a number of times, but the thing just glowed red. That meant somebody probably had it locked open on the second floor, and Bolan had a pretty good guess who that someone might be.

The Executioner found the stairwell almost by accident. It actually curved around the exterior walls of the elevator shaft, which proved a narrow and dangerous path to traverse. But Bolan figured if he couldn't see who was coming down they wouldn't be able to predict he was headed up, and that wouldn't put the enemy at any more advantage. Bolan would take equal odds over disadvantage any day of the week. He made the second floor unchallenged and was halfway down the hall when a man emerged from a door off the hall with none other than Inez Fuego in tow.

The man snap-aimed his pistol and squeezed off two shots that narrowly missed Bolan, who with his amazing reflexes sprawled onto his belly. The Executioner rolled, triggering a 3-round burst from the Desert Eagle before bumping into a door. He kicked up and out at a point just above the door lock and it gave under the force of his brute strength. Bolan made cover in time to avoid being ventilated by two more hasty shots from Fuego's escort.

The Executioner climbed to his feet and pressed his back to the door frame, keeping his body out of line of sight from the hallway. He was considering his next option when the hammer of feet on the winding steps reached his ears. Bolan dropped the magazine from the Desert Eagle and slammed in a fresh one. He crouched at the door, muzzle directed toward the stairwell landing, and triggered the weapon as soon as one of Fuego's house guards came into range. The Desert Eagle boomed and the round hit the guy in the abdomen. The impact drove him backward to crash into his partner coming up the stairs on his heels. Both men tumbled out of sight.

Bolan swung a one-eighty with the muzzle of his pistol and settled on an empty hallway. He heard the sound of breaking of glass coming from the room where Fuego and her bodyguard had first emerged. The Executioner rushed the door and continued past it before he stopped and pressed his back to the door. Two more shots sounded and bullets punched through the wall on the opposite side of the doorway. Just as he'd expected, whoever this guy was he'd expected Bolan to sidle up to the short side.

The Executioner counted to three, then kicked the door in and shoulder rolled inside. He finished on one knee and tracked the room with his pistol. He spotted the bodyguard easing Fuego out the window. As her head disappeared from view, the guy reached to a dressing table next to the window where he'd laid his pistol. It was a stupid move, to be sure, since Bolan had him dead to rights and the guy had to know it. There would be no turning back from that one.

Bolan squeezed off a double tap, the first one landing midchest and the second catching the guy on the chin. The bullet traversed an upward path, breaking teeth and bone on its way out the back of his head. Blood and gray matter spattered across the walls. The gunman's body twisted oddly before he flipped onto his back. His body twitched while what was left of his brain told the rest of him he was dead.

The Executioner rushed to the window and looked out. Fuego was descending via an emergency rope ladder and nearing the bottom. Bolan considered the distance, assessed the risks and realized he might have to fight his way out of the house. He couldn't risk that kind of delay, as it could buy Fuego a clean escape. This had to end here and now. Bolan spun and looked around the room until he spotted the unkempt bed, and a California king-size to boot. Those beds were seven feet in length, which meant sheets of eight feet end-to-end. This particular house was two stories, which put the distance from window to ground at about twenty feet.

No problem.

Bolan sprinted to the bed, ripped off the sheet and then grabbed a nearby coatrack made from mahogany. The thing would definitely hold. Bolan tied the sheet to the rack, then rushed back to the window and launched himself through it, dragging the sheet behind him. The impact should have yanked Bolan's arms from his sockets but his well-toned muscles held tight and he twisted his body so his feet would contact the side of the house first. He slowed his descent to minimize the friction burns to the palms of his hands, and dropped the remaining six feet to the ground.

Bolan reached out to grab Fuego as she hit the ground. She tried to bite his hand, but he got a fistful of hair and yanked her around. Fuego landed hard on the ground, the impact somewhat of a shock, and then the Executioner was on her before she could react. He hauled her to her feet and gripped her arm tightly, but she twisted from his grip and rocketed a punch into his kidney. The nerves around the nearby bullet wound screamed in protest and Bolan grunted, the pain driving him to one knee.

Fuego stepped in and executed a roundhouse kick that would have broken his skull if it had connected. Bolan stopped it short with an inside forearm block, then swept her leg out from under her. Fuego hit the ground with yelp but rolled out of his reach. The two opponents got on their feet simultaneously and then Fuego spotted a pistol near her— the one dropped by her bodyguard when the Executioner shot him.

Bolan drew the Desert Eagle. "Don't do it."

"You…" She spit, but her fury was so great she couldn't seem to finish.

Bolan remained silent and stock-still.

"I hate you, whoever you are! You ruined it all!"

"You ruined yourself," Bolan said. "You let guys like Andres and San Lujan manipulate you. And lots of people almost died because of that. Do you even care?"

"I cared about my husband," she replied with a sneer. "Where were you when they murdered him in cold blood?"

"Your husband made his choice, just like you. Every choice has its consequences."

"Go to hell, you bastard! You're not my judge!"

Fuego's eyes burned with hatred, one that had started with just a spark long ago but then it smoldered in the deepest and darkest recesses of her soul until it consumed her. And with all that fury and hatred, Fuego made her choice. Just like her husband had, just like Stein and Crosse, just like all of the poor and misguided souls who lose their way somewhere along the path of life and never seem to find redemption. Bolan watched with regret as Fuego lunged for the pistol and wrapped her delicate fingers around the grip. And then she came up with the muzzle, a look of pure bloodlust in her once beautiful features, a look that said she had killed before and she was ready to do it again.

And then the Executioner ended it.

EPILOGUE

"Nice job, Striker," Hal Brognola said to Bolan over the phone. "Hell of a job. The Man sends his thanks."

"Yeah," Bolan replied. "I only wish it could have ended differently for some."

Both men knew he was talking about Leslie Crosse. On his way out, Bolan had come across the two DIA agents. Fuego's goons had apparently cut down Stein, but Bolan found Crosse lying next to his partner with a gunshot wound to the head. Clearly it had been self-inflicted.

"Any word on Havana Five leadership?" the Executioner asked.

"Yeah. Looks the regime decided to finally take care of business. Famosa and Valdese were both killed during raids, and that led Armanteros to surrender peacefully. The trial was virtually nonexistent, most likely a farce for the press. Apparently the premier even made a personal appearance and claimed, and I quote, 'The heroic soldiers of the Cuban army in conjunction with our national police force put down these criminal dogs who were financing a private army to overthrow our government.'"

"Nice spin," Bolan said with a chuckle.

"Yeah. So, what's next for you, Striker?"

"I'm headed out on a fishing expedition."

"Sounds interesting. Anything we can help with?"

"Don't know," Bolan said, and he smiled. "Any good with wide-mouth bass?"

"Oh, you meant *real* fishing."

"I figured it was time for a bit of R and R."

"Rest will definitely do you some good."

"Let's hope." Bolan paused, and after some silence asked, "How's Rafael? He's been injured a lot over the past while."

"Grumpy as hell, but he'll get over it. David won't clear him for duty until the doctors are convinced he won't do more damage to that ankle. Guess it's taking longer to heal because it's an old injury. What about you?"

"Feeling pretty good," the Executioner replied. "This wound's just another reason I decided to take a brief rest."

"Yeah," Brognola said in a knowing tone. "Very brief, if I know you at all."

"Well, I'd better run, Hal. Give all my best."

"Wilco. Any idea when we'll hear from you again?"

"Not sure," Bolan said. "But you know how to reach me."

"You bet. Live large, Striker."

TAKE 'EM FREE

2 action-packed novels plus a mystery bonus

NO RISK

NO OBLIGATION TO BUY